I0781315

Strait Through the Heart
a Flip-Flop Detective novel

by Colin Conway

Strait Through the Heart: a Flip-Flop Detective Novel

Copyright © 2025 Colin Conway

ISBN: 978-1-961030-34-3

Cover Design by Rob Williams

Original Ink Press, an imprint of High Speed Creative, LLC
1521 N. Argonne Road, #C-205
Spokane Valley, WA 99212

Will you lend me a kiss?
I promise to give it back.

- pick-up line

Strait Through the Heart
a Flip-Flop Detective novel

Chapter 1

A dark-haired woman swam slowly across the pool. Nina Wilder's nearly perfect form caused little splashing and almost no noise. It seemed like practice in precision as much as exercise. She reached the deep end of the pool, briefly touched its ledge, then headed back. The flawless routine continued.

From behind his Ray-Bans, Sam Strait watched Nina glide through the water. He didn't bother counting how many seconds it took her to cross the pool, but he imagined there wasn't much deviation from when she started, roughly twenty laps ago. Nina's effortless style and unhurried rhythm created an almost hypnotic display.

An aquatic metronome, Sam thought. He smiled at the concept.

Overhead, the Hawaiian sun warmed the early afternoon. Its rays shimmered on the water and glinted off the aluminum legs of the furniture surrounding the pool. A white plastic fence enclosed the swimming area.

Sam lifted his arms and interlaced his fingers behind his head. He reclined on a chaise lounge with his bare feet crossed at the ankles.

From somewhere beyond the fenced area, a sputtering motor started. A lawnmower, Sam surmised.

Nina reached the shallow end of the pool and paused. She stood, brushed her long, black hair away from her face, then turned to Sam. "Coming in?"

"Not yet."

"The water's perfect."

"So's the view."

She playfully waved him off, then dipped her shoulders under the water. Nina headed back to the deep end, and the precise rhythm continued.

Sam and Nina were alone, the only two at the apartment pool. It wasn't always like that, though. Weekends were busy with families. Splashing children made getting in the water unenjoyable. The kids were most intolerable when they ran around the pool, laughing and screaming.

Almost no one came to the pool at this time of day, Monday through Friday. Thankfully, the children were in school, and their parents were at work. If both parents weren't employed, the one staying home was usually too busy to come down for a midday dip. At least, that's what Sam presumed. He avoided talking with any of the mothers and fathers, choosing to spend his time alone or in the company of single women.

That's how he met Nina.

She lived in the same complex, although her apartment was larger and recently remodeled. Nina was a nurse and worked the graveyard shift. They met a couple of weeks back on a beautiful winter afternoon, much like this one.

It started off as a casual conversation about the weather.

"Nice day," she had said.

"Nice day," he agreed.

The patter got better after that and culminated with a dinner she prepared. She was careful about what she ate. Nothing processed. No refined sugars. Her body revealed the results of her culinary discipline. Sam didn't tell her about the donut he'd eaten that morning.

Nothing deeply romantic happened after the initial dinner since Nina had to work. They saw each other a couple more times at the pool before she got a day off. That's when they had a date away from the apartment complex. It was the first time Sam spent the night with her.

Nina reached the shallow end of the pool again. She stopped, flipped her hair away from her face, then climbed out. Even though it was late January, her skin was deeply tanned. The red bikini she wore revealed almost every inch of her.

She walked with the grace of someone comfortable with her body and sexuality. Sam wondered if she had the same gait while in nurses' scrubs.

"What?" Nina grabbed her towel.

"Just wondering what kind of shoes you wear at work."

Nina spread her arms and looked down at herself. "That's what you're wondering?"

"Not anymore."

She dragged the towel over her arms. "What're your plans for the day?"

"You're looking at it."

Nina clicked her tongue against the back of her teeth. "Lucky."

Sam didn't bother correcting her. He corrected no one who considered his lifestyle lucky. It was probably hard not to feel that way about a man in his late thirties who followed the sun as his guiding principle in life.

Yet, several unfortunate events led Sam to live this way. None of which he shared with Nina. Their relationship hadn't reached that level of intimacy. Past hurts remained safely buried where they belonged.

Nina settled onto the chaise lounge next to him. She swung her legs up. Sunlight shimmered off the wetness lingering on her skin.

"I know that grin," she said.

He blinked, hoping he hadn't been leering from behind his sunglasses. "Sorry."

"Don't be. I wear this bikini for that exact reason."

"So I'll ogle you?"

"You and others." She slipped on her sunglasses and turned her face toward the sun. "Only you get to touch." A smile spread across her lips.

A phone rang. By the ringtone, Sam knew it was his. He reached underneath the chaise lounge and fumbled around for it.

"That's the first call I've heard you get," Nina said.

The phone rang a second time.

She was right—Sam didn't get many calls. It was a byproduct of his nomadic life. Plus, his parents were long dead. The paternal grandparents who raised him were gone, too. The only family Sam had were his maternal grandparents, and they lived in Southern Florida, a fact he knew only because of their annual Christmas card.

"Probably spam," Sam said.

The phone rang a third time.

He located the device and lifted it above his head, blocking the sun with his hand. The name and number on the caller ID screen didn't look right through his dark lenses. He sat upright and looked at the display from another angle. SONJA BOYD.

"Huh," he said.

Nina rolled onto her side. "Gonna answer?"

It rang a fourth time.

"Wrong number," Sam said. He silenced the ringer and set the phone down.

"I need a nap before work," Nina said.

"Okay."

She pulled her glasses to the end of her nose and stared at Sam.

"Oh," he said, "a nap."

***

Sam returned to his apartment around seven. Nina needed time to get ready, then make the drive to work. He didn't have an employer, so Sam often felt like he was in her way this time of night.

He set his keys and cell phone on the kitchen counter. Out of curiosity, he checked to see if Sonja had called again. She had. Four times in total.

It wasn't like her to call. Sam's head bobbled. That wasn't true. She used to call all the time when they were an on-again/off-again item. Sonja hated it whenever Sam left his Pacific Northwest home to head south. She wanted him to stay in Spokane County. She also wanted more of a committed relationship which he was unwilling to provide.

Sam stared at the phone for a few seconds, contemplating an action. He pressed a button on the side of the phone, darkening its display.

He headed for his bedroom, changed into a T-shirt, shorts, and a pair of orange running shoes. Getting some miles in might calm the thoughts banging around inside his head.

The cell phone remained on the kitchen counter when Sam stepped outside.

***

Sam left the apartment community, his stride slow and his breathing even. He wasn't running for any record; it was simply to get some exercise and free his mind. He headed west, toward the ocean.

Given enough time, he'd reach the water if he went in any direction. Oahu was an island, after all.

Sam didn't have a straight route to the beach since Daniel K. Inouye International Airport blocked his way. He could make it to the ocean by altering his route either north or south. However, he wasn't fascinated with the water. He'd grown up on Newman Lake in Eastern Washington. Being around water seemed second nature to Sam.

It was the heat he was after and the reason he escaped south every winter.

Sam had lived in Honolulu a couple of winters prior. He worked at one of the beach restaurants then. This was the first time Sam hadn't sought employment when he fled the snow. He usually worked in manual labor positions, something not requiring much experience or brain work. The jobs added a little money to his reserves, allowed him to meet some locals, but mostly kept him occupied. Truth be told, he felt restless not working right now. He never worked when he returned home for the summers, choosing to spend his time on the lake with the few friends he had. Therefore, his hands had been idle for almost nine months now. Too long by any man's standards.

He slowed at an intersection and let a convertible pass through. The blonde behind the wheel smiled in his direction. He waved back.

In Honolulu, Sam found a short-term apartment lease to assume—the former lessee had fled stateside, claiming island fever. The lease term would end around the time Sam usually returned to Washington State.

A sense of peace descended over him as the first mile

passed. He ran through various neighborhoods. Sam appreciated the variety of home construction. Some old. Others new. All packed closely together, much closer than the homes in Spokane County.

Thinking of home brought concerns about Sonja. Why had she called?

He didn't want to think about that now. He'd read somewhere that worry was wasted imagination. It seemed like good advice.

Sam pushed the meandering thoughts away and focused on his running. He matched his breathing to his footsteps. Breathe in for two steps; breathe out for three.

Unfortunately, he couldn't forget about Sonja Boyd.

He never could.

***

Sam slouched in a dining room chair. A glass of water rested near his right hand. In his left, he held his cell phone. He pressed the dial button. It never rang before she answered.

"About time. Where've you been?"

"Hi Sonja," Sam said.

"Don't 'hi Sonja' me. I've been calling." Her words ran together. "Why're you ignoring me?"

"I was on a run."

"For four hours?" Sonja's voice rose in panic. "What were you doing? A marathon?"

He shrugged, a gesture she couldn't see.

She didn't wait for him to respond. "I need you."

"I'm in Hawaii."

"I know. Don't you think I know?"

He didn't remember telling her his destination. Perhaps

one of his friends told her. Sam and Sonja had limited communication last summer because she had a new boyfriend. He should have been thankful Sonja found a new love, but Sam remained oddly jealous about it.

"Doesn't change the fact," she said. "I've been waiting for you to call me back."

Sam sipped his water.

"You still there?" she asked.

"What's going on?"

"Bruce's been arrested."

"The tooth mangler?"

She clucked. "This is serious, Sam. He's in trouble."

Bruce Bloom, DDS. The man Sonja decided checked all the boxes after Sam wouldn't give up his snowbirding ways.

"Did he over-whiten someone's teeth?" Sam asked. "Maybe a straightening wasn't straight enough?"

"Don't be that way. They say he murdered someone."

Sam sat upright and carefully set his glass on the table. "Bruce murdered someone?"

"No!" Her voice rose with panic. "He didn't murder anyone. Bruce wouldn't hurt a fly."

He didn't believe that. Dentists were licensed sadists. Forcing patients to keep their mouths open for unbearable amounts of time, or drilling into their teeth like they were searching for oil. The only thing separating dentists from psychopaths was a billing system.

"Wait, who's they?"

"The police," Sonja said.

"Oh." Sam winced slightly, recalling his own difficult dealings with law enforcement. Even though he had a pretty good idea as to the answer, he asked the next question anyway. "Why'd you call me, Sonja?"

"Why do you think I called?" Her question sounded accusatory.

Sam sighed. "I don't know. Can't you just tell me?"

"You're good at what you do."

"I'm not following."

Sonja muttered an expletive before saying, "You found the people who murdered that girl."

Sam absently waved his hand. "That was different."

"How?"

"It happened at my cabin," he said.

"What about the reporter? You cleared her name when she was accused of murder. That was the same thing as Bruce."

"It's not the same thing."

"Oh, that's right," Sonja said icily. "You were boinking her."

"You're sleeping with Bruce."

Sonja tsked. "Still."

"I don't know what I can do," Sam said as he glanced out his window at the night sky. "I'm in Hawaii." He'd already told her that, but it was a fact he believed needed repeating.

"If I had any other option, I wouldn't have called you."

"Since you put it that way."

"That's not what I meant," Sonja said, "and you know it."

Sam didn't know how to take it any other way.

She inhaled deeply, then exhaled slowly. Her breathing almost tingled his ear through the phone. Sam used to love how she did that when they were intimate. He shook the memory from his head. He didn't need that kind of stuff clogging the rational side of his brain.

"Listen," she said, "you and I have something."

"Had," Sam corrected. "We had something."

"Calling you is like playing with fire."

He didn't disagree.

"We need help."

"Eh."

"I need help," she clarified. "Me."

"Hire a lawyer."

"We did." Exasperation flooded her voice. "He can't do anything until a trial starts. I want someone to do something now."

"A private investigator, then."

"That's where you come in."

He started to protest. "I'm not a—"

"Maybe not licensed, but you used to be a deputy, and that counts for something."

"Not as much as you think."

"C'mon, Sam. I've never asked you for anything."

That wasn't true. She asked him for plenty. He just hadn't given her much.

Sam stood and moved to the window. The sky was nearly black, and he couldn't see any stars. However, he could see the lights on in the apartment community's pool and families gathered there. It was almost February now. Sam only had a couple more months to enjoy Hawaii before he returned home.

He occasionally kept tabs on the weather in Spokane County. It was a perverse habit—a reminder of why his decision to leave every winter was the right one. Earlier in the week, a heavy dose of snow fell in Spokane. The daily high temperature wasn't expected to crack the freezing level.

Sonja sniffled as if fighting tears. "Please, Sam."

His jaw tightened, and he shook his head. Crying

women were Sam's kryptonite. Not that he was comparing himself to Superman. The Man of Steel wouldn't get weak over some tears.

Sam remained quiet, though. Saying anything would likely result in him doing something he didn't want.

Leaving the island now would violate Sam's first rule—always be where flip-flops could be worn. It was a simple yet highly effective mantra. There were other rules Sam created to help live the life he wanted. He had trouble abiding by those, but he never violated the first rule. That one was sacrosanct. Breaking it was nonnegotiable.

Sonja's crying intensified. She took a stuttering breath and muttered, "I'm sorry for crying."

Sam looked down at his bare feet. His lifestyle was selfish, but it was his life. He didn't have a wife or a girlfriend to answer to. Sam had been careful to never have children. He could live mostly carefree because of his choices.

Perhaps he could call the agency which had arrested Bruce. If it was the Spokane County Sheriff's Office, the conversation probably wouldn't go well. Sam's reputation was still sullied because of the false accusation of drug dealing that his former employer leveled at him. Even though he was exonerated, the lawsuit he brought and won against SCSO didn't curry him any favors.

Maybe the Spokane Police Department was investigating the murder. Sam didn't have any friends in that organization, either. However, he went to the academy with a couple of guys who signed on there. If they were still around, perhaps they'd help him. Although that was many years ago, and the stink from his false accusation and subsequent lawsuit against the county might carry over to that agency.

"Please, Sam," Sonja said, snuffling now. "There's no one else who can help. We really need you."

Sam remained silent as his thoughts raced. He tried desperately to find a solution to this problem. The only one he could readily see was to say, "No," and hang up.

"We'll reimburse you for everything," Sonja said, amid her sobs. "If you want, we'll even pay for your time."

"You don't have to pay for my time." He cringed at the words, knowing what they meant.

"Really?" Sonja said, her voice filling with hope and pushing aside the tears.

A wild idea occurred to him. Perhaps it was the silver lining in this whole mess. Sam could become a travelling detective, bouncing from state to state, always avoiding the cold. How'd he find clients, though? They wouldn't consistently fall in his lap.

"Sam?"

"Yeah," he said, letting his thoughts of a wandering investigator fade into the ether.

"We'll figure out the money stuff when you get here."

"If I come…" He tried to sound more resolute than he felt.

"You're coming," she said. "I know it." The tears had almost stopped now. Determination replaced the hope in her voice.

"Know this. I'm helping you, not Bruce."

"I understand." She exhaled heavily. "Totally."

"I'll see if I can catch a red eye."

"Thank you." Sonja sounded stronger now, as if her worries had been pushed fully away. "Seriously."

"I'll let you know what I find."

"That's great. Really."

"Okay, I've gotta go."

"Oh, and Sam?"

"Yeah?"

"We're not in Spokane right now."

Sam stared into the dark Hawaiian sky. "Where are you?"

"Havre, Montana."

Chapter 2

Sam expected the Havre City-County Airport to be tiny, but its actual size surprised him. It had two runways, which Sam saw from the air. Passengers disembarked down a set of stairs built into the plane's door. Cold, snow, and darkness greeted him as he stepped onto Montana soil. By any measure, it was a rude welcome to Big Sky country, made worse since Sam only wore a hooded sweatshirt for protection from the weather.

He was the last off the plane, yet that hadn't been the worst part of the flight. His seat hadn't reclined. Neither had any of the other seats, it seemed. Eleven people were on the plane, including the lone pilot. There'd been no food service, no restroom, and no flight attendants. Everyone remained in their seats and held on as the twin-engine propeller plane had bounced its way through the night sky.

Sam wasn't a religious man. His grandparents hadn't brought him up that way. Regardless, he silently prayed that God deliver him and the other passengers safely to their destination. That's how he phrased it, too. *Deliver them.* Sam thought it sounded more biblical, which might help his request cut through the prayer clutter God likely dealt with surrounding sports teams, political affiliations, and unexpected pregnancies.

It was a quick walk into the terminal. Even so, Sam shoved his hands into his pockets. He leaned to the left to offset the weight of the backpack on his right shoulder. There wasn't much in the bag, but the ground was slick, and Sam took petite steps to avoid falling. It had been years since he walked on icy ground.

A cold wind nipped at him, but most of its impact was blunted by the tall, heavyset man Sam followed into the building.

Sam had visited many airports since he started snowbirding. The only nice thought he had about this one was it had heat. The waiting area consisted of low vinyl chairs with a mixture of colors dating back to the seventies—burnt orange, avocado green, and harvest gold.

The terminal was eerily quiet, almost as if a funeral was being conducted somewhere else in the building.

Sonja Boyd stood immediately outside the security gate. Her eyes anxiously searched the small crowd as it entered the building. Worry creased her face.

Strands of short red hair peaked from beneath Sonja's beige beanie. She wore a green coat with faux fur piping around its hood, faded blue jeans that revealed every curve, and clunky light brown boots. Even when dressed for winter, Sonja was a knockout.

Her eyes settled on Sam, and her expression eased. She breathed a visible sigh of relief and waved.

Sam returned the gesture.

When he cleared the security gate, Sonja hurried over. She slipped her arms around his waist, knocking his backpack from his shoulder. It dropped to the ground with a plop. Sam wrapped his arms around her. Even though she wore a heavy coat, Sonja Boyd felt natural in his arms.

The two remained embraced for several seconds, too long for a man and woman no longer involved with each other. Her perfume—a dark spicy aroma—floated up his nostrils and wreaked havoc in his brain. Countless images of them intertwined crashed upon the shores of his memory.

Sam vaguely understood the chemical reactions occurring inside his body. Oxytocin, dopamine, and serotonin coursed through his veins. Heck, adrenaline probably ran wild, too. He closed his eyes to fully enjoy the moment.

That's when Sonja broke the hug and leaned back. She grabbed his hands and forced a smile. There was no joy in it.

"It's good to see you," she said.

"You, too."

He desperately tried to push away the images of their past now clouding his thoughts.

Sonja shook her head. "I didn't think you'd ever get here."

"Me neither."

The journey from Oahu Island to northern Montana took almost nineteen hours. It consisted of three planes of diminishing sizes and increasing layovers in Seattle, Washington, and Billings, Montana. There was also a time zone difference that cost Sam three hours. He slept on the first plane, but sitting upright while snoozing isn't the most refreshing. On the flight out of Seattle, he was seated near the restroom and heard its door bang through most of the flight into Montana.

Sam had left Hawaii a few minutes after ten the previous night. It was shortly after 7 p.m. now. He was ready to crawl into bed and call it a day.

Sonja let go of him as she stepped back. Her gaze swept over Sam, from top to bottom and back up. She paused longer than necessary on his orange running shoes. It was a fashion faux pas, but Sam didn't care. This was the warmest outfit he could muster in the limited time he had.

Her eyes flicked to the backpack on the ground. "Did you bring another bag?"

"That's it." He grabbed the pack and slung it over his shoulder. "Socks, underwear, and other essentials."

Her face registered disapproval, and she thumbed toward the doors. "It's cold out there."

"I didn't have time to buy a coat. I came right away."

The tension in her features disappeared, and her eyes softened. "You did, didn't you?"

The way she looked at him caused another rush of chemicals through Sam's system much the way her hug did only moments ago. He'd go insane if he continued to experience waves of heightened emotions every six seconds. Sam needed to control himself. He cleared his throat. "So, Bruce?"

Sonja stiffened. "Right. Bruce."

She turned toward the exit, glancing back to make sure Sam was following. "I can't believe you're really here."

"Neither can I," he muttered.

The automatic doors slid open, and they stepped back into the Montana night. The icy breeze blasted Sam in the face. He turned away from it and hunched his shoulders up to his ears. Sam shoved his hands into his pockets. "You gotta be kidding me," he said.

"What's that?"

"Nothing." He shook his head.

If he had remained in Hawaii, he would have spent the day with Nina, likely by the pool again or rolling around in her bed. Or both. Sam had spoken with her on the phone before heading to the airport. Nina knew he was leaving in the spring, so her attitude had been to enjoy their time together. Even so, Sam was slightly disappointed in her blasé attitude about his sudden departure.

"Hit me up when you get back," Nina said, then ended the call.

He would have liked her to show at least some disappointment at his leaving. Sam and Nina had been an exclusive item since they met. Perhaps her apathetic response was due to their relationship coming with an expiration date. He always held something back of himself to avoid getting too close. It wasn't fair of him to expect a woman not to do the same.

Nonetheless, her response left him feeling oddly hollow.

"You'll get used to the cold again," Sonja said. She slipped her hands into her jacket. "We should probably get you a coat and some boots."

Sonja strode toward the parking lot as Sam shuffled across the icy ground behind her. His hunched posture and careful steps were not the confident picture he wanted to present to Sonja, even if there was no chance they'd ever get together again.

He stood up straight, pulled his shoulders back, and faced the cold like a man.

Then his backpack slipped off his shoulder, slid down his arm until it caught against the hand tucked in his pants pocket. It tangled with his leg, which caused his feet to collide. He stumbled, then fell. Sam sprawled in the parking lot, and his backpack slid away from him.

Sonja spun. "You all right?"

"Doing great," Sam grumbled as he struggled to his feet. "Just great."

***

"First things first," Sonja said from behind the steering

wheel. "We need to get you a coat."

"You don't want to talk about Bruce?"

Her cheeks slackened and tears welled in her eyes. "There's nothing we can do tonight."

"You're the boss." It was a stupid thing to say, but Sam didn't want her to cry. He could give her some time to talk about Bruce's arrest. He'd only just landed after all.

Sonja drove a black Range Rover with a loaded ski rack attached to its top. When they first climbed in, she called it, "Bruce's baby," a statement with a patina of sarcasm. Sam hadn't followed up on the statement since he wasn't there to rekindle a flame with Sonja, even though she looked and smelled wonderful.

There might have been an opportunity last summer to renew their relationship. However, he didn't think it right since he'd only go south again. If someone pressed Sam for the truth, he might admit he loved Sonja, yet he didn't want to give up his freedom to be with her. He also didn't want her to relinquish her dreams of acting and modeling to be with him. The right choice was maturity.

Adulting, as the media loved to call it, was stupid.

Hearing "Bruce's baby" in that tone of voice did give Sam a certain amount of satisfaction, though. He might have smiled if he wasn't so tired and hungry.

"You care what kind?" she asked.

"Of what?"

"A coat. Do you care what kind of coat we get you?"

Sam shrugged. "Not really."

They headed north on Airport Road through what appeared to be the countryside. No light poles illuminated the lane. The Range Rover's high beams provided the only light on the slippery road. Long continuous berms of snow lined their path. A breeze carried tendrils of wispy snow across the roadway.

There were no other full-sized vehicles on the road. Two snowmobiles, however, cruised south toward them, their low headlights oddly different than a passing car. Sam turned in the passenger seat to watch the snowmobiles go by. Their red taillights faded quickly into the distance.

"If you want something nice," Sonja said, "we could go to North 40."

"I don't know what that is."

Hot air blasted from the vents. No music played in the SUV. They rounded a bend in the roadway. Up ahead, occasional vehicle lights whizzed by left and right. An arterial, Sam thought.

"North 40 Outfitters," Sonja said. "It's an outdoorsman store." She shrugged. "Outdoorsperson. Anyway, you can get good stuff there. It's where the ranchers shop. We've picked up a few things. When Bruce is in Montana, he likes to wear Carhart." Her hand rolled off the wheel. "You know, to fit in."

"Sounds expensive."

"There's a couple boutique stores in town, although I don't think they cater to men."

"Nothing cheaper?"

"There's Walmart." Derision laced the final word.

Sonja had not, and would likely never, shop at the superstore. While at East Valley High School, she was the head cheerleader, a prom queen, and voted Lilac City Queen, the honorary leader of the city's annual parade. Roughly five years ago, she'd been named Miss Spokane. In Spokane County, she was a minor celebrity. She was the spokeswoman for a variety of local businesses, and she'd appeared in multiple movies made in the region.

Sam had no aversion to shopping at Walmart, however.

A guy bouncing north and south through the year needed to pinch pennies where he could. He did, however, have a propensity for winding up Sonja. It was something he relished and had done ever since high school.

"Let's find a thrift store," he said.

Her upper lip curled. "No."

"There's got to be a Goodwill around here," he said. "Maybe a Salvation Army or something."

"You're not getting a second-hand coat. Definitely not used boots. That's how people get foot fungus."

"They spray the shoes like the bowling alleys do."

Sonja slowed the Range Rover for a Stop sign but didn't bother coming to a complete halt. "Bowling." She clucked, then accelerated onto the arterial. "I'll buy you a coat and some boots. We're going to North 40."

"It's not about the money," Sam said. It was, though. He spent nearly eight hundred dollars on a one-way ticket to Havre. Beyond a return trip ticket, there were bound to be more expenses. Sonja promised to reimburse him, but Sam wouldn't have that. If Bruce covered his costs, that was fine, but Sam wouldn't make Sonja do it. "When I leave," he said, "I'll just get rid of the coat and boots."

"If we get you something nice, you could keep them." Sonja smiled. "You know, in case you ever stop doing what you're doing."

"Not a chance," Sam said.

She cast a sideways glance. "Not a chance?" Fading hope filled her question.

"Not a chance," he repeated with emphasis.

Sonja huffed. "In that case, we'll go to Walmart."

***

Sam tossed the large bag into the Range Rover's back seat. Sonja was already behind the steering wheel when he climbed in. Sam shoved his hands into the puffy orange coat he now wore.

Sonja started the engine, then glanced at him. "You look better than I expected."

"Are you talking about the coat or me?"

"The coat." She dropped the transmission into Drive, then accelerated forward. "Although I'm getting pretty jealous of your tan."

Sonja never tanned. Not only did she have a redhead's fairness, but she also slathered on sunscreen whenever outside to protect her skin from harmful UV rays. She didn't want wrinkles or more freckles. Sam adored the freckles she already had.

"Where now?" he asked.

"Our cabin."

Sonja paused at the edge of the parking lot before gunning the SUV onto the highway. A sign for US Route 2 zipped by. An abandoned car was parked on the shoulder and covered in snow.

"What cabin?" Sam asked.

"Bruce rented us a place." She momentarily took her eyes off the road. "He was going to propose."

Sam lifted an eyebrow. "That so?"

"Don't be that way."

"What way?"

"That way."

Sam eyed her now. "He told you he was going to propose?"

She shrugged a single shoulder, never taking her hands from the wheel. "He's a planner."

"Ah."

"Ah, what?"

"Nothing," Sam said. "Guy must be a keeper if he brought you all the way to the bustling metropolis of Havre to propose."

"It was to see his parents, if you must know."

"Keeps getting better."

"I should have told you," Sonja said. "Listen, I know, but I was afraid you wouldn't come."

Sam stared ahead, focusing on the yellowish lights hanging over the highway. He didn't want to ask if she planned to say yes. He likely knew the answer. If she planned to say no, Sonja wouldn't have come to Havre.

A silence descended over the car. The only sound was the rumble of the tires on the roadway.

"You can meet them," Sonja said, her voice soft and her words careful. "Bruce's parents."

"Why would I want to do that?"

"So you can get a picture of Bruce from someone other than me."

Sam rested his head against the seat. "Probably a good idea."

Sonja gripped the steering wheel tighter, inhaled deeply and said, "Bruce was accused of murder." She cast a sideways glance. "He didn't do it, by the way."

"Okay."

"He didn't." She glared at him.

"Eyes on the road." Sam pointed ahead.

Sonja reluctantly faced forward. "You don't sound convinced."

"If you're convinced, I'm convinced."

"He didn't," Sonja said resolutely.

"Then it's settled." Sam crossed his arms. "So who'd he kill?"

"What'd I just say?"

"Allegedly." Sam waved a dismissive hand. "Whatever."

Sonja pulled on the steering wheel and repositioned herself in her seat. "Topher Anderson."

"Who's that?"

"A high school bully."

Sam did a double take. "Bruce killed a teenager?"

Sonja threw her hands in the air. "He didn't kill anyone!" she shouted.

"This Topher guy is a teenager?"

"Don't be dumb." Sonja's face tightened. "Topher bullied Bruce in high school."

"Oh." Sam rested his arm on the passenger door. "Yeah, I can see that."

"What do you mean?" Sonja glanced at Sam twice. "You don't even know Topher."

"I know Bruce."

She clicked her tongue against the back of her teeth. "You don't know Bruce either."

"I've met him."

"For a minute."

"That's enough," Sam said. "In a bully-victim relationship, it's easy to know which side of the equation Bruce would fall on."

"Bruce is nice," she said protectively. "I don't care what you say."

"You shouldn't."

Since you're about to be married.

Sonja tapped the steering wheel. "We're meeting Bruce's attorney tomorrow morning."

"We?"

She nodded. "You need to meet with him so he can

deputize you.”

“He can’t do that.”

“Whatever it is.”

“So I can work on Bruce’s defense.” Sam didn’t like the way the words tasted in his mouth, especially not after the revelation of a planned marriage proposal.

“You’re helping me,” Sonja said.

“Yeah,” Sam muttered, “I’m helping Mrs. Bloom.”

“Soon-to-be,” Sonja whispered.

Sam rolled the back of his head on the seat so he could look directly at her. To hell with it, he thought. He was going to ask. “Do you plan to say yes?”

“I’m not telling you.” She shook her head. “Don’t ask again.”

His heart beat a bit faster. It was a bad sign. He didn’t need his feelings about Sonja to confuse him. She was with Bruce and that was the best for everyone. He turned forward and concentrated on the road again. “Anyone else at your cabin?”

“Just me.” As if reading Sam’s mind, she glanced at him. “No funny business.”

“I wouldn’t dream of it,” Sam said. He would, though. He’d more than dream about it. “I need a hotel room.”

“Don’t be ridiculous.”

“I’m not.”

Sonja looked at him; her eyes fully left the road again. “You’re not?”

The car drifted toward the shoulder.

“It’s safer that way,” Sam said. He pointed ahead. “Don’t drive us off the road.”

She looked forward and corrected the car’s path. A pleased smile creased her face. “A hotel it is.”

***

Sam checked in at Best Western, right off First Street and in the middle of Havre. After registering, he escorted Sonja out to the Range Rover, which was parked in front. His backpack remained over his shoulder, and he carried the Walmart bag with his boots in his left hand.

Off to the east—at least, Sam assumed it was east—was a lighted intersection. The traffic signal flicked from green to red, even though there wasn't any northbound traffic.

Sonja opened the SUV's door but didn't step inside. Instead, she turned and looked at him.

The cold bit at Sam and he shivered.

She smiled softly. "Thank you for coming."

"Still not sure what I can do."

Sonja leaned in, her eyes challenging him. "You'll do what you do."

"What's that?"

"Rescue the girl."

Sam's lips twisted. "Bruce needs the rescuing."

"Don't be too sure about that." She slipped her arms through his and wrapped them around his waist. Her head rested on his chest, and she leaned into him. "I'm glad you're here."

Sam hugged her, the shoe bag banging against the back of her legs. While her musky perfume invaded his nostrils, he did his best not to reminisce about his feelings. Images of them entwined washed up on the shore of his memory again.

She slipped out of his arms and lightly cleared her throat. When she looked up, tears filled her eyes. "I'll be back in the morning."

Sam felt himself slipping into the overwhelming effects

of the adrenaline, dopamine and other chemicals coursing through his veins. He hoarsely said, "Sonja."

Sensing the danger in that single word, Sonja stepped back and bumped into the car door. It slammed shut, and she jumped. She hurriedly said, "We're meeting the attorney at nine."

The memories of their past and the chemicals affecting Sam's body suddenly evaporated. He inhaled deeply and crinkled his nose.

"What's wrong?" she asked.

"Nothing."

It was a half-hearted denial. Sam didn't like lawyers. He didn't like a host of other careers either—accountants, IRS agents, politicians, real estate brokers, preschool teachers, and bikini baristas. He'd created a rule to avoid people with repulsive careers. Sam had valid reasons for listing each of those professions.

"Oh." Sonja frowned. "Your rules." She air-quoted *rules* which was unnecessary since she frowned and jerked her head at the same time.

He ignored her displeasure and said, "You still haven't told me the rest of the story with Bruce."

"You want to do that now?" She glanced around. "In the cold?"

Sam cocked his head toward the hotel. "We can go inside." Another surge of dopamine coursed through his veins.

"I'll tell you in the morning," Sonja said. "Get some rest."

"You're avoiding the subject."

"No, I'm not." She stood on her tiptoes and kissed him on the cheek.

"Sonja," he said.

"I'll pick you up a little before nine."

Sam sighed. "Fine."

She climbed into the SUV and started the engine. Sonja waved once, then zoomed onto First Street.

Sam Strait stood alone in the parking lot. A cold Montana breeze blew from the north. He glanced around. Hardly any cars traveled through the city now.

It was a long way from Honolulu.

Chapter 3

The phone beeped its alarm, and Sam groggily lifted his head from the pillow. He silenced the noise, ensured it was truly 7:30 a.m., then groaned. Time zone, he thought. It was 4:30 back on the island.

He'd been in the middle of a dream. Sam was lounging by a pool underneath the warm winter sun. Instead of Nina's rhythmic swimming across the pool, it had been Sonja. He watched her glide back and forth. She stopped in the shallow end and stood, water cascading from her naked body.

"Sam," she had said, "don't you want to swim?"

Before Sam could respond, Bruce Bloom, teeth mangler extraordinaire, walked to the edge of the pool with his hand extended. "Sam doesn't want to get in," Bruce said. "He's afraid of the water."

It wasn't true. Sam wasn't afraid of the water, but he couldn't find the words to argue with the dentist. He also couldn't find the words to tell Sonja he badly wanted to swim with her.

Bruce wrapped a towel around Sonja's bare body and escorted her away. That's when the alarm rang.

Sam flopped back to the bed.

Maybe he could sneak in another hour of sleep if he skipped breakfast. He'd still be ready for Sonja when she arrived. He closed his eyes, content with his plan for a little more rest.

Down the hall, a door opened and banged shut. A

second door opened and slammed closed.

Two men talked and laughed loudly as they passed Sam's room. It was a banal conversation about some report on government spending. Their voices faded in the direction of the lobby.

Sam pulled an extra pillow over his head. Sleep teased Sam, enveloping its arms around him, and gently pulled him into its warm blackness.

Another door opened and little footsteps hurriedly clomped down the hall.

"No running!" a woman shouted as the pounding continued past his room.

The door slammed, and the woman yelled, "What'd I say?"

Why were there kids in the hotel? Sam wondered. Shouldn't they be in school?

A whistle squealed from behind the hotel as a train rumbled slowly by. A BNSF maintenance facility sat north of the lodge. When Sam checked in, the night clerk made sure to let him know.

"It's not like they're roaring in and out all night," she had said, "but you'll hear them in the morning for sure."

Sam moaned, swung his feet off the bed, and stood. It seemed the world wanted him up and moving.

***

The elevator doors opened, and Sam stepped onto the first floor.

It was a few minutes before eight, and several guests gathered in the hotel's casino. It was a misnomer, since Sam always believed a casino should be like the large Las Vegas establishments with their endless games of chance, including those with dealers and pit bosses. Live entertainment, fancy restaurants, and trendy bars certainly added to the lure of the Sin City experience.

The hotel casino had none of that. Instead, eight electronic machines lined two walls of a small room. Several round tables, obviously filler, sat in the middle of the space. Pat Benatar's "Hit Me with Your Best Shot" rocked at a modest level, the volume appropriate for a hotel and the morning hour. Three players repeatedly tapped illuminated buttons on their respective machines.

It had been some time since Sam visited Montana. He never knew the gambling laws in the state. However, it seemed games of chance were at every bar, restaurant, and convenience store. Sam wondered how much money could really be made in a room this size.

A breakfast bar was set up off the hotel lobby. Biscuits and gravy were available, along with eggs, bacon, and other staples. A man in a brown Carhart jacket, blue running shorts, and scuffed work boots stood before the waffle maker. His hair was a mess and his face sagged with the bleariness of the day ahead.

The television hanging on the wall blared FOX news. Sam didn't have a political affiliation. He didn't care who led the government, so long as it didn't affect his ability to follow the sun. However, he hated the blather of news entertainment. He rarely watched TV and never in the morning. The broadcasters were as comforting as an incessant jackhammer.

He grabbed a plate, piled some food on top, then filled a Styrofoam cup with coffee. Sam didn't consider eating in the lobby. Not with the news blaring. He headed for his room.

As he passed an empty table, he noticed a worn copy of

the *Havre Daily News*. Above the fold was a picture of a smiling Bruce Bloom, likely taken from the website for his dental practice. A headline proclaimed, "Havre Son Accused of Murder." Sam looked around before grabbing the newspaper.

He slipped it under his plate and headed toward the elevator.

***

Sam sat at the desk in his hotel room. He ate slowly as he read the newspaper. The article was short on substance related to the murder, instead focusing on Bruce's history in the town.

The reporter identified Bruce's parents as Russell and Dorothy Bloom. Russell had taught at Havre High School. Dorothy worked in payroll processing at the local hospital. Bruce attended the dental school at the University of Washington before setting up practice in Liberty Lake, Washington.

The article named the victim in Bruce's alleged crime and included his picture, too. Topher Anderson owned a local handyman business and was a state wrestling champion during his time at Havre High. The short piece also mentioned an incident occurred between Bruce and Topher at a local watering hole, The Grizzly Den, prior to Topher's murder.

Topher and Bruce were a study in contrast. Bruce smiled while Topher smirked. Bruce's face was doughy and round, while Topher's was angular and gaunt. Bruce looked like the type of man a mother could entrust with her children's teeth. Topher looked like the type of man a husband wouldn't trust alone with his wife.

Law enforcement provided no comment for the article, which didn't surprise Sam. He reread the news piece to ensure he didn't miss anything.

Had he still had a book, Sam might have pulled it out. Unfortunately, he had finished the paperback he'd been reading while in the Billings airport. He left it behind for someone else to enjoy it. Hopefully, the cleaning staff didn't throw it away.

Sam read the rest of the newspaper while he continued eating. There was no other mention of Bruce or Topher. However, there was coverage about the high school's debate team win, an incoming winter storm, and a two-car collision that resulted in no injuries.

He returned to the front page. Sam used a hotel-provided pen and circled four names—Russell and Dorothy Bloom, Topher Anderson, and The Grizzly Den. It wasn't much to go on, but he had to start somewhere.

Sam was about to reread the Sports section when his phone rang.

The digital clock on the desk read 8:55.

Sam answered the call.

"I'm out front," Sonja said.

***

The Range Rover idled in front of the hotel's entrance. Sam opened the passenger door, but didn't get in. Instead, he studied two pairs of skis on the roof. He saw them last night, of course, but hadn't focused on them because of the activity surrounding his arrival. In the daylight, the colorful skis demanded more attention.

"What are you doing?" Sonja asked.

"Checking out your skis." Sam settled in the passenger

seat and pulled the door closed. "Didn't know you liked to hit the slopes."

"I do a lot you don't know about."

"I'll bet."

"Bruce wanted to show me the Bear Paw Ski Bowl."

Ski bowl, Sam thought.

"He said it's not as nice as the mountains around Spokane, but it's what he skied on when he was a kid." Sonja eyed him. "Seatbelt."

Sam secured himself and Sonja dropped the SUV into gear.

"How was your night?" Sonja asked.

"Went straight to bed."

The vehicle headed for the parking lot's exit. Immediately to the west was a stoplight. It turned green and a burst of traffic proceeded through the intersection and past the hotel.

A thick layer of white covered almost everything. Plows had pushed new snow onto the sidewalks, making foot travel additionally treacherous. The sky remained an oppressive gray, threatening to dump more powder on the community.

"Sleep well?" Sonja asked.

He shrugged and offered a noncommittal grunt. "You?"

"I haven't slept much since Bruce was arrested."

Sam found that hard to believe. Sonja's eyes didn't carry bags, and she seemed alert. Once again, she was put together. She wore a similar parka as the night before, but this one was black with faux white fur lining the hood. Her black pants were skintight, and her ankle-high boots were scuff free.

The traffic passed and Sonja was about to nose out onto the highway. However, she noticed Sam leaning as he checked out her clothing. "What?"

"Nothing."

A sad smile appeared at the edges of her mouth. "You like my boots?"

He avoided telling her how nice she looked because it might lead to complications. Maybe she wouldn't be swayed by any niceties Sam spewed, but he'd certainly cloud his own judgement. Sonja was with Bruce, and that's the way it was. His thoughts rang hollow in his own mind, though—he could already smell her perfume, and the musky scent caused his pulse to race.

Besides violating his first rule, Sam was now violating the fourth—*No drama!!!* The extra exclamations points were a reminder not to violate that rule, something Sam had done before for a woman and was clearly doing again.

He carried the list of rules in his wallet. Only two women knew about the folded piece of paper—Sonja and a former lover in Arizona. It wasn't something women in a relationship were likely to approve. Those two never did.

"I like your new boots," Sonja said. "Nice to see you in grown-up shoes."

Sam looked down the road. "How far is this attorney?"

"Less than five minutes."

"Not enough time for you to fill me in on what happened with Bruce."

"We'll get into everything when we get there."

Sam didn't like the answer. He got the feeling she was avoiding something.

Sonja swung the SUV onto First Street and accelerated westbound. She quickly crossed into the inner lane, then turned onto Seventh Avenue. A block later, Sonja slowed in front of a squat gray building with white trim.

A pylon sign announced The Law Office of Charles

Palmer with more flair than necessary. At least, it didn't list the attorney's specialties like a menu.

Sam started to get out, but Sonja lightly grabbed his arm. "Hold on."

He let go of the door handle.

"Chuck is an old friend of Bruce's."

"Chuck?" Sam already didn't like the attorney.

"Don't say anything bad about him."

"Why would I say anything bad about Chuck?" He refrained from adding extra emphasis to the man's nickname.

"You know what I mean."

"Relax," Sam said. "I'm not an idiot." He grabbed the door handle again.

"Chuck's an acquired taste."

"Like Bruce?"

Sonja's expression darkened. "I'm serious."

"Can we go?" Sam asked. "This whole affair is cutting into my Hawaii time."

"Yeah," Sonja said as she turned off the engine. "Your Hawaii time."

Chapter 4

"Chuck Palmer," the big man said with a toothy grin. "Damn glad to meet ya." He extended his hand. "Any friend of Brucie's is a friend of mine."

Sam didn't like Chuck. Not the man. It was still too early to tell. No, he didn't like the nickname. The only Chucks he'd ever met were older men—baby boomers or their fathers. A couple of older actors used the name, too, and he never liked their movies. Sam couldn't recall anyone else using the moniker. The younger generation seemed predisposed toward Charlie. However, now that he thought about it, he couldn't recall one Charlie from his generation. Charlie Sheen was older, like his dad should have been.

No one other than the British seemed to go by the stuffy name of Charles. All things considered, that was preferable to Chuck.

They stood in a small lobby. A brown couch sat along the wall across from two brown, low-back chairs. Hunting and gun magazines littered a wooden coffee table. A deer's head hung over a fake fireplace that blew warm air into the room.

A door blocked any view of the lawyer's inner sanctum.

Chuck wore a gray suit he must have purchased when he was twenty pounds lighter. The jacket strained around his chest, and his pant legs bunched above his snow boots.

Sam introduced himself and shook the attorney's hand. He didn't bother to say it was nice to meet the man. It wasn't, since it violated his fifth rule, the one about repulsive careers.

"Take a load off," Chuck said and directed them toward the couch.

Sonja sat at one end. Sam settled into the opposite.

Chuck unbuttoned his suit jacket before sitting in a chair. His stomach hung over his belt like a sack of potatoes spilling out of a grocery cart. Chuck's white shirt appeared more rumpled than normal for this time of day, and his collar was unbuttoned behind his red tie.

"We're on the clock." The attorney checked his watch. "I've got forty-five minutes before I head to court."

"Bruce's first appearance?" Sam asked.

Chuck shook his head. "Different client. Bruce already had his. They're holding him without bail."

That surprised Sam and the attorney must have read the expression on his face.

"Considered a flight risk," Chuck said.

Sam glanced at Sonja before saying, "He's a dentist."

Chuck spread his arms apart in a what-can-I-do gesture. "Prosecutor argued Bruce didn't reside here and had the means to escape extradition if he left the state. Wasn't hard for the judge to buy that load of horse pucky."

A heaviness descended over the room. Sam's gaze drifted up to the deer's head. The animal watched him with frozen curiosity. He wondered if the deer's eyes would follow him as he moved around the room.

"This little lady said you're from Spokane." Chuck grinned and motioned to Sonja. "That right?"

Sam's attention returned to the conversation. "More or less."

Sonja forced a polite smile. It was the same one she adopted whenever older men approached back home and said, "You're that pretty gal in that one commercial. Mind if I get a picture?" She did mind. However, she was too much of a professional to say anything about it.

"Nice town," Chuck said. "Bit big for my tastes." He slumped in his chair and repositioned his tie over his large belly. "To each their own, I guess."

Sam crossed one leg over the other and noticed the weight of his boots versus the flip-flops he normally wore. His eyes drifted back up to the deer's head. What exactly was a dead animal in a defense attorney's office supposed to signify? Was it symbolic of Chuck's clients? Or was it a representation of the prosecutors he bagged? Maybe it was nothing more than a trophy.

Sonja leaned forward. "I told Sam about you and Bruce being old friends."

"That's right." Chuck grinned at her, then flashed his big teeth at Sam. "Blue Ponies forever."

Sam's gaze dropped to the attorney. "Blue Ponies?"

Chuck nodded. "Havre High. It's our mascot."

"You met in high school?" Sam asked.

"Aw, heck no. Me and Brucie go all the way back to our days in short pants. We were in the same class from elementary through high school."

"So you knew the victim?"

"Yeah, I knew Topher." Chuck tsked. "Guy was a turd, you ask me."

"How so?"

"Used to be the big man on campus when we were in school. Played all the sports. Got whatever girl he wanted. You know the type."

Sam did. Unfortunately, he wasn't that guy.

"By the time we graduated," Chuck continued, "most of us boys had some sort of grudge against Topher. Maybe some girls, too. No one carried more hate for Topher than Brucie, though." Chuck glanced at Sonja. "This is between us, darling. I'd never say that when we're in the courtroom. Professional ethics and all."

"If it gets to the courtroom," Sonja said.

"Right." Chuck pointed at her and chuckled. "You got that right."

"Would others remember the rub between Bruce and Topher?" Sam asked.

The attorney's expression flattened. "I'd imagine so."

"Why'd Bruce have a grudge?" Sam asked.

"Why wouldn't he?" the attorney said. He shifted in his chair, struggling to cross one leg over the other. "Topher was everything Brucie wasn't. Tough, confident, full of reckless energy. Guy was a heck of an athlete. Won state in his junior year."

"Wrestling," Sam said.

Sonja turned slightly in her seat and eyed him.

"I read the paper this morning," Sam said. "The article mentioned it."

Chuck smacked his knee. "Did your homework. I like that." The attorney waggled his finger at Sam but spoke to Sonja. "He's a smart one, like you said." His attention swung back to Sam and continued. "Being a state wrestling champion from our town is a big deal. No matter how long ago. It's almost like being a rock star. Hell, Topher might've won state during his senior year if he hadn't torn his ACL playing football."

"Doesn't explain Bruce's grudge," Sam said.

"All the good stuff Topher had going for him, he was still kind of a louse in the human being department. Bullied Brucie to no end. Other kids, too. Took their lunches when we were little. Then copied their homework in junior high."

"If Topher did it to everyone," Sam said, "why'd Bruce hate him more than the other kids?"

"Grace Carlson." The attorney shrugged. "The love of Bruce's life." Chuck stiffened and smiled apologetically at Sonja. "Back then, I mean. It was a long time ago. You understand."

Her plastic smile returned. "It's okay."

"Still, I should be more careful about running off at the mouth."

"Everyone has a past," she said.

"Don't get me started." The attorney swung his attention back to Sam. "Remember how high school was? All those emotions roiling around inside." His fingers danced over his belly. "The heebie-jeebies. Not knowing what to do about them. What a time."

Sonja eyed Sam. She'd chased him throughout high school. He never got involved with her then. More than occasionally, Sam wondered what life might have looked like if they'd been high school sweethearts.

"Grace and Brucie were inseparable their junior year," Chuck said. "A real cute couple. Everyone thought they'd get married right after graduation." Once more, the attorney looked apologetically at Sonja. "There I go again."

She shook her head, not bothering with the plastic smile this time.

Chuck continued. "Come senior year, Topher snatched Grace away from Brucie. Torn ACL and all. Topher played the hurt puppy, and she ran to him."

"What happened after that?" Sam asked. "They get married and have some kids?"

The attorney rolled his lip down before answering.

"Nope. Topher trotted Grace around the school for a few weeks like a prized show pony. You know, just to make sure everyone saw what he'd done, then he dumped her."

"Nice guy," Sam said.

Chuck shrugged. "Different times, I guess. People weren't as worried about bullying then as they are now."

Sam didn't believe that was true. While growing up, bullying was addressed during every school year. It didn't stop the act from happening. Kids were kids, after all.

"Did they get back together?" Sonja asked.

Chuck cocked his head. "Topher and Grace?"

She frowned. "Bruce and Grace."

"Oh, heck no. Brucie was hurt and embarrassed by what Grace did and she pretty much avoided him for the rest of the school year." The attorney rubbed the crease of his pant leg. It had nearly disappeared as the cloth was pulled almost to a tearing point around his large thigh. "After graduation, Brucie couldn't wait to get away from Havre. Can't say I could blame him."

"Was it bad for you?" Sam asked. "You being friends with Bruce?"

"I had it great." Chuck laughed. "Those were my glory days. Probably hard to tell with what's happened to me since." He waved a hand along his length. "I used to be a hundred percent lean. Starting wide receiver. Did all right with plenty of girls." The attorney winked at Sam. "Know what I'm sayin'? They loved themselves some hunk o' Chuck." He eyed Sonja. "No offense."

She raised her hand in indifference. Her plastic smile remained holstered.

Chuck shifted in his chair and awkwardly recrossed his legs. "Brucie swore he'd never come home after high school graduation."

"But he did," Sam said.

"Oh yeah, sure." Chuck nodded. "It wasn't until years later, though. He went to U Dub and never came home during the summers. Got a part-time job in some Seattle pharmacy until school started back up. Brucie finally returned after he got his degree and started pulling teeth."

"After he made something of himself," Sam said.

Chuck scoffed. "Finally had something to hold over Topher's head."

"His degree?"

"A career and money." Chuck rubbed his thumb and fingers together. "Two things Topher never had."

"What happened with Topher?" Sam asked.

"High school was the pinnacle of his life. No scholarships waited for him after the ACL injury in his senior year. Maybe he could have walked on somewhere, but Topher seemed to lose his motivation to be a star athlete. He grew sullen by graduation."

Sam studied the attorney. He was obviously a smart man. After all, he graduated from law school and passed the bar. However, hearing him say "sullen" seemed like an odd word choice. Perhaps Chuck was smarter than he was letting on.

As if sensing Sam's unease, the attorney chuckled. "I'm just a simple man. What do I know?"

"Tell me what happened between Bruce and Topher."

Chuck cocked his head. "I just did. Grace Carlson."

Sam shook his head. "The night of the murder."

The attorney's eyes slid to Sonja. "You didn't tell him?"

"There wasn't time."

"There was time," Sam said. "She chose not to."

Sonja shifted on the couch to stare at Sam. "That's not

what happened."

"All I know is I traveled almost nineteen hours and spent a night in a hotel to hear about Bruce's childhood. We could have had this conversation over the phone."

"Fine." She faced forward and crossed her arms. She nodded once at the attorney. "Tell him."

***

In what felt like another life, Sam had been a deputy for the Spokane County Sheriff's Office. Working patrol was a job Sam thought he was good at. He responded to crimes in progress as well as investigated those that occurred sometime before. Often during his investigation, a witness or suspect would reveal facts or opinions that shocked Sam.

Keeping a straight face was an act of professionalism. A raised eyebrow or heavy sigh could signal disbelief and cause a witness or potential victim to clam up. An angry glance or a curled lip might tip his hand and cause a suspect to flee or fight.

He'd been away from the department for many years now, though. Remaining professional wasn't a skill required by a man whose life mission was to spend his days in flip-flops.

"Are you kidding me?" Sam said, throwing his hands in the air.

Sonja faced him. "What?"

"Bruce hit Topher?"

She pointed at the attorney. "That's what he said."

"Inside the bar?"

"Yes," Sonja and Chuck said simultaneously.

Sam snapped his fingers, trying to recall the name.

"Grizzly's."

Sonja nodded. "That's the one."

"The Grizzly Den," Chuck whispered.

Sam glared at him.

The attorney shrugged. "It's the legal name."

"There were witnesses," Sam said.

"A lot," Sonja nodded.

"Eight," Chuck corrected.

Sam's head flopped to the back of the couch, and he stared at the ceiling. His ears warmed as he tried to control the anger bubbling in his chest. "Topher made a move on you?"

"Yeah." Sonja glanced at Chuck, then back to Sam. "He was drunk." Her head bobbled. "Grabby, too."

"How so?"

"He put his hand on my hip." She mimicked the action.

"Topher did this in front of Bruce?" Sam lifted his head from the back of the couch and eyed her. "Like *right* in front of him?"

Sonja sighed. "It happened when Bruce went to the restroom. I went to the bar to get us another round. That's when Topher made his move."

"Hold on." Sam waved a hand. "Bruce knew Topher was in the bar?"

"I suppose so."

"Had to," Chuck said.

"And he chose to hang around?" Sam asked.

Sonja shrugged a single shoulder. "He didn't say anything to me about wanting to leave."

"Probably wanted to rub it in Topher's face," Chuck said. "You being so pretty and all."

"A show pony," Sonja muttered, clearly recalling the attorney's earlier comment about Topher and Grace

Carlson.

Chuck donned an apologetic expression. "We won't mention any of this in court."

Sam's lip curled. "So Bruce comes out of the restroom to find his old bully moving in on his new girl."

"That's when he hit him," Sonja said.

Chuck slapped his hands together, causing both Sam and Sonja to jump in their seats. His expression reflected a measure of pride. "Didn't think Brucie had it in him."

"He used his fist?" Sam asked. "Bruce makes a living with his hands. I'd have figured him smarter than that."

"He is."

"Meaning?"

She stared at Sam for a moment, then looked down at her hands. "He used a pool stick."

"A cue?" Sam asked.

She nodded.

"Right across the back," Chuck said. He mimed swinging a baseball bat. It's no doubt the same action a prosecuting attorney would demonstrate in court. "Like Babe Ruth."

"He hit him once?"

Sonja shook her head. "Twice. I think."

"The pool cue didn't break?" Sam asked. "Must not have hit him hard."

"He hit him hard," Sonja insisted.

"Probably don't say that in front of the jury," Chuck said. "Let's assume Brucie choked up on it like a baseball bat, which is why it didn't break. We'll argue differently, of course, to show he couldn't have hit him too hard."

Sam looked at the mounted deer's head. It stared blankly back at him for several seconds. Finally, Sam asked, "Did he fight back?"

"Nah," Chuck said with a satisfied chuckle. "I snapped him from three hundred yards. Sucker never knew what hit him."

"I meant Topher." Sam eyed Sonja. "Bruce hit him twice—"

"Maybe three times," Sonja interrupted.

That stopped Sam and he frowned, waiting for more information.

"I don't know," Sonja said. "Bruce swung the stick like a crazy man."

"Babe Ruth," Chuck mumbled.

"Then Topher hit the floor and cried for help." Sonja shook her head. "That's when the bartender dragged us outside."

"Eight witnesses," Sam said.

She nodded. "It got everyone's attention."

Sam groaned. He rested his head on the back of the couch and covered his face with his hands. "What happened after?" he asked between his fingers.

"We had a fight," Sonja said.

"Another one?" Sam didn't bother to hide the exasperation in his voice.

"Me and Bruce. We argued in the car all the way back to our cabin."

Sam's hands slid off his face and dropped into his lap. "About him fighting?"

"What else?"

He turned and studied Sonja. His gaze lingered on her skintight leggings. "Were you dressed like that?"

"Oh." Chuck grimaced and turned away. "Not good."

Sonja huffed, then scooched farther into the corner of the couch. "You, too?"

"Bruce asked the same?"

Sonja nodded curtly. "He said I caused the fight with how I was dressed."

Chuck shook his head. "Even I know better."

"Bruce was drunk," Sonja said. "What's your excuse?"

"Jet lag," Sam said. "Nineteen hours."

Her expression tightened. "You sound like a broken record."

"Time to stop the music." He stood. "I'll see my way out."

Sonja reached for him, but Sam pulled away.

"Where're you going?" she asked.

"To catch a flight. I'm not getting involved with this."

He opened the door and stepped outside.

Chapter 5

Sam shoved his hands in the pockets of his new jacket and headed north. He had a general idea of how to get to the hotel. It only took a couple of minutes to drive to the attorney's office, so the walk back shouldn't be that long. A cold breeze blew down the street and forced Sam to hunch his shoulders and bury his chin in his coat. Wisps of snow blew across the street. Flakes drifted down from the sky.

He admonished himself as he clomped along a sidewalk covered in ankle-deep crusty snow.

A waste of time. Just threw money down the toilet. Should never have fallen for Sonja's story.

The Range Rover's engine purred as the SUV pulled alongside Sam. Its tires crunched over partially packed snow, and the passenger window rolled down.

"Get in," Sonja called.

Sam ignored her and kept trundling through the snow, his legs churning to break free with each step.

The Range Rover crept alongside him.

"Please, Sam."

He refused to look at Sonja. He wondered if a city ordinance existed that required citizens to shovel their sidewalks. If so, he should call the municipality and complain. Jam these homeowners up. Let someone else feel the same kind of irritation he felt.

Although, it wouldn't take nineteen hours to shovel the sidewalk and a fine wouldn't likely cost more than a thousand dollars. Bruce wasn't going to reimburse him now. Sam stomped into the snow with his next step.

The Range Rover accelerated ahead, then the brake lights flashed. The vehicle briefly slid on the snow before Sonja hopped out. She ran around the vehicle, jumped onto the snow-covered sidewalk, and moved to intercept Sam.

He stopped walking.

"I'm sorry," she said. "Please don't leave."

"You could have told me what happened when we were on the phone."

"I couldn't."

"Sure, you could."

Her shoulders slumped. "If I told you Bruce hit someone with a pool stick and that guy later died, you wouldn't have come."

"You're right."

Sam tried to step around Sonja, but she blocked him. He stepped into the berm lining the road and sank up to his knee. His other leg hovered in the air. Sam had to commit now. Either stuff the second leg into the pile of snow and try to get into the street, or step backward and free himself.

"Here," Sonja said. "Let me help."

She reached for Sam and tugged him back to the sidewalk. The snow there was only ankle deep. Sam swatted at the snow clinging to his jeans. He should have bought gloves while at Walmart.

"After the incident at the bar," Sonja said, "Bruce and I went back to the cabin."

He looked at her. "Aren't you cold?"

"I'm fine. Like I said back there, he'd been drinking."

"You said he was drunk."

She shrugged. "I was mad at you. We'd been drinking. Neither of us was drunk. I promise." Her eyes begged for him to believe her.

"Then you had an argument," Sam said.

"One I wish we could both take back."

Sam straightened. "Showed his true colors, huh?"

Sonja frowned. "Not now, okay? I'm being serious."

He shoved his hands in his pockets. A chill worked its way up his pant legs.

"I yelled at him," Sonja said. "Yelled at him good."

Sam wanted to smile but he didn't. Sonja had yelled at him before. For a moment, Sam felt some empathy for Bruce. Only for a moment, though. Bruce was a dentist, after all. Plus, he was with Sonja, which bothered Sam in an unreasonable way. The charge of murder almost seemed the least offensive thing about Bruce.

Sonja looked toward the gray sky. "I don't know what he was thinking."

"I do. You're out of his league."

Her gaze dropped to Sam. "No, I'm not."

"Keep telling yourself that." The cold worked its way inside Sam's jacket, and he started to shiver.

"He's got a successful practice," Sonja said. "He owns his home. He's got a boat. Two cars." She held up as many manicured fingers. "Two. How many do you own?"

"One."

"Your grandfather's old clunker doesn't count."

"It's not a clunker." Sam shuddered from the cold. "I've got a boat, too."

"Also your grandfather's."

"Doesn't matter." Sam glanced at the SUV. Exhaust drifted from the tail pipe. He imagined it was warm inside. "Want to get in the car?"

"Not yet," Sonja said. "I'm not out of Bruce's league. If anything, he's out of mine."

Sam rolled his eyes. "Please."

"I'm serious. Don't dismiss my feelings."

"Whatever." Sam hopped up and down. "You're made for each other. Can we finish this in the car?"

She eyed him. "Are you still leaving?"

"Yes." Sam's head bobbled. "But not right now."

***

Sam bent forward and held his hands in front of the heater vents. Hot air blew out with full force. They were parked alongside the berm now.

Sonja turned in her seat and watched him.

"It's really not that cold," she said.

"Says you." He eyed her. "How are you not freezing in those leggings?"

"They're fleece lined. You wouldn't believe how warm they are." She straightened her body and rolled the top of the pants down away from her waist. "See?"

All Sam saw was pale naked skin near the pelvic region. One thought blasted through the morning's drama—*she's not wearing panties*.

"Anyway." Sonja let go of the waistband and the leggings snapped into place. "Back to Bruce."

Sam faced the heater vents. "Bruce," he muttered, still thinking about Sonja's lack of underwear.

"Didn't take him long to realize he should never have hit Topher with the stick. No duh, right?"

Sam rubbed his hands together as he studied the glove box. Was he an idiot for chasing the sun? He imagined an alternate version of his life in which he stayed with Sonja a couple of years ago. If he'd done so, Sam and Sonja could be together now. *Would* be together was more likely.

She'd have seen to that.

Sonja faced forward and put her hands on the steering wheel. "After saying he was sorry for how he acted, Bruce decided to go back to The Grizzly Den to apologize to Topher. I told him to wait, but he insisted."

They'd probably have gotten married, Sam thought. He and Sonja that is. If he'd stayed. Initially, they could've lived in the cabin he inherited from his grandparents, but surely, she'd want to move into something larger. Sonja owned a condo on Liberty Lake that was as small as his place.

"I wanted to go with Bruce to the bar, but he wouldn't let me." Sonja's hands tightened around the steering wheel. "Said he embarrassed himself enough. He didn't want me to see him groveling for forgiveness from his high school bully."

Once they got the new house, Sam thought, Sonja would want kids. They'd never get a vacation after that. There'd be children with them always, clamoring for attention. Sam flopped back in his seat. That settled it. He was right to continue chasing the sun.

"Bruce was the one who found Topher," Sonja said.

What he needed to do, Sam realized, was follow his rules more rigidly.

"Are you listening to me?" Sonja asked.

"Yes," Sam said, even though it was only half true. "Was Topher still drinking?"

"No," she said. "He was dead."

Now, she had Sam's full attention. "Bruce found Topher dead at the bar?"

"In the parking lot, yeah."

"Did he call the cops?"

She nodded.

"But there were still witnesses inside who'd seen him crack the pool cue across Topher."

Her head continued to bob. "See the problem?"

Sam thumbed over his shoulder. "Let's get back to the attorney before he heads to court."

***

Charles Palmer stepped out of the small gray building as Sam and Sonja pulled alongside the curb. He wore a red parka over his suit. Its hood dangled from his shoulders. Chuck noticed the two, held a single finger in the air, then stepped back into the building.

The Range Rover's heater continued to blast hot air.

"Done being mad?" Sonja asked.

Sam eyed her. "It's been two minutes."

Her eyes flicked to the front of the building. "That's enough time to get over it."

"Are you serious?"

Sonja's gaze slid back to him. "What?"

She'd been angry with him plenty over the years for a variety of real and perceived slights. Sonja never got over anything quickly. Sam happily applied sweeping generalizations to people like dentists, attorneys, and bikini baristas. However, he usually refrained from doing so with people because of their color, national origin, or religion. Yet the old joke about crazy redheads had a ring of truth whenever it came to Sonja. He might not have believed it if he'd spent any time with a ginger blessed with a Stoic's calm. He never had.

Sam shook his head, then turned to look at the gray building. "I'm over it," he muttered.

"Told you it was enough time."

Chuck exited the building again with a white envelope in his hand. He locked the door before trotting out to the curb. Chuck's winter boots altered his gait, making him look like an astronaut jumping awkwardly across the moon's surface.

Sam rolled down his window.

"This is for you," Chuck said, extending the envelope. "It's the initial report from the police department. There's also an authorization letter that says you're in my employ. Anyone gives you grief about asking questions, show 'em that."

Sam took the envelope. "Will the authorization letter stand up?"

"Probably not," Chuck said. "You're not licensed, not a resident, and not family. So don't use it as an anvil. Smile a lot and be nice. Being courteous goes a long way in these parts."

Playing the heavy was never Sam's style. Even when he wore a deputy's badge, he chose to talk arrestees into handcuffs rather than fighting with them. His reasoning had two parts. First, the department scrutinized any use of force. Second, Sam didn't like to fight. Getting hit hurt— a lot.

"Don't you have a guy for investigations?" Sam asked.

"I do." Chuck nodded. "A retired cop who does it as a side gig, but he's in Hawaii with his wife right now."

"Hawaii?"

"Waikiki for two weeks. Crazy he's over there and you're here, huh?" Chuck patted the door. "Hate to run, but I gotta get to court."

Without waiting for a goodbye, the attorney spun and clomped away toward an older Ford Bronco.

Sam slowly turned to Sonja. "His normal investigator

is in Hawaii."

"I know, right? What are the odds?" She dropped the transmission into gear, and the Range Rover pulled away from the curb.

He sulked for several blocks. Finally, he looked at Sonja. "Where're we going?"

"To see Bruce."

Chapter 6

The Hill County Detention Center sat just west of Havre, south of US Route 2. The single-story green building had a military feel to it, made only more prominent by the communications tower looming over it.

Next door, a small warehouse housed the Coca-Cola Bottling Company.

Once Sonja parked, Sam climbed out of the SUV.

A thumping sound drew his attention to a helicopter hovering over a large brick building to the south.

Sonja walked around the car to stand with Sam.

"What's back there?" Sam asked.

"Border patrol."

Havre sat just south of the Canadian border. The helicopter slowly descended until it landed. Sam turned to say something to Sonja, but she had already walked off toward the building.

He hurried to catch up.

****

Sam waited alone in a small room. It was big enough for a steel table and two plastic chairs. The concrete walls were painted gray, an unnecessary color as far as Sam was concerned. A window faced the hallway.

Overhead, a fluorescent light buzzed and flickered. The room smelled funny, almost like mildew but not quite. Sam glanced about the small confines but didn't find any water leakage. Perhaps the funk was latent body odor that settled into the crevices of the concrete wall.

He'd been in the room several minutes now. The letter from Charles Palmer did the trick. Sam still had to remove everything from his pockets, walk through a metal detector, and get patted down by an overly eager guard. It was a jail, after all. Attorneys or their agents surely had attempted to smuggle contraband inside before.

Sam tapped his fingers on the table and mumbled the words to one of his favorite songs, "Round and Round." It was an old Ratt song and something most in his generation would never know. Sam grew up with his father's record collection. Since his parents died in a collision shortly after his birth, it was one of the few ways Sam could connect with his dad. He had listened to all his father's albums so many times that he knew the words to every song.

The door opened and interrupted his muted performance.

Bruce Bloom stepped into the room. He wore an orange jumpsuit over a white T-shirt. He was a thinner man, but not athletic as his potbelly revealed. A personal trainer Sam once dated called the body type "skinny fat." Bruce's hair was mussed, his eyes were red, and his face puffy.

The deputy behind him said, "Ten minutes," and closed the door. The overhead light flickered several times.

Bruce forced a smile and revealed unnaturally white teeth. "Sonja said you were on the way."

Sam motioned toward the empty seat.

"Good flight?" Bruce asked as he sat.

"It was fine."

"Honolulu was it?"

Sam nodded.

"You go there a lot?"

"We should probably talk about your problem," Sam said. "We only have ten minutes."

Bruce grabbed the table with both hands, hooking his thumbs over its top. "Just looking to establish something between us."

"There's already something between us."

"Right," Bruce said. "Sonja."

"I'm here for her." Sam leaned forward and rested his arms along the table's length. "Now, how about you tell me what happened?"

Bruce licked his upper lip, then looked down. "How much do you know?"

"Topher made a move on Sonja, and you hit him with a pool cue. The bartender broke up the fight and threw you out. You took Sonja back to your cabin, then decided you should apologize. That's when you found Topher dead in the parking lot."

"That's pretty much it."

"There's a big hole in the story."

"What's that?"

Sam bent slightly to get Bruce's attention. "Where was Topher in the parking lot, and how did anyone else not find him?"

"He was off to the side."

"Near any cars?"

Bruce nodded. "Some."

"Any lights?"

"Not really."

"What were you doing when you found Topher?"

"The truth?"

"No, I want you to lie to me."

Bruce's face paled. "It's a stupid thing to say."

"Especially now."

"Right." Bruce leaned back in his chair and his thumbs slipped off the edge of the table. "I had to pee."

"Why not do it inside?" Sam crossed his arms. "No offense, Doc, but you seem the type of guy who likes indoor plumbing."

"No offense taken." Bruce waved a hand before continuing. "I should have gone before I left our cabin, but I was hellbent on talking with Topher. When I got there, I felt I was going to burst. If I went into the bar, I might run into him right away and not have a chance to go. I didn't want to apologize with a full bladder."

"Wouldn't want a full bladder if Topher took a swing at you, either."

"I honestly wasn't even thinking that way."

"Honestly," Sam said.

Bruce stared at him for a moment, likely replaying their conversation in his head. He winced. "Gotta stop saying stuff like that."

"So you go into a dark corner of the lot and found Topher?"

"Actually, I relieved myself first, then found him."

"You peed at a crime scene?"

Bruce cringed. "That's the same question the policewoman asked me."

"It's not normal," Sam said.

The buzzing of the fluorescent light increased as its flickering worsened.

"Can I ask you something?" Bruce leaned forward. "What's really with you and Sonja?"

"There's nothing with us."

The dentist waved a dismissive hand. "Not now. Back before. She said you were best friends in high school."

That wasn't true. Sonja had pursued him in high school,

but he never relented until they were older. That's when their on-and-off-again romance started. However, Sam wasn't going to say that now. He had no trouble supporting Sonja's story. Besides, the truth about their troubled relationship wouldn't help Bruce now. It'd only make his stay in jail worse.

"What about it?" Sam asked.

"She mentions you a lot."

"I don't know what to say about that."

Bruce's lips twisted. "It's just…" His thought trailed off.

"You're planning to propose."

"She told you?"

Sam nodded. "We should stay focused on Topher."

"This is important, Sam. I love her. I want to marry her." Fear laced his words.

"You don't want another Grace Carlson moment."

Bruce stiffened. "How'd you—?" His face tightened. "Chuck."

"He had to tell me," Sam said. "I need to know everything. You went after Topher with a pool cue. That's an extreme reaction for a guy hitting on your girlfriend." Sam cocked his head. "Unless there was already history of such behavior."

Bruce looked at the floor.

"It's exactly what a prosecuting attorney is going to find. They will, too. I promise." Sam waggled his hand. "When they find that connection, it's one more bullet in their chamber."

Bruce hugged himself. "Grace was my high school girlfriend." Wistfulness filled his words.

"The love of your life."

"Chuck said that, too?"

"He did." Sam nodded. "In front of Sonja."

"Oh, God." Bruce scoffed. "She probably hates me now."

"It was high school," Sam said. "She understands."

"You think?" Bruce's brow furrowed. "Is that what happened between you and Sonja? Were you two high school sweethearts?"

"No," Sam said. "We weren't high school sweethearts."

Outside, the deputy stepped into view. He tapped on the window and held up five fingers.

Sam nodded, then turned his attention back to Bruce. "When's the last time you talked with Grace?"

Bruce's lips squeezed together.

"You talked with her recently?" Sam asked.

"Not in real life."

"What's that mean?"

"She friended me on Facebook."

Sam wasn't on any kind of social media. He'd always thought it seemed like an engine for envy. Folks posting only the best photos and stories of their lives, which forced others to post their best pictures, so they didn't look less successful than their friends. The cycle spun round and round.

He never considered it might be a way for old lovers to connect.

"Does Sonja know about you reconnecting with Grace?" Sam asked.

"No," Bruce said. His shoulders hunched, and he glanced around as if he was afraid someone might eavesdrop on their conversation. "I wasn't trying to do anything. I just wanted to see how she was. See what she looked like now. You know."

"You connected with an old girlfriend." Sam's smile

was crueler than necessary. "Sonja won't take that well."

Bruce's expression melted into one of panic. "Please don't tell her."

The guy was accused of murder, an act he most likely didn't commit, and he was worried about Sonja discovering a Facebook connection.

Sam smirked.

"I swear," Bruce said, "I didn't do anything wrong." He clasped his hands. "You've got to believe me."

Sam held up a hand. They were getting off track. As much as he loved getting some dirt on Bruce the tooth jockey, that wasn't why he'd flown to Montana.

"Back to your arrest," Sam said. "Are the cops assuming you're involved with the murder because of the fight in the bar?"

"Mostly."

"What's that mean?"

Bruce sighed. "I picked up the rock."

"What rock?"

"The rock that someone hit Topher with."

Sam closed his eyes and lifted both hands now. "Wait. Hold up." A moment passed as he considered the ramifications of what Bruce just said. He opened his eyes. "Someone bashed in Topher's head with a rock and left him lying in the snow."

"That's right." Bruce nodded.

"When you found him, the first thing you did was pick up the rock?"

"No, the first thing I did was to see if he was breathing."

"Was he?"

"No."

"Why'd you pick up the rock?"

The color drained from Bruce's face. "I don't know."

"Were you wearing gloves?"

"No," he whispered.

The guard banged on the door a moment before it swung open. "Wrap it up."

Bruce leaned in and lowered his voice. His words ran together as he whispered, "Don't let Sonja meet Grace."

Sam cocked his head. "You're charged with murder."

"This is important."

"Yeah, it is," Sam said, fully convinced the two men weren't seeing the gravity of the situation in quite the same way.

"Up," the jailer said. He hooked a hand into one of Bruce's armpits and tugged him to his feet. "Hands behind your back."

Bruce did as the guard ordered. He stared at Sam, silently pleading. The jailer snapped handcuffs around Bruce's wrists, then pulled him away from the table.

The two walked out of the room leaving Sam alone with the flickering fluorescent light.

***

Sonja waited in the lobby. She bowed her head over her phone, her thumb hurriedly swiping over its display. Sam's winter coat lay in the chair next to her. When he approached, she lifted her head.

"How'd he look?" Sonja asked.

"About normal."

"That's not funny." She stood and tucked her phone into a side pocket of her leggings. "What'd he say?"

"What you'd expect." Sam picked up his coat and slipped his arms into it. "He didn't do it. He's innocent. Please help." Sam shrugged the garment over his shoulders. "The same thing every guy in jail says."

"He is innocent," Sonja said. She poked Sam in the chest. "He didn't do it, and he needs your help. Me, too. I need your help."

"I know."

"What part do you know?"

"Why do you think I'm here?" Sam asked. "It's not for the weather."

"You were about to leave."

"That was before." He zipped up his coat.

Sonja cocked her head. "Going outside?"

"Not waiting in here while you lovebirds have a conjugal visit."

"I'm seeing him the same as you did."

"Whatever." He held out his hand. "I'm gonna wait in the car."

Sonja handed him the keys. "Don't leave me."

"What kind of guy do you take me for?"

"I know exactly what kind of guy you are." She scowled before turning. She paused a moment before looking back, her expression softening. "Thank you for believing him. It means a lot."

Sam nodded but remained quiet.

Sonja headed toward the jail's service window.

***

Sam opened the envelope Charles Palmer had given him. Inside were the initial police report and an affidavit of arrest. That was it.

Perhaps that's all that had been filed so far. It'd only been three days since Topher's murder. The responding officer—Riley Malone—developed enough probable cause to detain and arrest Bruce for the crime. If the Havre Police Department was anything like the Spokane County Sheriff's Office, a homicide detective was assigned the case and responsible for developing further evidence. However, the Major Crimes investigator was not listed. Sam imagined his or her reports would remain inaccessible until the investigation was complete.

Sam looked up and glanced around. The sun peeked through a pack of thick, gray clouds. Its rays reflected off the snow covering almost everything. Sam hadn't thought to bring his sunglasses on this trip.

Hot air blasted through the vents as the engine idled. The stereo remained silent. He had scanned it when he first got in. Sam hated country stations and found Christian rock too sugary for his liking. An oldies station held promise, but its disc jockey seemed bent on playing mostly sixties tunes. Sam chose quiet over those options.

The first two pages of the report listed the particulars: where the incident occurred and who the suspect and victim were. Eight witnesses were identified. None of the names meant anything to Sam.

He flipped to the third page and began reading Officer Riley Malone's narrative. Sam immediately assumed Riley was a woman because of the flowery signature. Perhaps he shouldn't assume. Men could sign their names with large looping letters, too. He didn't, and he didn't know any guys who did, but it was a new world. Sam shrugged. He'd continue with the assumption Riley was a woman.

Prior to her arrival, the listed witnesses had been drinking at The Grizzly Den. An altercation occurred between Bruce Bloom and Topher Anderson earlier in the night. The bystanders' stories were similar.

Bruce approached Topher from behind and hit him with a pool cue. When Topher fell to the floor, Bruce swung the stick again. It was the same tale the attorney and Sonja had relayed earlier.

The only differences in the bystanders' accounts were how many times Bruce clubbed Topher after the local man was on the ground. Six witnesses said Bruce hit Topher once more. One said Bruce hit the downed man twice. The last witness claimed Bruce hit him three times, then kicked him twice for good measure.

All the witnesses were very clear the attack appeared unprovoked while Topher was talking with an unidentified woman. The bartender/owner claimed the woman had arrived with Bruce and left after the altercation. No one seemed to know the name of the woman. She was described as tall and thin with short, red hair. Bruce Bloom denied being at the bar with anyone.

Sam stopped reading the narrative and returned to the page of witnesses. He quickly scanned the document. Sonja wasn't listed anywhere.

How could that happen? Sam wondered. He wouldn't have to speculate long since Sonja would soon return to the car. He'd ask her then.

Sam flipped back to the narrative and continued reading. Officer Malone responded shortly after midnight to The Grizzly Den on a report of a dead man. She found Bruce Bloom standing near the body. A bloody rock lay near Topher's still form and blood was on Bruce's left hand. Bruce confirmed he'd held the rock but did so out of reflex. He denied killing Topher.

Officer Malone checked the victim for signs of life and discovered him cold and unresponsive. A large contusion was on the right side of Topher Anderson's head.

After her initial investigation, Riley detained the out-of-state dentist and subsequently arrested him for Deliberate Homicide. She secured the scene until the Montana Department of Criminal Investigations arrived and took control.

Movement caught Sam's eye, and he looked up. Sonja crossed the parking lot.

He watched her with the appreciation of a former lover. Even though she wore a heavy black parka, he remembered every curve underneath. The black leggings didn't leave much for Sam's imagination, but he didn't need the help. He knew every inch of Sonja.

They made eye contact through the windshield, and she smiled. Her expression was devoid of warmth. It was an automatic response. Something she did to show her bravery.

She opened the car door and dropped into the driver's seat. "It's killing me to see him that way."

"I know what you mean."

"Are you making a joke?"

"I'm talking about you," he said.

Her eyes softened. "Oh."

Sam held up the report. "Did the police interview you?"

She suddenly looked guilty. "You think I'm in trouble?"

"How'd you find out about Bruce's arrest?"

"When he called me from jail."

"Just so you're aware, there's no expectation of privacy in a jail. They can record the calls."

Sonja said, "That doesn't seem legal."

Sam waved the letter. "No one has tried to contact you yet?"

"I've had some calls from a blocked number the past

couple of days."

The phone numbers from the Spokane County Sheriff's Office were blocked when Sam worked for them. So was the Spokane Police Department's. "That was probably the cops," he said.

"I didn't know."

Sam flipped back to the first page of the report. Bruce's address was listed in Liberty Lake, Washington. "They didn't note where he's staying in Havre." Sam looked up. "You think he was trying to keep you out of it?"

"Probably."

"He had to give them an address where he was staying, but nothing's in the report."

"Maybe he gave them his parents' address," Sonja suggested. "We hadn't seen them yet. I'm not sure if Bruce told them where we were staying."

Sam gnawed on his lower lip as he thought.

"What's wrong?" she asked.

"You're not in trouble since you technically didn't do anything wrong. However, a detective is going to want to talk with you. You're listed as 'unidentified woman' in the report."

"An uncredited role," Sonja said. "I think I'm okay with that this time."

"You want to read the police report?"

She stared at the papers in Sam's hand. "I don't think I could bear to do it."

"It's not as bad as you think."

"It's not?" Sonja jerked her head toward the jail. "Then why is Bruce in there?"

"The details aren't as bad," Sam said. "That's what I meant."

Sonja inhaled deeply. "You've read it. I trust you."

Sam folded the papers. "All right, then."

She dropped the transmission into Drive. "Where to?"

"The police department."

Her mouth dropped open. "I don't want to talk with the cops. Not now while I'm so emotional. I'm afraid I'll say something stupid and get Bruce in more trouble."

"You're going to have to talk with them sooner or later."

"I choose later."

"Take Chuck with you. He'll run interference with them."

"Later," she said.

Sam sighed. "Fine. You'll stay in the car, and I'll go in."

Chapter 7

Havre's City Hall Complex sat at the corner of Fourth Street and Fifth Avenue. Sonja used the car's GPS to guide them to the location. She dropped Sam off a couple of blocks east of the center.

An open-air walkway connected two buildings made of yellowish brick. The front building contained the police and fire departments. The rear structure held the administration offices related to running a city government.

The sidewalks were freshly shoveled, and a deicer had been applied.

Entries to both the police department and the city administration were in the open-air walkway. Sam put his hand on the south door's handle.

A receptionist with short, graying hair sat behind a desk. She looked up from her computer when Sam entered. A nameplate at the edge of the desk read *Althea*. A smile spread across the receptionist's lips.

The experience was distinctly different than visiting Spokane's Public Safety Building where security officers watched the entry. Visitors to the building proceeded through metal detectors. Officers and police administrators hid behind locked doors. Only with pre-approved access could a visitor enter the holy sanctum of Spokane law enforcement. Sam imagined visiting Spokane's Public Safety Building was much like any other large city— intimidating.

On the other hand, Havre's police department had a certain charm to it. Behind the receptionist's desk were four cubicles. Only the tops of the occupants' heads were visible.

Glass-walled offices lined the outer ring of the large room. No one sitting behind glass wore a uniform. In fact, Sam didn't notice a single person in police attire.

It was mostly quiet in the offices of the Havre department. A heating system whirred as hot air pumped into the room. A phone rang somewhere but was quickly answered.

"Help you with something?" Althea asked.

Sam said, "I'd like to speak with Officer Malone."

Althea's smile dampened but didn't fully leave her face. Her eyes took Sam in fully now. "Officer Malone is off duty. Can I have someone else help you?"

"I'm working on Bruce Bloom's defense," Sam said. "I need to talk with Officer Malone about her report."

The receptionist straightened. "Bloom?"

"Yes, ma'am," Sam said. "He was charged with murder."

"I know." The remnants of the smile slipped from the receptionist's face as she reached for the phone.

Before she could dial anyone, a tall man exited a corner office. "I heard, Thea."

The man appeared to be in his early fifties. He had the broad shoulders of a former athlete and the bulging stomach of a man who sat behind a desk for too many years. He wore blue jeans and a plaid shirt. Scuffed cowboy boots were tucked underneath his pant legs. A badge was clipped to his belt next to the holstered gun on his hip. "Working with Chuck Palmer?" the man asked.

"That's right," Sam said.

"Got proof, sunshine?"

Sam unzipped his puffy coat and reached into the inner pocket.

The tall man turned his body, and his right hand hovered over the butt of his gun.

Sam slowly pulled out the attorney's letter and extended it. "Can I ask who you are?"

"You can ask." The tall man snatched the document from Sam's fingers.

While the new arrival read the letter, Sam's attention drifted to the nearest wall. A placard announced *Our Officers*. Underneath the heading were eighteen oval pictures of men and women in uniform. Sam knew the number because he took the time to count them.

The man reading the attorney's letter had the top picture. Below that were three other photographs, likely supervisors of some sort. Two rows of seven revealed how many line-level cops were in Havre.

Names didn't identify who were in the pictures but there were only three women on the department. Before Sam could study the oval photographs, the tall man said, "Sam Strait?"

He turned his attention to the man he believed was Havre's Chief of Police.

"That's right," Sam said.

"You're not from around here." It wasn't a question.

"I'm not."

"The tan gives you away." The chief's lip curled. "Which means you're not a licensed investigator."

"That's correct."

"What kind of malarky is Chuck pulling?" The chief handed back the letter. "He's got a normal guy for this type of thing. Retired cop from Missoula."

"I used to be a deputy," Sam said reflexively.

"Where was that?"

"Spokane County."

"Friend of the suspect?"

"Not really."

The chief crossed his arms and rested them on his belly. "What do you want Malone for?"

"To ask some questions. What she saw, how people acted when questioned, that sort of thing."

"If I say no?"

Sam shrugged. "I'll interview the witnesses. Start checking into Topher's life."

"You're likely to wear out your shoe leather and come up with nothing."

"Is there a detective assigned the case?"

"There is." The chief nodded. "Agent Dale Hathaway."

"FBI?"

"DCI. Division of Criminal Investigation." The chief motioned toward the window. "They're based out of Great Falls. DCI handles murder investigations in these parts."

"Is Hathaway around?"

"Great Falls, like I said."

"How far is that?"

"What do I look like? Google Maps?"

Sam forced a smile. "Should I hope for a call from Officer Malone?"

The chief jerked his head toward the receptionist. "Leave your name and number with Thea. I'll have Malone call you when she comes in for her shift. I'm doing this because Chuck and I are in the same gun club. Otherwise, you'd get nothing."

"I appreciate the help," Sam said. He relayed his information to the receptionist.

As Sam turned to leave, the chief said, "Hold on."

"Yeah?"

"Your buddy was supposedly with a woman the night he was arrested. We're having trouble locating her. Know where she is?"

"I'll ask Bruce about her and get back to you."

The chief smirked. "Of course you will."

***

"What'd you learn?" Sonja asked after Sam climbed into the SUV.

"You need to talk with the cops."

"I will."

"The chief of police asked about you," Sam said.

"Did he know my name?"

"No, but he'll figure it out soon enough. Surely after the investigators talk with Bruce's parents."

She glanced at him from behind the wheel. "Think they'll follow you?"

"I don't think they've got the manpower."

They were headed toward The Grizzly Den which, according to the GPS system, was located in a northern neighborhood just across the train tracks.

Sonja weaved her way through Havre's side streets. The GPS flashed with each course change she made, desperately trying to keep up with her erratic turns.

"How do you know they don't have the manpower?" Sonja asked.

"There's a roster board in the lobby," Sam said. "Shows eighteen commissioned personnel all the way up to the chief. If I had to guess, they're running three shifts—day, swing, and graveyard. Figure twelve to fourteen officers are spread over those times. Excluding the chief, that leaves three to five positions open for leadership—sergeants, lieutenants, and whatnot."

Sonja stopped zigzagging through the side streets and the GPS course corrected itself. They were only a couple of minutes away from the bar.

"What about detectives?" she asked. "Who's investigating the murder?"

"Montana State Division of Criminal Investigation."

"DCI?" She glanced at him. "Like the British shows?"

Sam didn't know what she was talking about, so he shrugged.

"They're really good in those programs," Sonja said. "Do you think they'll straighten this out without our involvement?"

"We can stop right now, and I'll head home."

She slowed the Range Rover and looked at him. "That's not what I asked."

"There are a lot of good people in law enforcement, but it only takes one crooked or lazy cop to put an innocent man away."

"Look who I'm asking." She stepped on the accelerator. "I should have expected that."

She should have. Sam's career was derailed by a dirty sergeant. It might have been avoided had some in the department's upper echelon asked the right questions sooner. As it was, luck played a large part in Sam's exoneration. The lawsuit and resulting payout weren't good fortune, though. It was simple restitution for the pain and mental anguish Sam suffered during that time. As a result, he harbored some trust issues where law enforcement was concerned.

The Grizzly Den hunkered at the edge of a mixed-use

neighborhood on the corner of Twelfth Avenue and Third Street. Wood paneling covered the small, single-story building. Large black letters announced the bar's name.

A car repair business sat across the street sandwiched between two houses. To the west was a small mobile home park. Two trailers huddled together to the east, on the other side of the bar, looking like wayward children.

No cars occupied the parking lot, but Sonja entered it anyway.

"Probably too early," she said.

"Don't be so sure." He motioned toward a lit Open sign. "Park and let's go in."

Sonja nudged the Range Rover into a stall and turned it off. Before leaving the car, Sam pulled the police report from his inner pocket and reviewed it. When he found the name he wanted, he folded the document and got out.

"Do you know where Topher was killed?" Sonja asked.

"It was somewhere dark and away from the bar's entrance."

There was a single overhead light near the road. Sam tried to imagine the parking lot at night. Some illumination would come from the bar's sign and the windows.

At the eastern edge of the parking lot was a group of Evergreen trees. Sam wandered over to the area. If the parking lot was full, this section of the lot might have been difficult to see. Also, the single overhead light wouldn't brighten this portion of the property.

"How full is the moon right now?" Sam asked.

Sonja shrugged. "I don't know."

Sam couldn't recall the fullness of the moon either. He'd need to look it up online later.

He turned and headed for the bar. Sonja fell in step with him. As he neared the building, Sam searched for exterior cameras. He didn't notice any.

Sam held the door for Sonja, and they entered the business.

Because of the establishment's name, Sam expected mounted animals on the walls, much like Charles Palmer's office. Perhaps a wilderness painting or two. Definitely good ol' boy country music pumping out of some speakers. Maybe even a Confederate flag.

There was none of that, however. He felt silly for his preconceived notions.

Instead, there was maroon and silver paraphernalia everywhere. The University of Montana was the state's biggest school and a perennial powerhouse in the Big Sky Conference. The grizzly was their mascot. Several helmets—their design indicating their vintage—lined an upper shelf. Signed jerseys were enshrined in glass cases. Large photos of passes, catches, and tackles adorned the various walls.

A cluster of gaming machines took up a corner of the bar behind two billiards tables. The Who's "Won't Get Fooled Again" played through a neon jukebox.

Sam searched the upper corners of the bar. There were no cameras inside, either.

A man in his late fifties stepped out of a backroom, wiping his hands on a small towel as he walked. He wore a U of M jersey, blue jeans, and snow boots. "Howdy, folks," he said. "Sit anywhere."

"We're looking for Darrol Hartill," Sam said. He was listed as The Grizzly Den's bartender/owner in the police report.

The man stiffened. "You bill collectors?"

"Private investigator," Sam said. He didn't see the harm in embellishing the truth.

"My ex-wife send you?"

"Mr. Hartill?" Sam asked.

"I suppose so." Darrol Hartill frowned and put his hands on his hips. "Although everyone calls me Darry. What's this about?" His gaze bounced to Sonja. "Wait. I know you."

"A few nights ago," Sam said, "there was an altercation in your bar."

"Yeah," Darry said, wagging his finger at Sonja. "Started because of you, didn't it?" His attention whipped back to Sam. "Hey, I already spoke to some detective about this. Why are you sticking your nose into it?"

"I work for Bruce Bloom's attorney." Sam wished he'd found a more acceptable way to describe their arrangement since it violated the fifth rule, the one regarding associating with seedy types, like lawyers. However, he didn't have time to find one. "We're trying to prove Mr. Bloom's innocence."

Darry snorted. "You're joking, right? I saw that fella swing a pool stick like a Louisville Slugger. Knocked Topher right to the ground." He pointed to a spot in front of the bar. "Over there."

"Did you see any conversation between the two men before that?"

"Topher and that Bloom fella?" The bartender shook his head. "Nope. All I saw was Topher trying to make time with the lady here. Next thing I know, my man's on the floor and I'm kicking your client out." He thumbed at Sonja. "Her, too."

"What happened with Topher after?" Sam asked.

Darry wiped his hands on the towel. "What do you mean after?"

Sam didn't think it was that hard of a question.

The bartender must have realized it because he shrugged and continued. "Topher dusted himself off, climbed back on his barstool, and ordered himself another beer."

"Anybody with him?"

Darry shook his head. "He's usually alone. Lots of people came up to commiserate with him, though."

"Topher's a regular?"

"Was long before I took over the bar from my father. More than five years now."

"How often is he in?"

"Almost every day. Comes in, has a few, heads home. Like clockwork."

"He ever fight with anyone else?"

"Listen here," Darry said, "I'm gonna let you in on a secret since that tan of yours makes it obvious you ain't a local. We don't mind fights in this part of the country, but we do it fair. Square up on a guy, announce your intentions, that kind of thing. Smacking a man across the back without warning is dirty pool."

"No pun intended."

The bartender cocked his head. "How's that?"

Sam waved away the comment. "The others here that night. Anyone else have a problem with Topher?"

"I don't know." Darry crossed his arms and his gaze drifted toward the ceiling as he thought.

The song ended on the radio and a new one started. It was a seventies song; the one about "All the Young Dudes."

Darry continued. "Not everyone dug Topher. Know what I'm sayin'? The ladies loved him for sure, but he rubbed almost every guy wrong at one time or another."

"Even you?"

The bartender nodded. "Even me." He held up a hand to stop Sam from speaking. "Before you ask, it's because he was behind on his bar tab. Guy got that way every few months. As long as I've known him, he's never been smart with his cash. I cut him off now and then until he brings his account current."

"Is he current?" Sam asked.

"Luckily, yeah. He squared his tab the night he was killed."

"How much was he behind?"

"Hundred bucks. He didn't pay for the drinks he had before he was murdered, but not much I can do about that." Darry motioned toward the kitchen. "How many more questions? I gotta get ready for the lunch rush."

Sam glanced at Sonja who shook her head.

"Thanks for your help," he said.

"Do me a favor." Darry stuffed the towel into his back pocket. "Don't come back unless you're gonna do some drinking. I don't need you botherin' the customers."

***

"This is all you do?" Sonja asked as the Range Rover pulled away from the curb. "Ask questions."

"Mostly."

Sam turned up the car's heater. Cool air blasted through the vents.

"Gotta let it warm up," she said, snapping it off. "Won't be long."

"Warm up," he grumbled and shoved his hands in his coat pockets.

The SUV weaved its way through the neighborhood.

"What'd you think?" she asked.

"About?"

"The bartender."

Sam shrugged, his hands still in his pockets. "Seemed truthful."

"What could he have lied about?"

"People lie about everything."

"I guess."

They fell quiet for a moment until they reached the intersection at US 2. A semi zoomed by. A grocery chain logo was splashed across the trailer's side.

Sonja eyed him. "You ever lie to me?"

He probably had. Nothing serious, though. A white lie, perhaps. Something likely to avoid hurting her feelings. He certainly omitted comments in their conversations so as not to upset her. Sonja hated that he left Spokane County during the winters. She certainly didn't need to know about his relationships while he was away.

"Well?" Sonja asked, not letting him avoid the question about lying.

"No, never," he said. He had no intention of admitting that lie.

Sonja looked left and right but didn't enter traffic. "Where to next?"

Sam pulled his hands free of his pockets and removed the police report. "We've got eight witnesses. A couple of them have the same last name, so probably husbands and wives."

"We're not too far from Bruce's parents," Sonja said.

"Are we far from anyone here?"

"Probably not. Why don't we run over there so you can meet them?"

"What do you think that's going to get us?"

"I need you to do it for me."

He cocked his head. "It's not the best use of our time."

"Their son is in jail. I need to show them we're trying to get him out."

"I see. You need to let them know I'm no threat to their son's marriage plans."

"Something like that."

She stepped on the accelerator and the car lurched onto the highway. They sped westbound.

***

Russell and Dorothy Bloom lived off First Street across from Eagles Park. A sign stood at the southwest corner of the small park. A thick layer of snow covered what Sam assumed was grass. Besides a merry-go-round and a restroom, there didn't appear to be any other amenities.

Sonja turned off the street and took a winding driveway up to a modern two-story home. It was painted tan with brown accents. A purple University of Washington Huskies flag hung from the side of the house and fluttered gently in the breeze. Smoke wafted from a chimney.

A gray-haired woman stood at the second-floor window, watching their arrival.

"Russell and Dorothy are nice people," Sonja said, as she slipped the transmission into Park. She reached for the ignition button but stopped when Sam spoke.

"You've met them before?"

"A few times." She pulled her hand back. "Why?"

Sam unbuckled his seatbelt and studied Sonja. "You're gonna go through with this, aren't you?"

"Meeting the parents?" She bent slightly so she could better see the Bloom house through the windshield. "Why not?"

"I mean you're gonna marry Bruce."

"You had your chance," Sonja said.

"I don't want to get married."

"So you've told me." Tears welled in her eyes. "Sam Strait, the perpetual bachelor."

He leaned his back against the passenger door. "Why are you making this about me?"

"This isn't about you." She flicked her hand at him. "It's about me and Bruce."

Sam glanced at the Bloom house. A gray-haired man now stood with the woman at the window. They watched the Range Rover with interest.

"We should go in," Sam said.

Unfortunately, Sonja wasn't ready to end the conversation. "Why do you care?"

"Because they're watching us."

"I mean if I marry Bruce," she said, wiping the tears from her eyes. "Why do you care? You're the one who left. You're the one who always leaves."

"It isn't easy to leave."

"You make it look that way." Sonja bent slightly and waved up at the older couple. They returned the gesture.

"It takes courage," Sam said. "A lot of courage if you must know."

"Whatever. Now I'm crying. Great."

"I'm serious," Sam said gently. "Had I stayed through the winter, I'd have given up my dreams."

"People give up their dreams all the time." Sonja bowed her head. "That's life. It's part of being an adult."

"You think people are happy when they give up their dreams?"

Sonja nodded. "When they do it for someone else, yeah. It's called love."

"Being unhappy is love?"

She inhaled deeply and held the breath. Tears again welled in her eyes, and she settled back in her seat. Sonja glanced at the Blooms who remained standing in the window. She waved at them, and they returned the gesture.

"Sonja," Sam said.

She exhaled when she turned to him. Sadness masked her face. "I wasn't enough for you, Sam, but I'm more than enough for Bruce."

He didn't like the words. They sounded defeatist, like a woman resigned to a future she wasn't ready to embrace. However, perhaps he filtered those words, sifting any tone of happiness out of them, so it would sound as if she was lost without him.

If he was honest with himself, Sam didn't want to know Sonja could be happy with Bruce Bloom, Captain Toothbrush, which was an idiotic way to feel. Sam hadn't worried about Sonja the past few months while enjoying the sun in Hawaii. He certainly never considered her feelings while in bed with Nina. Now that he was near Sonja, Sam wanted her to feel regret over them not being together.

Perhaps he was a narcissist. He didn't like that idea and turned away.

The Blooms continued to watch them from the second floor, concern clearly etched on their faces. It appeared they were talking to each other.

Sonja stopped the SUV's engine. "You are who you are." She forced a smile. "I have to accept you for who you are." She nodded once before adding, "Thank you for coming to my rescue."

Before Sam could think of anything to say, Sonja opened the driver's door and slid out of the vehicle.

Chapter 8

Russell Bloom met them at the door. He was in his early seventies with thinning brown hair, large round glasses, and an acceptable paunch for a man of his age. Russell wore faded blue jeans, a purple Huskies sweatshirt, and white socks. He smiled broadly as he hugged Sonja, taking care not to step over the transom and into the snow.

"Everything okay?" he whispered in her ear, just loud enough that Sam caught the words.

"Everything's fine," she said. She embraced the older man for a moment. When she graciously slipped out of his arms, Sonja turned to Sam and introduced him.

Russell extended his hand and Sam accepted it. The older man had a firm but brief shake.

"Sonja's told us a lot about you," Russell said as suspicion filled his eyes.

"All of it bad, I assume." Sam smiled.

The older man's skepticism seemed to deepen as he furrowed his brow. "Why would she say something bad about you?"

"He's kidding, Russ."

"My son's in jail," Russell said, his lips puckering in frustration. "This isn't a time for jokes."

"I understand," Sam said. He plastered on a contrite expression. At least, Sam hoped he looked contrite. As far as he knew, he might appear constipated.

Russell studied Sam a moment longer before harrumphing and turning his attention to Sonja. "Let's get you out of the cold."

The older man ushered them into the house, then guided Sam and Sonja up a set of stairs into the living room.

A wood stove huddled in the corner of the room. Behind a glass door, a fire blazed. Feeling the warmth immediately, Sam unzipped his coat but didn't take it off.

Two burgundy recliners sat side by side in the main portion of the room while a similarly colored couch was positioned under the window. Pictures of Bruce cluttered the top of a floor-model television. A wooden cross hung on the wall.

A woman in her late sixties stood with her hands clasped in front of her. She was thin with short, gray hair and plain features free of makeup. She wore blue slacks and a beige sweater.

"Dorothy," Russell said, "this is Sam Strait." Disapproval laced the introduction.

Sonja crossed the room and hugged the woman. Dorothy looked at Sam during the embrace. He smiled politely and nodded. Eventually, Dorothy broke the hug and stepped away from Sonja. "It's nice to meet you," she said to Sam with all the warmth of a snowball.

"Sit," Russell said, motioning toward the couch.

The Blooms settled into the recliners as Sam and Sonja sat on the couch. Sonja looked at Sam and raised her eyebrows. He was next to her, their legs touching. It was too close for a meeting with her potential in-laws. It was definitely too close given their history.

Sam scooched toward the farthest end of the couch. The Blooms watched him with curiosity that bordered on hostility.

"We saw Bruce a little earlier," Sonja said.

Dorothy's expression softened as she turned to Sonja.

"How's he doing? We're going to see him after lunch."

"He's staying strong."

Russell leaned forward and rested his elbows on his knees. "What were you two talking about in the car?"

"Nothing," Sam said.

"Don't lie to me, son. I know an argument when I see one."

"Sam wanted to keep interviewing witnesses," Sonja said, "but I insisted we come see you."

Russell's face relaxed slightly. "That so?"

Sam nodded.

"Well, I appreciate that." The suspicion didn't leave Russell's eyes when he glanced at his wife. "We won't take too much of your time, will we?"

"Not too much," Dorothy agreed, her voice flat.

Russell's gaze swung back to Sam. "You used to be a deputy. That right?"

Sam nodded again.

"How come you aren't one anymore?" Russell's eyes filled with a teacher's suspicion, an ingrained distrust in younger people.

Sam wasn't going to share his history with the Blooms, so he used an excuse he often pulled out in moments like this. "It didn't work out."

"Couldn't hack it, huh?" Russell flopped back in his chair. His eyes remained focused, like a poker player searching for an opponent's tell.

"Didn't like blood," Sam said.

Dorothy smirked. "Could never have been a dentist like our Bruce."

"Nope," Sam agreed, though he suspected his reasons for not being a dentist were different than the ones the Blooms imagined.

Russell crossed his arms. "You're living in Honolulu?" He jerked his head toward Sonja. "She told us."

"That's right."

"Why don't you live on one of the nicer islands?"

"It's the same sun no matter which island I'm on." Sam glanced between the Blooms. "Is this really what you want to talk about?"

Russell's upper lip curled. "We just want to know what kind of man agrees to fly a full day to help out in a situation like this."

Sonja reached across the couch toward Sam. "He came because Bruce and I asked him."

Dorothy cocked her head as she studied Sonja's gesture. "You're not trying to move in on Sonja, are you?"

Even though Sonja didn't touch Sam, she pulled her arm back as if her hand grazed a hot stove.

Russell's eyes flooded with distrust as he focused on Sam. "You know what the bible says about coveting thy neighbor's wife. Goes for their fiancées, too."

Sam eyed Sonja. Maybe Bruce had told them about his plan to propose.

Sonja said, "Sam's not that kind of guy."

Dorothy scoffed. "He looks like the type."

Russell asked, "What have you got to say about that?"

Sam was about to deny any attraction to Sonja, which would have been an obvious lie, but she blurted out an excuse.

"Sam's taken the abstinence pledge."

"Oh," the Blooms said simultaneously. They looked at each other and repeated, "Oh." Russell seemed relieved and Dorothy appeared almost ecstatic by the news.

Sam eyed Sonja, but she ignored him. "He took it back in high school," she said.

"That's impressive," Russell said. "Wish we could have gotten Bruce to take it."

Dorothy shook her head. "Probably would have saved him some heartache over the years." Her eyes drifted to Sonja. "Present company excluded of course."

Sonja appeared uncomfortable under Mrs. Bloom's gaze.

"Haven't heard about the pledge in years," Russell said. "For a while, it seemed to be the rage in the youth group. Times change, I guess."

"Not for Sam, apparently," Dorothy said with an approving smile.

Sonja shifted her position, obviously uncomfortable with the way the conversation turned. "Sam has some questions." Her eyes locked with his. "Don't you?"

Sam turned to the Blooms. Their earlier distrust was gone, replaced with friendliness.

"What can you tell us about Topher Anderson?" Sam asked.

Dorothy waved her hand. "*Him.*"

"Bullied our son," Russell said. "I tried to protect Bruce when he was in high school, but I probably made it worse. Teacher's kid and all."

"They had friction?"

"Almost everybody had friction with Topher as far as I remember."

Dorothy nodded. "Bruce couldn't wait to move away."

"You ever run into Topher?"

"Around town you mean?" Russell glanced at Dorothy before continuing. "We've seen him around, sure. Not much. We're a bigger city than you think. Over the years, though, we've seen him at the grocery store or a restaurant."

"A couple of times at the fair, too," Dorothy added.

"That's right." Russell nodded. "The fair."

Sam was out of questions then. He could have asked if the Blooms thought their son capable of murder. It would have been a waste of breath, though. They certainly wouldn't think that. The question was likely to upset them, too.

He looked at Sonja. "I'm good."

"That's it?" Russell asked. "You can ask anything you want."

"I can make us some coffee," Dorothy offered. "Do you like cookies? I just made some snickerdoodles. They're Russ's favorites."

"Happy to share," Russell said. He forced a smile, but any real joy was gone.

Dorothy hurried into the kitchen.

Sam stood. "We've got a lot of ground to cover. Best to do it while there's still sunlight."

"Back to the witnesses," Mr. Bloom said as he left his recliner. "Good for you."

Sonja got to her feet. "I'll come by later after I drop Sam off."

"We'd appreciate seeing you again," Russell said. He turned to Sam. "I'm sure you'll do a fine job."

"A fine job," Dorothy echoed from the kitchen. "I'm sending you with a bag of cookies."

***

"These are great," Sam said, his mouth full of snickerdoodle. He wiped away the crumbs that had fallen on his coat.

"You couldn't wait until we left the driveway?"

"Didn't know I should."

"You're eating like a starving man."

Sam wasn't hungry since he had breakfast. However, he hadn't eaten sweets while dating Nina. Her health consciousness hadn't rubbed off on him. Rather, he didn't want her to think less of him because of his weakness for treats. The donut he ate the morning they met was the last goodie he'd had since their relationship started. Realizing he was acting this way after only a short time abstaining from desserts made the cookie in his mouth taste less appealing but only slightly. He pulled another cookie from the plastic bag and studied it appreciatively.

"Dorothy Bloom sure knows her way around an oven," Sam said, shaking the baked treat for emphasis.

Sonja stopped at the edge of the Bloom's driveway, prepared to turn onto First Street. She glanced at him with a disapproving look. "You're spilling crumbs everywhere."

"Let me guess." Sam shoved the entire second cookie into his mouth. The treat held down his tongue and distorted his words, creating a dry lisp. "Bruthe doethn't like people eating in hith car?"

"You're gross, and it's a very nice, expensive car."

"It'th hith baby," Sam said mockingly.

"I don't like people eating in it either."

"Fine." Sam swallowed the remaining bits of cookie and closed the large Ziploc bag. He held it high for her to see. "For you."

"Thank you."

The Range Rover accelerated onto the snowy road and headed east.

"What'd you think?" Sonja asked.

Sam thought he wanted another cookie, but he didn't

voice it. Instead, he asked, "About the Blooms?"

"What else?"

"The cookies were a nice touch." Sam's eyes remained on Sonja as he discreetly reopened the Ziploc baggie.

"They're nice people, aren't they?"

"Yeah," Sam said. "Nice." He removed a cookie from the baggie, then tapped it over the floorboard like a smoker removing ash from a cigarette. Crumbs rained down.

"It's too bad you couldn't have met them under nicer circumstances," Sonja said. "This whole situation with Bruce is weighing on them."

"Uh-huh." Sam took a bite of the cookie and more crumbs fell onto his coat. He hastily stuffed the entire treat into his mouth. The baked goodie tasted even better than before.

Sonja's attention snapped to the rearview mirror. "I'm being stopped."

Sam turned in his seat for a better look. A dark blue police car with its lights whirring followed them.

"Are you eating another cookie?" she asked as she glanced at him, the rearview mirror, and the road ahead.

He smiled like a guilty squirrel—lips closed and cheeks full.

"What'd I do?" she asked, her eyes locking onto the rearview mirror again.

Sam flopped back into his seat, then casually wiped the crumbs from his coat. "Pull over and find out."

Sonja guided the Range Rover to the side of the road. Due to a snow berm, the vehicle remained partially in the lane of travel. She slipped the shift into Park.

Sam extended the bag to her. "Want a cookie?"

Her expression strained. "Look at the crumbs."

"I think I'm addicted." He bit into another

snickerdoodle, spraying crumbs everywhere including the center console. "I prawbably need countheling."

Someone knocked on the window, and Sonja jumped. She rolled down the window.

A handsome man in his late twenties leaned to look inside the vehicle. He had dark hair, a square jaw, and a dark blue coat with a silver badge on the left breast. His gaze jumped from Sonja to Sam and back.

"Morning, ma'am. I'm Officer Pitner with the Havre Police Department. May I see your driver's license and registration?"

"What'd I do?" Sonja asked.

Pitner's gaze hopped to Sam. "Do you have any identification, sir?"

Sam nodded as he continued to chew his cookie. He dropped the large baggie onto the floorboard and reached into his back pocket.

Sonja turned to Sam. "What'd we do?"

"They want to know who we are."

"Who's they?"

Sam reached past Sonja to hand his license to the cop. "Who wants us stopped and identified?"

Officer Pitner took the ID card from Sam. The cop studied him for a moment before saying, "DCI."

Sonja briefly turned to the cop, then whipped around to Sam. "That's the detective."

"Yes, it is," Sam said. He picked up the bag of cookies. "Give him your ID. We're gonna be here a while."

***

"My stomach hurts," Sam said.

"It should." Sonja scoffed. "You ate the whole bag."

He moaned. "You could have helped."

"I don't eat cookies." She looked in the rearview mirror. "Besides, I'm too nervous to eat." Sonja settled into her seat. "What's he doing back there?"

"Running our names."

"It's been like five minutes."

"He's got to wait for the detective to arrive." Sam closed his eyes and rested his hands over his aching stomach. "It feels like I'm gonna have a baby."

"You're so gross."

"I'm never doing that again."

"I don't know how you stay fit with the stuff you eat." She clucked. "Look at what you did."

He opened his eyes and leaned forward. Even that small movement bothered his stomach. Cookie crumbs were everywhere on the floor. The Ziploc baggie lay crumpled in their midst. He flopped back. "It's not so bad."

"You're a pig."

"Oink," he muttered.

She turned in her seat. "This is about Bruce, isn't it?"

"What is?"

"The mess you made. You're jealous."

"Me?" Sam turned in his seat, his gut aching with the slight movement. "Jealous?" He touched his chest as if offended by her accusation. "Of a dentist?"

"Exactly."

"A dentist who's in jail, let's not forget."

"How can I forget?" Her eyes briefly went to the rearview mirror, then landed back on him.

"Jealous," Sam muttered, shaking his head in disbelief.

"Totally." Sonja nodded emphatically with a self-satisfied smirk. "Admit it."

"You're crazy."

"You know I'm right."

"Whatever." He faced forward and slumped in the seat. "Oh," he moaned. "My gut."

A knock on the window caused Sonja to jump again. She rolled it down. "Yes?"

Officer Pitner leaned so he could see them both. "Would you step out of the car, ma'am? You, too, sir."

Sam popped open his door. It didn't open fully since it caught on the side of a snow berm. He wriggled out of the vehicle and shimmied down its length. Standing brought some relief to the pain in his stomach.

A large man in a puffy red coat, black slacks, and winter boots stood with Officer Pitner and Sonja. Parked behind the patrol vehicle bearing the markings of the City of Havre was an unmarked Ford Bronco.

"This is Agent Dale Hathaway," Pitner said. "He's got some questions for you."

Hathaway smiled before he spoke. It was the same cruel way that Sam's physical fitness instructor grinned when the new recruits lined up for their first morning at the academy. "I'm investigating the murder of Topher Anderson," the agent said. His eyes settled on Sonja. "I've reason to believe you may know something about that."

She swallowed and glanced at Sam. When her attention returned to the investigator, she asked, "Should I have my attorney present?"

"I don't know. Should you?"

Sonja shrugged. "I'm thinking yeah."

"In that case, we'll do this down at the station. I'll have Officer Pitner give you a ride."

Sam held up his hand. "Just tell him the truth, Sonja. You'll be fine."

Her eyes searched his. "All right. I'll tell you what I

know."

"In a minute," Hathaway said. His gaze slid to Sam. "Where's the beach?"

"Sir?"

"Nice tan."

"Uh, thank you?"

Hathaway frowned. "Word is you're poking your nose into my investigation."

"I wouldn't say poking."

"Yeah, handsome? What would you say?"

"Well," Sam said, "I've been asked to look into it."

"Asked?" Hathaway's eyebrows rose. "By whom?"

"The accused's attorney."

"Oh, boy, I can't wait to hear this."

Sam started to respond, but the agent lifted a finger. "Nope, not your turn." His gaze cut to Sonja. "Right now, Miss Boyd and I are gonna talk. We can do it here in the cold, or we can sit in my rig."

Sonja pursed her lips before saying, "I guess we'll sit in your car."

"Excellent choice." Hathaway thumbed over his shoulder. "Passenger door is unlocked. Grab a seat."

She walked away.

"You, handsome, are gonna wait in Officer Pitner's car."

"Why can't I wait in ours?"

"Because I said so." Hathaway turned and headed for his vehicle.

***

Sam reclined on the backseat of Officer Pitner's patrol car with his shoulders pressed against the door on the driver's side. His hands rested on his aching stomach, and his feet were up on the seat and crossed at the ankles. There wasn't room to sit with his feet forward like a normal passenger, otherwise his knees would press into the steel partition separating the front seats from the rear.

When he was a deputy, Sam often recommended this position for those he transported to jail. He wasn't uncomfortable, just miffed. Interference by the cops was to be expected. Solving Topher's murder was their responsibility after all. Sam was simply trying to prove Bruce wasn't involved.

Pitner sat in the driver's seat with his head bowed over a clipboard. Hot air blew through the small opening in the steel partition, and country music played through the stereo. The song about patriotism tried to sound tough with its references to drinking whiskey, shooting guns, and hunting deer.

Sam looked through the back window. Agent Hathaway faced Sonja as she spoke. He occasionally nodded, and she gestured now and then. It was like watching a silent movie. Sam hated silent movies.

He shifted his seating position and the plastic cover on the backseat groaned. Pitner glanced over his shoulder.

"This gonna be a while?" Sam asked.

"No idea." Pitner's attention swung back to the clipboard.

"Mind if I have my phone?"

Sam's cell rested on the dashboard. The officer had taken it after searching him prior to putting him in the backseat. It was standard procedure, so Sam didn't get ruffled by it. Officer safety dictated many items be removed from a detainee's pockets before they were placed in the back of a patrol car. Pitner hadn't removed his wallet or cash, though.

"Who you wanna call?" the officer asked.

"Does it matter?"

Pitner looked back again. This time with a raised eyebrow. A cop would never suggest Sam call his lawyer, even when employed by one.

"I want to call—" Sam struggled to find an appropriate word before finally settling on, "my girlfriend."

The cop faced forward. "Girlfriend, huh?"

Sam nodded even though he didn't like the word he chose. It sounded too permanent, and he'd never risk saying it in mixed company.

Pitner looked at Sam in the rearview mirror. "You'll end the call when Agent Hathaway steps out of his vehicle."

"Got it."

"I'm gonna listen in." Pitner turned in his seat to eye Sam. "Make sure you're not planning an ambush or something."

"I just want to call a girl."

Officer Pitner clicked off the country music, then handed the cell phone through the small opening in the plastic shield.

Sam mumbled his thanks before dialing Nina Wilder's number. She answered on the fourth ring.

"Well, well," she said. "Look who it is. I thought maybe you forgot about me."

"Not possible. What're you doing?"

"Relaxing by the pool, enjoying my day before I have to go into work."

"Sounds nice," Sam said.

"Would be better if you were here."

"Tell me about it."

She chuckled.

"I'm serious," Sam said. "Tell me about it. How's the weather?"

"Oh, right, you're where the buffalo roam or some such thing. Well, the sky is blue, and it's going to be a warm day. Supposed to get to eighty."

Sam whistled. "That's about eighty degrees warmer than here."

He looked out the back window again. Sonja continued talking with Hathaway. The agent seemed to pay close attention to what she was saying.

"What're you doing?" Nina asked. "Tell me you're wearing cowboy boots."

"I'm sitting in the back of a police car."

"You're *what*?"

"All things considered," Sam said, "it's not so bad."

Some of the patrol cars he'd driven smelled horrible in the backseats. Bodily fluids of all sorts were spilled back there. Whenever he had transported a prisoner, it was Sam's duty to ensure the back was clean. Not only for the next passenger or the next deputy to drive the vehicle, but to make sure no evidence was left behind. In his short time with the department, Sam had cleaned vomit, blood, and feces from plastic-covered seats. That was the glamorous part of the job no one talked about.

"What'd you do to end up there?" Nina said.

"Asked some questions."

"That's all?"

"That's all," Sam said.

It was Nina's turn to whistle. "They don't mess around in Montana, do they?"

Sam looked forward now. Officer Pitner stared straight ahead, obviously eavesdropping on the phone call.

"Hey," Nina said, "you think you might get strip searched?"

"Why?"

"Wanted a reason to think about you naked."

"Got to be better reasons than a strip search."

Pitner's gaze rose to the rearview mirror, and he made eye contact with Sam. "Strip search?" the officer asked, suspicion clearly in his voice.

"My girlfriend," Sam said with a dismissive shake of his head. "She wants to know if you're going to strip search me."

The officer rolled his eyes, then looked away from the mirror.

"I'm your girlfriend now?" Nina asked.

Sam winced and remained quiet.

"Didn't know we were labeling this thing of ours."

He never wanted to label his relationships. It brought too many expectations, too many feelings. Once a man referred to a woman as a girlfriend, his options for happiness were limited solely to her expectations. His decisions, plans, and dreams had to coalesce with hers. Sam didn't want to change his life for anyone.

He eyed Agent Hathaway's car. Besides, if he was going to change for anyone, it probably would have been Sonja. Yet, he hadn't stayed in Spokane when she wanted him. Sonja smiled apologetically at him through the windshield.

"Listen," Sam said, "I gotta go."

"Oh, I see. Drop that hot potato, then hang up. Is that how you operate, Mr. Strait?" Nina's words sounded playful, which Sam hadn't expected. He thought for sure there'd be a hint of seriousness after letting "girlfriend" slip from his lips.

"It's not like that."

"It never is," Nina said.

"I'm about to be interviewed."

It wasn't a lie. The DCI agent opened his car door and stepped out. Sonja did the same.

"This person you dropped everything for must be pretty special," Nina said. "Another woman, perhaps?"

"A friend," Sam said.

"That didn't answer my question."

"For real. I gotta go."

"You didn't go home to your wife, did you?"

Sam scoffed. "I'm not married."

Officer Pitner's gaze returned to the rearview mirror. "Get off the phone."

"Don't worry," Nina said. "I'm not jealous."

"Neither am I."

"I won't hold that girlfriend comment against you."

"It's okay," Sam said and cringed. He shouldn't encourage the word to fester any longer than necessary.

"I don't want a boyfriend," Nina said.

Sam stiffened. "You don't?"

"I like my life, Sam. A boyfriend would just muddy it up."

"Oh." He wished he'd said more, but he was oddly bothered by her relationship reluctance at that moment.

Hathaway and Sonja headed toward the car.

Officer Pitner turned in his seat and glared at Sam through the partition. His lip curled in a nasty snarl. "Hang up. Now."

Sam nodded at the cop and tried to smile as politely as he could. "I've gotta go," he said.

"I heard," Nina said. "Take care, all right? I don't want you getting eaten by some bear or something."

"I'll call you later."

He ended the call and handed the phone through the small window in the Plexiglas partition.

***

"Samuel Roy Strait of Newman Lake, Washington," Agent Hathaway said as he studied Sam's driver's license. "That near Spokane?"

"Uh-huh."

Hathaway put the license on the dashboard, then jotted the information into his notebook. When he finished writing, the agent turned in his seat so he could better study Sam. "Where'd you get the tan?"

Sam thought about lying. Maybe tell the investigator he got the tan from a local salon. However, he didn't know what Sonja had said. Perhaps Hathaway asked the same question of her. Detectives often ask questions for which they already knew the answers. There didn't seem to be any harm in telling the truth.

"Got it in Hawaii."

"Yeah?" Hathaway's eyebrow rose. "Where?"

"Honolulu."

"That's Oahu, right? I've never been. Been to Maui, though. You?"

Sam shook his head.

"What were you doing in Honolulu?"

"Avoiding the snow."

Hathaway motioned toward Sam's face. "Chasing the sun. Why not stay at one of the nicer islands? Why be in the big city?"

"Stayed there before and liked it. Didn't get to do everything I wanted, so I went back."

The agent's nose crinkled. "Next time, stay in Maui. You'll like it better."

Sam didn't know how Hathaway could make that promise since he'd just admitted he'd never been to Honolulu or Oahu Island.

"I hear you were a deputy," Hathaway said. "Sonja confirmed it."

"Five years."

"Why'd you quit?"

Sam leaned his back against the passenger door. "Was accused of something I didn't do. Won a lawsuit as a result."

"Lots of hurt feelings on both sides, I suppose."

"Something like that."

Hathaway looked forward. Sonja wasn't sitting in the patrol car. She was allowed to wait in the Range Rover. "Sonja said you flew in to help prove her fiancé's innocence."

"You could say that." However, he wished Hathaway would never say fiancé again when talking about Sonja.

"That was nice of you," the agent said. "Leave the sun, jump on a plane. Must be old pals with Bruce."

"He's a good guy." Sam tried to force some conviction into his voice.

"That so?" Hathaway asked but didn't face Sam. "Known him long?"

"About a year."

"A year?"

"That's right."

Now, Hathaway faced him. "What'd a plane ticket cost?"

"Bruce is reimbursing me."

"Guess that's to be expected. Still, you've got to

account for the lost time on the island, right? That's a long flight, too. I know."

"Maui," Sam said, showing the agent he'd paid attention.

"That's right." Hathaway nodded. "If you go there, stay near Baldwin Beach. It's excellent for families."

"I'll remember that," Sam lied.

"Nineteen-hour flights each way is a lot of loyalty for a guy you've only known a year. Technically, not that long since you've been on the islands part of that time. Am I right?"

"Doesn't mean we didn't get to know each other."

Hathaway waggled his hand. "So you and Mr. Bloom have stayed in touch?"

"Through Sonja."

The agent's eyes cut toward the Range Rover. "I see the connection now."

Sam didn't want to go down whatever road Hathaway thought he saw. "Are we going to talk about what I've learned, or we gonna keep talking about Hawaii?"

"We're talking about Miss Boyd now."

"Let's not."

The agent smirked, seemingly pleased to find a weak spot in Sam's armor. "All right," Hathaway said. "Before you share what you've learned, let me tell you what I know. You arrived late last night via plane. This morning, you've been by the county jail, the local police station, and the suspect's parents." He lifted three fingers, one by one, as he listed the places Sam and Sonja had visited. "What could you have learned that I don't know?"

Sam shrugged. He didn't bother telling Hathaway about visiting The Grizzly Den. Besides, if he did, Sam would have to admit he really didn't learn anything there.

Hathaway rested his arm over the steering wheel. "All I see is a pretty boy wannabe playing detective."

"Pretty boy?"

"Wannabe," the agent clarified. "My suggestion is you hop the first plane out of here and stop sticking your nose into my investigation."

"Are we done?" Sam shifted in his seat and put his hand on the door handle.

Hathaway reached out and grabbed him by the shoulder. "You reading me, Strait?"

"Stay out of your investigation," Sam said. "Is that reading you right?"

"Grab a flight home. Today." The agent grabbed the driver's license from the dashboard and held it out. "Understand?"

Sam took the license. He didn't like being pushed but he didn't need to offend a guy who could drum up charges for interfering with an investigation. "Message received," Sam said and popped open the door.

Chapter 9

Sonja turned on First Street and headed west toward the heart of Havre.

"I'm hungry," Sam said.

"I thought your stomach hurt."

"I'm over that."

She shook her head in disbelief. "Aren't we going to talk about what happened back there?"

"What's there to say?" Sam unzipped his coat and pulled out the initial police report Chuck Palmer had given him. "The cops don't want us interfering with their investigation."

She glanced at him. "You think they're covering up something?"

"I doubt Hathaway even knew Topher Anderson existed before the case landed on his desk." He pointed ahead with the folded report. "Wasn't there a McDonald's or something up there?"

Sonja clucked. "That's really going to make your stomach hurt. There are better options."

"If they got a drive-through, great."

"We're not eating in the car."

"Why not?" Sam looked at the cookie crumbs on the floor. "It's not like someone hasn't eaten in here before."

"I should make you clean that."

"We don't have time." Sam unfolded the report. "We've got witnesses to interview."

"And you want to stop for lunch."

"A drive-through," he corrected.

"If you want to eat, we're stopping." She glanced at him. "We're not eating like teenagers."

"I'd like to wrap this up fast." He scanned the report. "Get back to Hawaii while there's still some winter left."

"That's what this is about." Sonja's tone turned icy.

"I figure you'd want to get Bruce out in a hurry."

"I do."

"Eating at a sit-down restaurant isn't the best use of our time. I bet if you asked Bruce, he'd rather have us eat in his car and work on his defense, then take a break at a nicer restaurant."

"Fine," she muttered. "McDonald's."

The Range Rover bounced into the parking lot of the hamburger franchise. Sonja guided it into the drive-through. They quickly ordered, paid at the first window, and crept forward to the second window.

She eyed him. "Who are we seeing first?"

"I don't know my way around this town. I say we start at the top of the list and work our way down. Use the GPS to guide us."

"So I repeat, who are we seeing first?"

"Carl and Pamela Buckenberger."

Sam held the report so Sonja could see the address on Eighth Street. She plugged the information into the GPS. The drive there would only take a few minutes.

The drive-through window slid open, and an employee held out a paper bag. Sonja took it and handed it to Sam. The Range Rover accelerated back onto First Street.

***

The Buckenbergers lived in a quiet neighborhood.

Eighth Street seemingly dead-ended into First and Second Avenues. Their house was a two story, pitched-roof affair. It was painted white with gray accents. The structure's bland color scheme was washed out by the snow.

An older beige GMC pickup sat in the driveway next to a purple PT Cruiser. Both vehicles were dented and scratched. A thick layer of snow remained on top of the car. A thin coating of snow covered the truck's roof, while a heavy wool blanket protected the windshield.

Sonja parked the Range Rover along the curb and underneath a leafless tree. "What'd these people see?"

"Same as everyone else," Sam said. "Topher and you flirting, then Bruce hitting Topher."

She clicked her tongue against the back of her teeth as she turned off the engine. "Topher tried to flirt with me." Her eyes cut to him. "I certainly wasn't flirting back."

Sam held up a conciliatory hand. "Flirting doesn't have to be a two-way street."

"It most certainly does." Sonja nodded vigorously. "That's what flirting is. It goes both ways." She motioned between herself and Sam. "If one side doesn't engage, then the other person has to stop. That's why guys come off clumsy and creepy."

He stared at her, refusing to bring up the many unwanted advances she made while they were younger. Sam also didn't mention her continued harassment whenever their relationship wasn't on.

Sonja cocked her head. "What?"

"Nothing," he said and left the vehicle.

Neither the sidewalk paralleling the street nor the pathway to the home were shoveled. Repeated footsteps had tamped down some of the snow, but it made for a gawky, inelegant walk.

On the front stoop, Sam pressed the doorbell. Almost immediately, a dog barked—a single, half-hearted warning that a canine was present inside. A woman yelled, "Shut up, you."

"I'm gonna let you do the talking," Sonja said.

Sam lifted an eyebrow. "You sure?"

"Only seems right."

The home's main door opened, and a woman appeared behind the heavy glass of the storm door. She was a shorter woman, in her late fifties with wiry gray hair. A large sweater drooped around her neck. Her red, bulbous nose almost pressed against the glass as she leaned in. Suspicious brown eyes darted between Sam and Sonja. "What do you want?" The words were mushy and ran together. Her breath fogged the glass.

"Are you Pamela Buckenberger?" Sam asked.

"No charity," the woman announced and closed the door.

Sam immediately rang the bell again. From inside, the dog barked another lackluster warning.

The door sprang open, and the woman jammed her finger into the storm door. The glass rattled in its aluminum frame and popped free of the jamb. "Stop riling up my dog and get off my property!" Spittle flew from her mouth as she yelled her sloppy demand.

The storm door relatched.

"Ma'am," Sam said calmly. "We're investigating the assault you saw a few nights ago." He motioned in the direction he thought The Grizzly Den was. "At the bar," he added, just in case the woman might have seen more than one fight.

"I already spoke to some police." The woman's gaze drifted to Sonja. "You don't look like the cops."

"We're working for the defense," Sam said.

"You could've made that up to get inside my house."

Sam could have simply pulled open the unlocked storm door if he wanted to enter. Instead, he reached into his pocket for the letter.

The woman yelped and slammed the door.

"She's a keeper," Sonja said.

Sam rang the bell a third time and was rewarded with an indolent bark.

"Knock it off, you!" the woman hollered before pulling the door back a crack. A single eye peered through the opening. "You gonna shoot me?"

Sam unfolded Chuck Palmer's letter and pressed it against the glass.

"What's that?" the woman asked, looking over the letter at Sam.

"Authorization from a defense attorney," he said. "It proves who we are."

The inner door opened fully now, and the woman stepped forward to better see the letter. She squinted as she read, and her lips moved with each word. When she finished reading, the woman looked up, "Why didn't you say so sooner?"

She slapped the latch, popping the storm door open. "Guess you better come inside."

✳✳✳

Carl Buckenberger slept on the couch. His mouth drooped open, and his feet extended over the top of the armrest. An orange crocheted blanket covered most of his body. He snored heavily, almost angrily. Empty beers cans gathered on the floor, standing guard for an ashtray stuffed full of cigarette butts.

Pamela's lip curled as she studied her husband. "He could sleep through a world war." Her gaze moved lazily to Sam and Sonja. "Me? A mouse farts, and I'm awake." Her words continued to slush together.

They stood in the living room since there was no other place to sit. There was another chair, but an old black labrador with a white face was curled in it. The dog watched Sam and Sonja with tired eyes.

"Don't mind Jeb," Pamela said. "He's harmless. He only moves when its chow time."

"Ma'am," Sam said, "we'd like to ask you and your husband some questions about that night."

She shook her head. "Leave Carl be. He's about as friendly as a rattlesnake when he's got a hangover."

To emphasize the point, Mr. Buckenberger snorted, then resumed his enraged snoring.

"Do you go by Pam?" Sam asked.

"Why? You trying to get fresh?"

"Pamela it is," Sam said. "Did you know the victim?"

Mrs. Buckenberger smirked. "Topher?" She bent and shook the beer cans near her husband's head. Finding one with some liquid left in it, Pamela straightened. "Everybody knew Topher at the Griz."

"You went there often?"

"It's our place." She leaned back and swallowed what was left in the can, then smacked her lips.

"You liked Topher?"

"Man was a dog." Pamela dropped the can, and it clattered when it hit the other empties. The ashtray lost the soldiers guarding it. "Not a good dog like Jeb, neither. Topher was always on the make."

"I know the type," Sonja muttered.

Sam eyed her, but the comment didn't seem directed at him.

Pamela sniffed. "A woman's curse, am I right?" She wiped her thumb across the bottom of her nose. "Topher fancied himself a ladies' man. Even put the moves on me once." Her eyelids drooped as she swayed. "Carl wasn't having none of that nonsense and almost strangled the living daylights out of Topher."

"So this altercation wasn't the first Topher had?"

Pamela's pshaw sounded like a slow tire leak. When she ran out of air, she inhaled heavily, started to speak, but paused. "What was the question?"

"The altercation with our client wasn't the first Topher had over a woman."

Mrs. Buckenberger pshawed a second time, but this leak expired quicker. "Not even close."

Sam and Sonja exchanged glances.

"You could throw a rock in this town," Pamela said, "and hit some fella Topher crossed because of a woman. It ain't no secret."

Jeb yawned in his chair, and Carl pulled the crocheted blanket over his head.

"Got any names of people we should speak with?"

Pamela put her hands on her hips and leaned forward. "What do you take me for? A rat?"

Sam cocked his head. "Who'd you be ratting on?"

"Don't get wise," Pamela said as she studied Sonja. "You look familiar. You were making time with Topher that night."

Sonja shook her head. "I wasn't making time with him. I barely said a word to the man."

Pamela curled her upper lip. "Could've fooled me." She waved off Sonja's look of denial. "Don't be too hard on yourself, though. Plenty of women prettier than us have fallen for Topher's line of garbage."

Sonja raised an eyebrow.

Sam jumped back in the conversation. "No one comes to mind who might've wanted to hurt Topher?"

Pamela's attention remained on Sonja. "Your boyfriend walloped ol' Topher a good one. I'll give you that." She chuckled. "Nobody deserved it more. Too bad your boyfriend had to go and kill him, though."

"Bruce didn't kill anyone," Sonja said.

Pamela turned her head slightly and winked. It was an exaggerated gesture and about as graceful as a ballerina falling down a set of stairs.

Sam crossed his arms. "Are you avoiding my question?"

"What question is that?" Pamela asked.

"Who else wanted to hurt Topher?

Pamela grimaced. "I don't think I like your tone."

"I apologize," Sam said, trying his best to recall the diplomatic skills he learned while a deputy. "I didn't mean to offend."

Her eyelids sagged. "I'm done talking."

"Ma'am, please," Sam said, "I'm just trying to get an answer."

"You want an answer?" Her eyes popped open, and anger flooded them. "I'll give you an answer." Pamela kicked the couch. "Get up."

Carl stirred underneath the crocheted blanket.

"You're in for it now," Pamela said.

"What'd I do?" Sam asked.

Mrs. Buckenberger pointed at her husband. "No one threatens me."

"I didn't threaten you." Sam looked at Sonja. "Did I

threaten her?"

She shook her head. "I don't think so."

"Hey, you." Pamela kicked the couch harder. "This guy's bothering me."

Jeb slid out of the chair and slunk into the next room.

"Sam," Sonja said, watching the dog leave. "Maybe we should go."

Pamela slapped the crocheted blanket where her husband's head should've been. Carl snatched the covering from his head and bolted upright. "Good Lord, woman!" he shouted. "What is it?"

"Them two." She pointed at Sonja and Sam.

"What about them?"

"They won't leave."

Sam grabbed Sonja, and they backpedaled toward the front door. "We're going," Sam said. "Thank you for your time."

Carl stood now. His gaze bounced about the room, obviously confused by the moment. "What'd they want?"

"They're asking about Topher's murder."

"That's it?" Carl flopped back to the couch.

Sonja stepped out of the door, but Sam paused, emboldened by Carl's change in demeanor.

"Mr. Buckenberger, can I ask you a few questions?"

Carl extended himself across the couch and pulled the blanket back over himself. "Step in my house again, and I'll beat the snot out of you."

"Have a nice day." Sam pulled the door closed behind him.

Chapter 10

"Norlan Wisner," Sam said. He read the address from the police report.

Sonja tapped the GPS screen and a destination immediately popped up. She dropped the Range Rover into gear and accelerated away from the corner.

Sam's phone rang, and he removed it from his pocket. It was a 406 area code which the phone identified as belonging to Montana. He swiped his thumb across the screen. "Hello?"

"Sam Strait?" a woman asked.

"Yes."

"This is Officer Malone. You left a message at the station."

Sam pulled the phone from his ear and checked the time. If Malone was at the station to start her graveyard shift, she was early—extremely early. "That's right," Sam said. "I'm working with Bruce Bloom's attorney."

"I heard." Malone's voice was flat, bordering on annoyed.

Sonja weaved through neighborhoods, following the directions provided by the GPS system. On one corner, she gunned the engine, causing the tires to slip on the snow-covered ground.

Sam grabbed the door handle for support. He said into the phone, "Is there a place we can meet?"

"For?"

"I'd like to ask you some questions about what you saw

that night.”

“This is bordering on interfering with a police investigation.”

“I’m not interfering,” Sam said. “I’m just asking questions.”

Malone clucked. “I arrested the right guy.”

“Then you won’t mind talking with me for a few moments.”

Sonja took another corner, this one slower. She jammed on the brakes and the Range Rover slid to a stop. A long-haired orange cat stood in the middle of the road. Balls of snow clung to its fur. It didn’t seem frightened by the looming vehicle.

“Aw,” Sonja whispered. “Poor kitty.”

Malone sighed in Sam’s ear. “I’ll meet you in an hour.”

“Done.”

“The Four Oh Six Roastery on First Street.”

Officer Malone ended the call before Sam could thank her.

Sonja pulled to the curb in front of a small blue home. No vehicles were in its shoveled driveway. The sidewalks were bare and wet. Bits of deicer remained on the concrete, standing vigilant against the new-falling snow.

No one answered the door when Sam rang the bell, so he knocked.

“Probably not home,” Sonja said.

“Report listed where he worked. Let’s try that.”

***

Western Welding sat on Main Street. The beige metal building butted up against the railroad tracks. Several graffiti-covered rail cars waited on the tracks.

Sam and Sonja entered a small office which was extraordinarily warm, almost nauseatingly so. The rest of the structure was visible through interior windows, one of which appeared capable of sliding open. Several men in welding helmets worked on various projects, and sparks flew from their torches. Loud rock music reverberated through the office walls.

"Can I help you?" a younger woman asked from behind a gray metal desk. She might have been thirty, but she could just as easily have been twenty-two. Brown roots showed under blond hair, and her fake eyelashes looked heavy. Bright white teeth contrasted mightily with her tanned skin and ruby red lipstick. She wore a faded Nirvana T-shirt with its sleeves rolled up to her shoulders. The office's temperature appeared to be tailored toward her fashion choice.

Sam unzipped his coat. "We're looking for Norlan Wisner."

The receptionist eyed Sonja, her gaze cooly appraising. "Can I ask what for?"

"We want to ask some questions," Sam said.

Sonja took a business card from the plastic holder at the corner of the desk.

"What questions?" The receptionist rose from her seat slightly to check out Sonja's boots.

Sonja forced a smile and batted her eyelashes. Sam had seen that look on her before. It never ended well. Sonja didn't look away from the receptionist when she tapped Sam's arm and extended the business card.

Sam took it. *Rebecca Wisner, Executive Assistant.*

He tried to recall Norlan's age from the police report. "How are you related to Norlan?"

The receptionist dropped into her seat, and her gaze

flicked to Sam. "Why's it matter? What's this about?"

Sam said, "Norlan witnessed a fight a few nights ago. We're here to follow-up on what he saw."

Distrust filled Rebecca's eyes. "You're not cops."

"We're with the defense. Is he here or not?"

"Yeah," she said with a tsk. "He's here."

Rebecca stood and slid the window to the side. Van Halen's "Panama" blared through the opening. The receptionist leaned into the warehouse and shouted, "Dad!" over the deafening rock music and sounds of welding. Rebecca waved and hollered once more. "Dad!"

One of the men stopped working and looked up. He flipped his visor open.

Rebecca jerked a thumb over her shoulder. "Visitors!"

Nolan Wisner nodded and put down his welding torch.

Rebecca slammed the window closed and the rock music was once again muted. The dolled-up receptionist dropped into her chair and pulled herself closer to the desk. "I heard the guy did it."

"He didn't," Sonja said frostily.

"Like he beat up the guy inside the bar, right? Then finished it in the parking lot." Rebecca cocked her head and mockingly said, "Guil-ty." Her finger bounced twice in the air along with each syllable.

Sonja put her hands on her hips. "Thank you for your input."

"I call it like I see it."

"Were you there?" Sonja asked.

"Nope." Rebecca's upper lip curled. "I know what happened, though." Her eyes cut to Sam. "Nice tan. You get it over at Sunny Buns?"

Before Sam could reply, the door to the welding shop opened, and Norlan Wisner stepped through. He was a big man, standing more than a head taller than Sam. His handlebar mustache was flecked with gray, and long black hair cascaded down his broad shoulders. He wore heavy black overalls and a long-sleeved T-shirt. The welding helmet remained kicked back on his head.

Norlan's lips pressed together as he appraised Sam.

Rebecca flicked her hand at Sam. "These people wanna ask you some questions."

"About?" Norlan's gaze swung to Sonja and his face relaxed. He flashed a smile that he likely assumed was charming but bordered on creepy.

"Topher Anderson," Sam said.

Norlan's smile melted as his attention drifted back to Sam. "What about Topher?"

"According to a police report, you witnessed an assault."

"Uh-huh." Norlan studied Sam again. "You clearly ain't the cops, so you're what? A reporter?"

"We're working with the defense."

"Maybe you, but not her." Norlan lifted his chin toward Sonja. "She was the cause of the whole mess."

Sonja took a half-step back, offended. "I didn't do anything."

"Honey," Norlan said with a dismissive shake of his head. "A woman like you comes into The Grizzly Den, she's there to cause a stir."

"He ain't lyin'," Rebecca said.

Norlan glared at his daughter as he continued to speak. "Topher wasn't causing no harm, but your boyfriend had to go and hit him with a pool stick."

Sam crossed his arms. "What happened after the fight ended?"

"What do you think happened?" Norlan smirked.

"Those two got tossed out, and the rest of us went on drinking. Fighting at the Griz ain't abnormal, you know?"

"That's what we've heard."

Norlan put his hands on his hips. "Listen, Topher wasn't a model citizen, but I'm not sayin' nothing that's gonna help his murderer get away with it."

Sonja stepped forward. "Please, Bruce wouldn't hurt anyone."

Norlan chuckled. "Seems you're forgetting how your boyfriend made like Sammy Sosa and swung for the fences with that pool cue."

"He was jealous," Sonja said.

Norlan's eyes swept over her length, and his creepy smile returned. "Looks like he had good reason."

Sam raised a hand. "No one is saying Bruce didn't hit Topher. You saw it."

"You bet I did," Norlan said. "I had a front-row seat. I was at the bar next to them."

"You go to the Griz often?"

Rebecca muttered, "Like clockwork."

Norlan's hands slipped from his waist and he frowned at his daughter. "I'm a grown man, Becky. I can drink when and where I like. You on the other hand."

"I'm a grown woman," Rebecca said defensively.

"That remains to be seen."

The daughter glared at her father. "I can do what I want."

"Not while you're living in my home. Not while you're eating my food."

Embarrassed, Rebecca glanced at Sam, then looked down at her desk.

"As for your question," Norlan said as he turned to Sam, "once your lady friend and her big hitter was tossed out, the fight was over.”

“You never saw them again?”

Norlan lifted his chin at Sonja. “She came back in later.”

Sonja shook her head. “No, I didn’t.”

“Pretty sure it was you. From what I heard, it sounded like you were apologizing.”

“I didn’t.” Sonja looked at Sam. “I swear.”

Sam said, “You didn’t mention her coming back inside to the cops.”

Norlan seemed confused. “I’m pretty sure I did.”

“It wasn’t in the police report.”

“You were probably drunk,” Rebecca said poutingly. Her head remained bowed.

“Watch it,” Norlan said to his daughter.

Sam asked, “How was Topher after the altercation?”

“Sore. The man got smacked with a pool cue.”

“I mean,” Sam said, “how’d he act? What did he do?”

Norlan shrugged. “He continued drinking. Like I said, fights aren’t unusual there. Folks came up and talked with him. Even me. Message was the same. If he wanted to press charges, we’d all stand by him. Topher said to forget it.”

“Was that like him?”

Norlan cocked his head.

Sam clarified his question. “Would Topher normally let a fight like that slide?”

“I already told you—”

“Fighting at the Griz isn’t abnormal.”

“That’s right.” Norlan nodded. “To your question, I don’t know if Topher would let something like that slide.”

“You knew him well though?” Sam asked.

“It’s not like we hung out or nothing.”

Rebecca clucked. "You were at the bar enough."

Norlan glowered at his daughter. "Zip it."

She smirked. "I'm just saying."

"It's not like you two hung out," Sam prompted.

Norlan reluctantly tore his attention away from his pouting daughter. "Right. We didn't hang out." He pulled the welding helmet from his head. "We were bar friends. You know how it is. We told some stories, shared some laughs, but I really didn't know him aside from a few things."

"Like what?"

"You writing a book or something?"

"Trying to learn all I can about Topher."

Norlan put the helmet on the corner of the desk. His daughter seemed put out by the intrusion into her territory.

"What'd I know?" Norlan asked. "His favorite beer was Rainier, he had a handyman business, and some chick was giving him grief."

"He ever say this woman's name?"

Norlan's eyes drifted toward the ceiling as he thought. "Don't think as he did." His gaze drifted down to Sonja. "Far as I know, it was her."

Her jaw dropped. "It wasn't. I never met Topher before that night."

"You didn't tell the police about the woman giving Topher grief," Sam said.

"You sure?" Norlan shook his head. "I could've sworn I did."

"See?" Rebecca said. "I told you. You forget stuff when you drink."

Norlan Wisner rolled his eyes. "Got kids?" he asked Sam.

"No."

"Lucky you."

"You're no picnic either," Rebecca said.

Norlan thumbed himself in the chest. "I pay for everything."

"I work around here, too."

"Doing your nails." Norlan flicked his hand. "Running my heat bill up."

Sam eyed Sonja, then jerked his head toward the door. They left without saying goodbye. The Wisners were too busy bickering to notice.

***

The aroma and sounds of coffee production hung in the air of the 406 Roastery. An espresso machine hissed as a barista worked it. In the kitchen, a woman hastily made some sandwiches.

Overhead, a syrupy ballad played. It sounded like a newer song with soulless instrumentation, angsty lyrics, and over-modulation of the male singer's voice. Sam hated it.

At the cashier counter, a customer chatted about the dog at her side. The golden retriever wore a red vest that read *Service Dog in Training. Do Not Touch.* The animal looked around with what appeared to be a grin.

Sam watched the dog from his table.

Sonja turned in her chair to see what caught his attention. "Snowbirds can't have dogs."

"Sure they can." He sipped his coffee. "It would take some planning, but I could have a dog if I wanted."

"Let me clarify." Sonja turned in her chair, and her expression hardened. "You can't have a dog."

"Why not?"

"It requires commitment."

Sam saluted her with his cup. "Straight through the heart. Nice shot."

Her face relaxed. "I'm sorry."

"What's eating you?"

"Besides Bruce being in prison?"

"He's in jail."

Anger flared in her eyes. "Don't play semantics."

The difference between jail and prison was a pronounced one, but Sam could tell she was in no mood to hear about it. He set his cup on the table. "What's got you wound so tight?"

She moved her coffee out of the way and leaned forward. "I didn't go back in the bar."

"Okay."

"Well, I didn't. I don't like people saying I did something when I didn't."

Sam nodded. "None of us like that."

"Look who I'm talking to. Of course you understand it."

"So we're clear, you didn't make Bruce hit Topher either."

Earnestness filled Sonja's eyes. "I'd never want anyone to do something like that."

"I know."

"*They* don't." She motioned absently out the window. "Everyone keeps accusing me like I do."

"It's not everyone," Sam said. "It's only a few people."

"Still hurts."

"Who cares what they say?"

"I do." She flopped back in her chair. "Even though I know I shouldn't."

An athletic woman entered the business and looked

around. She wore a tight-fitting sweatshirt over yoga pants. Her long brown hair was tucked behind her ears. She glanced around the establishment, her gaze lingering on Sam for a moment, before walking toward the cashier.

"People will say what they wanna say," Sam said. "You're not the type of woman who wants a guy fighting for her."

Sonja bristled at the comment. "I never said that."

"What?"

"I want a guy to fight for me, not over me." Sonja leaned forward. "Something you never did."

"Here we go. You came after me, remember?"

"Repeatedly," she said. "Clearly, I made it too easy."

The athletic woman inserted her credit card into the payment machine. In a moment, she signed the screen with her left hand, ending it with a flourish. She said a couple of friendly words to the cashier before walking over to Sam and Sonja's table. Her expression hardened as she approached.

"Sam Strait?" she asked.

He stood and offered his hand. "Officer Malone?"

"Call me Riley." She shook Sam's hand, then her eyes shifted to Sonja. Riley's eyes widened briefly before narrowing once again. "Hello," she said, flatly.

Sonja introduced herself but didn't bother standing or to offer her hand.

"The missing woman," Riley said. "Agent Hathaway said you were Mr. Bloom's fiancée."

"Not yet," Sam and Sonja said simultaneously. He said it with a bit more vigor than she did, however.

Riley's eyes cut questioningly to Sam, then back to Sonja. Her face relaxed a bit further. "Hathaway said you were cooperative during your interview."

Sonja shrugged a single shoulder. "I tried."

Sam motioned toward an empty chair, and Riley sat next to Sonja.

"I'm not sure how much I'm going to share," the officer said. "I'm here more out of curiosity than anything."

"Why's that?" Sam asked.

"Never had a defense investigator want to interview me."

"A murder allegation is pretty serious."

Riley's brow creased briefly but quickly returned to a relaxed state. She had an excellent poker face. Her gaze bounced to Sonja, then back to Sam. "You two look friendlier than a client-investigator should."

"We're old friends," Sam said.

"Friends," Sonja clarified. "We're not old."

"I'm not buying it." Riley's eyes filled with skepticism. "There's something else going on between you two."

"There's nothing going on," Sonja said. Splotches of red blossomed on her cheeks. "Sam's here because he was a deputy."

Riley rested her arms along the edge of the table as she studied Sam. "You're not from around here."

"What gave it away?"

"The suntan." A smile hinted at the edges of Riley's mouth. "Where you from?"

"Hathaway didn't tell you?"

"Must've forgot."

"Just flew in from Hawaii."

"Yeah?" Her voice rose with appreciation. The smile broadened slightly, but her lips remained tight together. "Is it nice? I've never been."

"It's wonderful." His grin was bigger than necessary. "The weather. The sites. The new friends."

"Don't let him fool you," Sonja said. "He's from Spokane." Her expression tightened as she waggled her thumb between Sam and herself. "We both are."

"I snowbird," Sam blurted, then chuckled self-consciously. "I snowbird."

Riley's smile grew a bit larger. "That's how you guys became friends?" Her gaze bounced to Sonja but lingered less than a second before returning to Sam. "Spokane?"

Sam nodded.

"I like it there. Often thought about trying to get on with their police department or the sheriff's department."

"I'm probably not the best guy to ask."

"Why's that?" Riley asked.

Sonja sighed heavily. "Are we going to talk about Bruce or what?"

"That's the reason I'm here." Riley leaned back in her chair and her smile vanished. "Fire away, Mr. Defense Investigator."

Sam asked, "Can you tell us how Topher Anderson was murdered?"

"Agent Hathaway said you had a copy of my report. Courtesy of your employer no doubt."

Sam dipped his chin in acknowledgement. "You didn't describe anything more than it appeared Topher suffered blunt force trauma to the head."

"I'm not a medical examiner," Riley said.

"You've been a cop long enough to make an educated guess."

Sonja shifted in her seat. "Even a citizen can make an uneducated one."

The barista brought over a cardboard cup and a brown paper bag. She set it on the table in front of Riley. "Here you go. Have a safe night."

The off-duty officer smiled at her, then wrapped her hand around the cup. She pushed the bag to the side. "Hathaway said you were a deputy."

"For a few years."

Riley sipped her coffee. "Is that why you don't want to talk about the cops in Spokane?"

"My experience wasn't the same as most."

"Bruce," Sonja said. "Can we focus?"

Riley looked at her. "Right, sorry. Where were we?"

"How was Topher murdered?" Sam asked.

"His brains were bashed in."

Sonja grimaced.

"With a rock." Riley lowered her cup and stared into the coffee. "It was pretty gruesome."

"Took some anger," Sam said.

"I'd imagine," Riley agreed.

Sonja asked, "Could it have been a robbery?"

Riley shook her head, then looked up from her cup. "His wallet and keys were still in his pockets."

"What can you tell us about the rock?" Sam asked.

"The rock?"

Sam opened his palm. "How big? How heavy? That sort of thing."

The off-duty officer's eyes slanted. "It was big enough to crush a man's skull. What more do you want?"

"I'm just wondering…" Sam let his thought trail off.

Riley sighed, then nodded. "Sorry. Second-guessing bugs me."

"We're trying to find answers."

"The answer is I didn't weigh the rock. It was this big." She held open her palm. "That's all I know."

"You picked it up?" Sam asked.

He couldn't see any reason for a patrol officer to pick

up a rock at a murder scene. Also, it wasn't mentioned in her report. Had an officer inadvertently contaminated a piece of evidence with their fingerprints or DNA, standard practice dictated he or she noted such in their narrative.

Riley shook her head, though. "I didn't touch it."

"Then how do you know the size?"

"I'm guessing."

"Sure," Sam said, "but the rock was in the snow, right?"

"You calling me a liar?"

"I'm trying to understand how everything went down."

"It looked this big." Riley opened her palm again. "Like a baseball. You want to know more than that, I'm sure your employer will get a copy of the evidence report soon enough."

Sam rested his forearms on the table. "I'm sorry. I wasn't saying you were lying."

Riley looked around the restaurant. "How much longer is this going to take? I'd like to eat and hit the gym before work."

"Just a minute longer," Sam said. "Only a few more questions."

Another angsty song started on the radio. Sam also hadn't heard this one before, and he was thankful for it. He stopped listening when the singer mentioned leaving her scarf at someone's sister's house.

He asked, "On what side of the head was Topher hit?" He couldn't recall that information being in the police report.

Riley faced him. "Right."

"Huh," Sam said.

Sonja's gaze bounced between Sam and Riley. "What's that mean?"

"It means," Riley said, "a lefty smacked him with the

rock."

Sonja's face slackened and her eyes darted to Sam. "Oh."

According to the police report, Bruce was discovered with blood on his left hand, likely the one he used to pick up the rock. Only ten percent of the population was left-handed. It was a fact Sam had read in a book at some time, or perhaps he learned it while a deputy. Regardless, if the prosecutor could show Topher Anderson was killed by a left-handed assailant, it diminished the pool of suspects by quite a bit. In a stressful situation, most people are likely to default to using their dominant hand. He was pretty sure he read that in the same place he'd gotten the ten percent factoid.

Riley toasted them with her cup. "You see why we arrested the fiancé."

"You didn't mention it in your report."

"Didn't mention what?"

"The side of Topher's head."

"I didn't?" Riley seemed surprised. "I'm sure I put it in." Worry flashed across her face. "Don't think that'll get your guy off on a technicality."

He didn't. If anything it was a harmless omission. Agent Hathaway would certainly add it in to his report. He was the detective, the professional homicide investigator. Even if he failed to include it, the medical examiner's report would detail all the important facts. Sam wondered how many murders Riley had responded to in her career. He imagined there weren't many opportunities for such a thing in Havre.

Riley continued, "Mr. Bloom had means, motive, and opportunity. What more do we need to prove?" Her eyes challenged Sam, then moved to Sonja.

"Bruce is innocent," Sonja said.

"That's one story." Riley slid the brown bag in front of her. "If that's all?"

Sam asked, "When will the medical examiner have their results?"

The off-duty cop shrugged. "That's a good question. The body was transported to the Montana State Crime Lab pending an autopsy. Those results don't come to us."

"Right," Sam said, "they'll go to Agent Hathaway."

"My part of this investigation is done." She cocked her head. "You being a former deputy remember how it is."

Sam did. As a first responder, his duty was to contain whatever situation he found. If he was sent to an assault, he ensured danger to all was mitigated. Then he conducted an initial investigation. If Sam determined who was at fault, he'd make an arrest. His report would make its way to a detective who'd continue the investigation until he handed it to a prosecuting attorney. Officers and deputies were rarely involved after the initial contact.

He said, "You arrested Bruce Bloom for deliberate homicide."

"Are you asking me to explain the probable cause? Do I look like your Criminal Law instructor?" Riley squinted. "I'm sorry. That was uncalled for."

"It's okay," Sam said. "All states are different. In Washington, we've got multiple levels of homicide. Is it the same in Montana?"

"It is," Riley said, "and I charged Mr. Bloom with the appropriate crime. There was more than enough evidence to do so."

Sam stared at the off-duty cop as he thought. Witnesses saw Bruce attack Topher inside the bar. The bartender then tossed Bruce and Sonja outside. In the eyes of the law, that likely gave Bruce time to ambush Topher. The call to the police was Bruce's attempt at building an alibi. It was a simple story, but that's the way cops liked them. At least, that's the way Sam liked them when he wore a uniform.

Riley stood and picked up her items. "This has been fun." Her voice was as flat as her expression. "Let's not do it again." She glanced at Sonja before spinning on her heel and leaving the coffee shop.

Sonja muttered an expletive. "I hate her."

"Because she did her job?"

"Because she arrested Bruce."

Sam asked, "What else was she supposed to do?"

Sonja's face tightened. "Why are you defending her?"

"I'm not." He stood. "I'll tell you this much."

"What's that?"

"Things are worse for Bruce than I thought."

Sonja stood now. "How can it get worse than being arrested for murder?"

"When the evidence looks airtight."

Chapter 11

"Willow Dawson," Sam said, then read her address from the police report.

Sonja entered it into the GPS system. "Another witness?"

"Unless you've got a better idea."

"I don't." When the system located the address, Sonja dropped the Range Rover into Reverse and backed away from the angled parking on the side street.

"Stop," Sam said.

She hit the brakes and pulled the car back to the curb. A truck behind them honked, then sped past.

He stared at the report.

"What is it?" Sonja asked.

"Maybe we're going about this the wrong way."

"How's that?"

Sam waggled the report. "We're getting the same information Riley reported."

"Haven't we found something not in her report?"

"We have." He scanned the report as he spoke. "Nolan said a woman was giving Topher grief."

"That's something, even if I don't know what that means."

He cast a sideways glance.

"What?" she asked.

Sonja gave him plenty of grief over the years. She had wanted a relationship when Sam didn't. Could the mystery woman Norlan Wisner mentioned have desired the same from Topher Anderson? Or was it another type of grief?

"*What?*" Sonja repeated.

"How can a woman give a man grief?"

Sonja's face slackened. "I feel like this is going to be an attack on my gender."

"It's not."

"Or me specifically."

Sam waved a hand to clear the air symbolically. "Maybe she wants a relationship."

"Uh-huh," Sonja muttered slowly, undoubtedly suspicious of the direction the conversation may take.

"Maybe they *had* a relationship."

"Uh-huh," Sonja repeated, her apprehension not dissipating one bit.

"What if," Sam said, "it was about money?"

"Oh." Sonja brightened some. "Like maybe he owed her something."

"Child support, you think?"

"Do we know if he has kids?"

Sam shook his head. "He's our age. Sounds like he's been active."

"A dog," Sonja interjected.

"Not improbable that he has a child somewhere."

"Do you?"

"Do I what?"

Sonja crossed her arms, and her eyes hardened with a judging look. "Do you have a child somewhere I don't know about?"

"I don't."

"You don't have one, or you don't know if you might?"

He rolled his eyes. "Let's not make this about me."

"Seems like a reasonable question."

"Not from a woman about to be married to someone

else."

Sonja's jaw tightened. "If you do—"

"I don't."

"—would you tell me?"

"Of course, I would."

She stared at him. "I probably wouldn't want to know."

"Fine. I won't tell you."

"You'd keep secrets from me?"

Sam might not have been the smartest man, but Sam knew sharing details of his love life with any woman never produced positive results. The outcome was always predictable—disastrous.

"Focus on Topher," he said.

"Nice way to avoid my question."

"I'm not, but we're on the clock, remember? Bruce is sitting in jail."

Sonja dropped her arms and her expression relaxed. "Okay, so we need to know a little more about Topher's background."

"A lot more."

"Then where do we go from here?"

Sam's gaze fell to the police report in his hand. "I guess we talk with Willow Dawson."

"So we're staying the course."

"I don't see a reason to change yet. We just have to ask some more questions when we get the opportunity."

"Whatever you say."

Sonja checked the rearview mirror before backing out of the parking stall. She dropped the gear into Drive, then proceeded half a block before flipping a U-turn and heading back to First Street. She accelerated into the arterial and headed eastbound.

****

Willow Dawson lived in a small rancher on Seventeenth Street. Not much stood out on the house except it was made of brick. Snow covered its roof and lawn. A red Honda Accord idled in the driveway. Most of the snow and ice had been scraped free of the windows. Any remnants had turned to water courtesy of the heater running inside the car. An MSU-Northern sticker resided in the bottom left corner of the back window.

Someone had shoveled the sidewalks at some point, but a dusting of snow covered the concrete now.

The front door opened and a thin woman in tight jeans and a puffy burgundy coat stepped out. A similarly colored beanie covered the top of her long blond hair. In her left hand, the woman carried a hardback book and a notepad. She pulled the door closed behind her and carefully stepped off the stairs. She shuffled hurriedly toward the driveway, careful not to lift her boots too far from the ground.

The woman stopped, surprised, when she realized Sam and Sonja blocked her from reaching her idling car. Her mouth opened, and she clutched her belongings to her chest.

"Willow Dawson?" Sam asked.

The woman's eyes darted to Sonja. "What's this about?"

"We're looking for Willow so we can ask about a fight she witnessed a couple nights ago."

"I'm headed to class."

"This'll only take a minute."

"I don't have a minute. I'm already late." She lifted her chin toward her car. "Now, if you'll excuse me."

Sam backpedaled. "Can we talk with you at another time?"

Willow opened the Honda's door, then turned around. "Are you the police?"

"We're working with the defense."

"In that case," Willow said, her upper lip curling, "no. You can't talk with me at another time."

She dropped into the driver's seat and pulled the door closed. The engine whined as the Honda accelerated away.

"Friendly," Sonja said, watching the car disappear. "Think she might be the woman Norlan mentioned?"

"Who knows?"

They headed toward the street. Sam checked the time on his cell phone. It was nearing two, but the sun was already beginning its descent toward the western horizon. Darkness would likely arrive around five.

"What's wrong?" Sonja asked.

Sam looked up.

She motioned toward his face. "You're frowning. What's wrong?"

"It'll be dark soon."

"So?"

"Showing up at someone's house when it's dark sets a different tone."

"You did it when you were a deputy."

Sam opened the passenger door to the Range Rover. "That's different. It was official."

"This is official," Sonja said as she climbed into the SUV.

"Official-ish." He settled into the passenger seat.

"Are you saying we stop asking questions when the sun goes down? That seems silly if you ask me."

"I'm saying things take on a different tone. That's all."

"You're overthinking it." Sonja started the car. "People won't have a problem with us coming by at night."

He wasn't sure about that. Sam would like to think most folks would be open to talking with them later in the evening. However, he believed many didn't want to be disturbed when the sun went down. After work, many retreated to the safety of their castles where the world couldn't reach them. They hadn't liked it when Deputy Strait came by to follow up on a witness statement or some other matter. It certainly meant they'd be less inclined to talk with Citizen Strait.

"Where to now?" Sonja asked.

Sam pulled the police report from his pocket. "Enough with the witnesses. Let's see what we can find out about Topher's life."

***

Topher Anderson lived in a rundown home on Second Avenue. A blue tarp hung over the edge of the roof, a tale-tell sign of a temporary repair. Several inches of snow covered the house. The brown wood siding was in desperate need of new paint. The screen door was opened and clung to the house by its bottom hinge. A line of yellow POLICE—DO NOT CROSS was taped across the front door.

"The cobbler's children have no shoes," Sam said.

"What's that?" Sonja asked as she slipped the Range Rover into Park.

A carport extended off the side of Topher's house. Underneath the flat roof was a pile of wood, an upside-down dirt bike, and an ATV missing its fourth wheel.

On the lawn sat a rusty Camero and an equally oxidized

Dodge truck. Snow covered both.

"Topher was supposed to be a handyman," Sam said, "but he didn't take care of his home."

Sonja eyed him. "What's that got to do with cobbler?"

"A cobbler is a shoemaker."

"Who says?"

The question surprised him. "The dictionary."

"I thought cobbler was a dessert."

"It's both."

Sonja smirked. "You're making that up."

"If you say so." Arguing about homonyms now didn't make sense when there were more important tasks to do. He opened the passenger door.

"Wait," Sonja said. "Where're you going? We can't go inside the house."

That wasn't necessarily true, Sam thought. He'd entered an apartment once after the police had secured it. The entry was illegal, of course, but he still gained access. He had no intention of doing that today, though. Not only did Agent Hathaway and Officer Riley know he was snooping around, but Sam wasn't sure if breaking into Topher's house was worth the trouble.

"Let's talk with his neighbors."

"I guess that's okay." Sonja silenced the engine, and they left the SUV.

***

No one was home at the first three houses Sam and Sonja visited.

The fourth house they approached sat kitty-corner from Topher's. Even though it was covered with snow, the small yellow rancher appeared to be well maintained. The sidewalk and driveway were both shoveled and covered with deicer. A Buick LaCrosse sat in front of the garage. Its windows were scraped clear, and snow had been brushed from its top.

"This isn't working," Sonja said as they walked toward the front door.

Sam glanced over his shoulder. "We can come back."

"When it's dark?"

"What other choice do we have?"

"You said that was bad for interviews."

He shrugged. "No one wants to be interrupted during dinner."

There wasn't room for them both on the steps, especially if the homeowner opened the storm door for them to enter, so Sonja remained on the sidewalk. A *No Solicitors* sign hung above the doorbell. Sam rang it anyway.

From inside, someone grumbled something. Heavy footsteps crossed the house.

A man in his mid-seventies opened the main door but stood safely behind a sturdy storm door. Thick glasses covered a considerable portion of his face and magnified his eyes, giving him an almost bug-like appearance. He wore blue slacks and a brown sweater, but he had bare feet. A cigarette dangled between his lips; its rising smoke caused his left eye to squint.

"You read?" he asked and pointed toward the *No Solicitors* sign. He started to shut the door.

"We want to ask about your neighbor," Sam blurted. He thumbed over his shoulder toward Topher's house.

The older man stopped. "What about him?" His cigarette bounced as he spoke, and the squint worsened.

"What can you tell us?"

"You ain't the cops."

"No, sir," Sam said while shaking his head. "We're not."

"This ain't the church social." The older man snatched the cigarette from his mouth and pointed its butt at them. "Even if it was, I wouldn't gossip, especially about my neighbors." He started to close the door again.

"Wait," Sonja said from behind Sam. She climbed the steps now, standing next to him. "The police arrested my boyfriend."

"So?" the older man asked. "What's that got to do with the price of fish?"

Sonja's smile was sad and apologetic. "They think he murdered your neighbor, but he didn't. He couldn't."

The older man stuck the cigarette between his lips as he studied Sonja. He didn't eye her in an appreciative way that so many others did, but rather in a calculating manner—the same way a parent might try to discern if a child was telling the truth. "You know the Blooms?" the older man asked.

Sonja nodded. "Russell and Dorothy. They're wonderful people."

"Guess that counts for something." The older man pushed the storm door open slightly. "C'mon in."

***

Harvey Mayer's living room was impeccable. A loveseat, two wingback chairs, and a television were the featured pieces in the room. A small coffee table sat in the middle of the room. The only things it held were a green glass ashtray, a box of cigarettes, and the TV remote.

Family photos hung on the wall. At least, Sam assumed

they were family, but Harvey wasn't in any of them. The pictures were in a hodgepodge of frames. No knickknacks gathered dust anywhere.

It was a clean and functional room. Beyond the photographs, the space was devoid of emotion. Sam's appreciation for the setup was only marred by the heavy cigarette smoke lingering in the room.

"I'll put this out," Harvey said as he crushed his cigarette in the ashtray. It was nearly full, but the older man managed not to knock any ash or butts onto the coffee table. When he straightened, his glasses slid down his nose. With a single finger, he pushed them back into their correct position. "Plant yourselves."

Sam and Sonja each sat in a wingback chair and Harvey settled onto the middle of the couch. His hands rested on his knees.

"I don't get many visitors." Harvey's magnified eyes narrowed. "Don't have anything to offer except water."

"We're good," Sam said.

Sonja cocked her head. "You know the Blooms?"

"A little," Harvey said. "We go to the same church, but they're involved in the programs and the leadership. Never tended toward any of that stuff myself." His head bobbled. "Other than that, they seem like decent folks."

"Have you met Bruce?" Sonja asked.

"When he was younger. Nice-looking boy. Haven't seen him in quite some time. You two have been together a long time, though, huh?"

Sonja smiled kindly. "About a year."

"Only a year?" Harvey looked at the ground. "I could've sworn you two were high school sweethearts."

"Must've been another redhead," Sam offered with a slight chuckle.

"Perhaps." Harvey lifted his head. A worried look filled his enlarged eyes. "A number of my friends have dementia. Old timer's disease, I call it." His smile contained no joy.

Sam and Sonja exchanged glances.

"I always worry the sickness might catch me, too." Harvey rubbed his palms on his pants. "When I forget something or make a mistake like that, it bothers me something fierce."

"Only natural," Sonja said. "I think you're fine."

Sam scooted to the edge of his seat. "About Topher."

The older man's gaze slid to Sam, and he sat up straighter. "What about him?"

"We're looking for anyone who might've wanted to hurt him. Since the cops have their man, even if he is the wrong one, that's who they'll stay focused on. It'll take a pretty big reason for them to consider anyone else."

"That's what you're after?" Harvey asked. "Someone else to throw under the bus?"

"We're looking for the truth," Sam said. "The cops have the wrong guy."

Harvey stared at him skeptically.

"We're not trying to muddy anyone's reputation," Sonja said. "We only want to learn what we can about your neighbor."

The older man blinked several times as he watched Sonja. "I hate gossip," he told her.

"So do I," Sonja said. "We're not looking for gossip. Just a clearer picture of the truth."

Harvey considered her words. "When you put it that way," he said finally, "I guess I can speak to matters of the truth. As long as it ain't gossip, you understand?"

"We understand," she said.

Harvey turned slightly on the couch to look through the window. "Never did like Topher much. The way a man lives tells you a lot about what's inside him." He motioned across the street. Sam and Sonja followed his gesture and looked out the window. "Guy was a dadburn slob. Junkers in the yard. House falling apart. Swore like a drunken sailor." Harvey faced them again. "I used to be in the Navy, and Topher made me blush on more than one occasion."

"Did you ever see him get into it with anyone?" Sam asked.

"You mean fisticuffs?" Harvey waved his hands around in a poor imitation of a boxer. "Never saw anything like that. Did see him arguing with a woman once. Nothing physical, mind you. Looked like it might have gone that way had she not left."

"You catch her name?"

"Topher called her plenty, but nothing her parents would have named her."

"What'd she look like?" Sonja asked.

"Can't really tell you." Harvey appeared embarrassed. "Didn't have my glasses on." He patted the couch with both hands. "I was taking a nap right here when I heard them."

"Must've been some argument," Sam said.

"It was." Harvey looked toward Topher's house. "I heard them out there but couldn't see their faces. It could've been you two, except I knew what Topher sounded like."

Disappointment crossed Sonja's face. "So you didn't see anything?"

"By the time I got my glasses on, she was turned away."

"Did you see any hair color?" Sam asked.

"Can't say as I did. She sported a baseball hat—a red one. I can tell you that much. Probably not a lot to go on, but almost everyone else wears a stocking cap this time of year."

"So it was recent?"

"Last month, I suppose. Winter hangs around a while in these parts." Harvey's bug eyes danced behind the thick glasses as he studied Sam. "You been on vacation or something? You're mighty tan for this time of year."

"What about her car?" Sam asked, ignoring the older man's question. "How'd she get to Topher's house?"

Harvey waggled a finger. "There you go. That's a good question. Now, you're thinking. She drove a pickup. One of those foreign jobbers. A Toyota something or other."

"Tacoma?"

"Sounds about right." Harvey shrugged. "I'll never get used to women driving trucks. Seems as unnatural as them riding motorcycles."

Sonja's expression remained passive. She didn't drive a truck or ride a motorcycle, so Sam imagined the slight to the sisterhood didn't bother her much.

"What color was the truck?" Sam asked.

"Red like an apple."

Sam felt a zing of excitement. Maybe things were breaking his way, and they could quickly end the investigation. He asked his next question. "Was Topher ever married?"

"Not a chance." Harvey smirked. "Look at those toys in his yard. Motorcycle, four-wheeler, cars. He was a perpetual child. Something's wrong with a man who won't settle down with a woman and start a family."

Sonja's eyes cut to Sam, but she refrained from commenting.

Sam asked, "Is there anything else you can recall about Topher?"

"No, but I didn't really know the man. You check with the other neighbors?"

"You're the only one home," Sam said. He heard the disappointment in his voice.

"Guess they're all at work." Harvey rubbed his chin thoughtfully. "Maybe you should check with his customers."

Sam didn't know how he'd go about finding Topher's clients unless he broke into the man's house. He didn't want to do that and risk getting himself into deeper trouble.

"I could never imagine Topher doing good work," Harvey said. "Look how he kept his house."

Sonja leaned to look out the window. "Sam said it could have been the cobbler wasn't focusing on his children's shoes."

Harvey clucked. "That's the dumbest thing I ever heard."

She glanced at the older man, and Sam felt the need to rush to her defense. "That's not how I said it."

"What kind of advertising is that for a man not to take care of his family or home?" Harvey waved his hand toward the window. "If you saw Topher's house, would you hire him to fix yours? If I saw the cobbler's children in worn-out shoes, I sure as heck wouldn't buy a pair from him."

Sam didn't feel like getting into it over a fictional shoemaker. "Have the police been by to talk with you?" Sam asked the older man.

Harvey nodded. "Day after it happened. Tall fella from the DCI. Hathaway, I think, was his name."

"You tell him about the girl?"

"I did."

"The truck, too?" Sam asked.

Harvey's lips pursed. "Don't think he asked. Maybe he did, and I forgot what I told him." He motioned across the street. "I remember he was in a hurry to get inside Topher's house and search the place. What do you wanna bet it's a pigsty in there?"

Sam stood. "Thank you for your time."

Sonja and Harvey rose as well.

"If the Bloom boy really had nothing to do with the murder," the older man said, "I wish you the best. Russell and Dorothy are good folks. They don't deserve this blight on their reputations."

Chapter 12

Sonja weaved through traffic, following the directions the GPS system provided.

"We're doing pretty good," she said, then glanced at Sam. "Right?"

"I guess." Sam shoved his hands in his coat pockets. The heat pumping out of the vents wasn't warm yet. Beyond that, he was still feeling stymied. He wasn't sure why the sentiment rolled over him, but it left him in a funk.

Sonja slowed the Range Rover at an uncontrolled intersection before speeding through, after ensuring it was clear. "I think we're doing well." She nodded twice, convincing herself of their good fortune. "Really well."

Sam eyed her. Sonja tried to hide her worry, but she wasn't completely successful.

"We'll figure it out," he said. The resolve in his voice surprised him and helped cut through his emotional malaise.

Sonja raised her eyebrows. "You think so?"

"Yeah, sure," he said and faced forward.

"I'm not sure if I've said it today, but I really appreciate you helping us."

"You," Sam corrected sullenly. "I'm helping *you*."

She slowed the car at another uncontrolled intersection. "I don't know anyone else who would do what you're doing."

"Me either," Sam muttered. He wasn't patting himself on the back. What had he learned that the cops hadn't?

Hardly anything.

Thanks to Harvey Mayer, Sam knew the color and make of the vehicle that an unidentified woman drove to Topher Anderson's house to argue with him out front. Norlan Wisner mentioned Topher complained about some woman giving him grief. Supposedly, the cops didn't know those two pieces of information.

Neither was the proverbial silver bullet—the clue that would allow Sam to solve the mystery of who killed Topher Anderson. Those pieces of information wouldn't even get Bruce's charges dropped. They were circumstantial, at best. They might even be worthless.

He felt like a dog chasing its tail. A car spinning its wheels in mud. He mentally searched for another metaphor for hopelessness but couldn't find one. Sam grunted. Even that felt hopeless. His head flopped against the seat.

Sonja pulled alongside a curb and stopped the engine. A snow berm several feet high loomed outside the passenger door. "What's wrong?" she asked.

"Feeling sorry for myself."

"You just said we'd figure this out."

"I know."

Sonja's expression dimmed. "Unless you're missing Hawaii, and what's her name?"

"That's not it."

"So there is a what's her name."

Sam rolled his head on the seat to face her. "Sonja."

"I'm sorry," she said, gripping the steering wheel tighter. "It's your life, but if you're not missing Hawaii, what is it?"

Sam shrugged and looked ahead. "It feels like we're not getting anywhere."

"I thought you said—"

"I know what I said," he said gloomily. He flicked his hand at the falling snow. "Maybe it's the weather."

"I doubt that."

"You don't know."

Her expression softened. "Let me ask you something. Did you solve those other murders in a day?"

He thought for a moment before shaking his head.

"Then give yourself a break. You're doing great." She reached out and squeezed his shoulder. "I believe in you."

"I'm glad someone does." Sam forced a smile.

She turned and looked at the brown split-level across the street. Two cars sat in the driveway, both with their tops mostly free of snow. "Who are we seeing here?"

***

"Jerrold retired from the railroad several years ago," Louanna Dellar said, patting her husband's leg. She was in her early sixties with short silver hair and bright ruby lips. Louanna wore a beige turtleneck sweater and blue slacks. "We spent the first couple of winters RVing through the southwest."

"Should be doing it now," Jerrold said grumpily. He also had short silver hair, but it resided only on the sides of his head. His pate shone like it was freshly buffed. Jerrold wore a plaid flannel shirt and blue jeans. "I had a health scare, though."

Louanna lifted her hand to the side of her mouth as if telling a secret. "His heart," she whispered.

"Getting old ain't for sissies," Jerrold said. "Stay young as long as you can."

They were seated in the Dellars' living room, a warm and inviting place that Sam imagined had hosted many gatherings. Pictures of friends and family hung on the wall. Knickknacks were strategically placed about the room. The television was on the FOX News channel, but the sound was off. A newscaster team blathered silently on.

The Dellars huddled side by side on a couch, while Sonja and Sam sat next to each other on a loveseat. Her hip and leg pressed against Sam's. He tried to ignore the endorphins flowing through his veins.

Louanna cocked her head as she studied Sonja. "You look so familiar. Doesn't she look familiar?"

Jerrold shrugged. "I suppose."

Sonja smiled. "I've been in some commercials. Maybe they're showing them in this market."

"That's not it," Louanna said. "You got family around here?"

"Just my boyfriend's."

"You're working with Chuck Palmer," Jerrold said. "Isn't that what you said?"

Sam nodded.

"He's an all-right fella, I suppose." Jerrold eyed his wife. "He palled around with our son during his school days."

"They were thick as thieves back then," Louanna said. "Charles was such a nice boy. Always so polite."

Jerrold smirked. "He was a harmless goofball back then. Thin as a rail and always hungry. Our youngest daughter had a crush on him. We dodged a bullet with those two not dating. I'm open minded about a lot, but I wouldn't want a lawyer sharing my Thanksgiving turkey, if you get my drift."

Sam did. It was rule number five.

"Plus," Jerrold continued, "I get the feeling Chuck leans Democrat. Talk about a double whammy."

Louanna leaned forward slightly, her eyes narrowing as she studied Sonja. "Did you know our daughters?"

"No, ma'am." Sonja smiled. "I promise. I'm not from around here."

"If your son hung out with Chuck," Sam said, "he probably knew Bruce Bloom."

Jerrold's brow creased. "You mean the guy arrested for murdering that fella in the parking lot?"

"That's the one."

"Can't say as I remember him," Jerrold said. He looked at his wife. "What about you?"

Louanna shook her head. "I tried to recall him after reading the name in the paper. Couldn't seem to place him either."

"That's who Chuck's trying to get out of jail?" Jerrold asked.

Sam nodded.

Jerrold turned to his wife. "Remind me to ignore Chuck the next time we see him."

Louanna shushed him. "Our kids probably knew Bruce in school." She turned to her husband now. "I should call and ask."

Jerrold waved off his wife's suggestion. "Leave them be. They've got their own lives to think about. They don't need to be worrying about some murderer."

Sonja leaned forward, pressing her hip and leg harder into Sam. "Bruce is innocent," she said. "He wouldn't hurt anyone."

Sam held his tongue on dentistry's natural tendency toward sadism.

"Who are his parents?" Jerrold asked.

"Russell and Dorothy Bloom," Sonja said.

The older man looked at his wife. "Ring a bell?"

"Can't recall them." She looked apologetically at Sonja. "Maybe we met them at some school function way back when."

The interview had quickly gotten off track. Sam needed to get everyone focused on the task at hand. "How often do you go to The Grizzly Den?" he asked.

A sly smile appeared on Jerrold's lips. "I see what you're after." He waggled his finger between his wife and himself. "Why're a couple of fogeys hanging out at a happening place like the Griz?"

Sam nodded once as he struggled to believe anyone would refer to The Grizzly Den as a happening place.

"That used to be my spot," Jerrold said, "when I worked for the railroad. Back when Cyrus was behind the bar."

"That's Darry's father," Louanna said. "The man who owns the bar now."

"We've met him," Sam said.

Jerrold continued. "I'd stop at the Griz for a beer before heading home. On Friday nights, Lou and I would get a babysitter for the kids when they were little and go have ourselves a real time."

Louanna patted her husband's leg. "Those were the days."

"That's for sure." Jerrold nodded. "Crowd's different now. Less working man, more angry man." He shrugged. "Guess that's a commentary on the whole dang country."

"Did you know Topher?" Sam asked.

"Not personally, no," Jerrold said. "Saw him at the bar, of course. Seemed like he was there whenever we stopped in."

"We knew him by reputation," Louanna added. "Our kids talked about him during their school days. Sounded like a bully."

Sam wanted to shift his position on the couch, since he was slouching and his back was starting to ache. However, he didn't want to pull his leg and hip away from Sonja. Perhaps he could scoot back and sit up straighter. If he did so, maybe she'd notice they were touching and she'd move away. Sam decided he could put up with the pain in his lower back a little longer.

He said, "You told the police you saw the fight."

Jerrold nodded as he looked toward his wife. "We missed what caused the ruckus, but we saw that Bloom fella hit Topher with a pool cue. Swung it like Reggie Jackson. Surprised the cue didn't break."

"I thought the same," Sam said.

Sonja cast a sideways glance at him.

"As quick as it started," Jerrold said, "it was over. Darry tossed him out." He lifted his chin toward Sonja. "You, too, I think."

"I was there," Sonja admitted.

Jerrold thumbed at Sonja while he looked at his wife. "That's probably where you saw her."

Louanna's brow wrinkled. "Maybe, but I don't think so."

"You didn't leave the Griz after the fight?" Sam asked.

"Because of a couple hotheads mixing it up?" Jerrold laughed. "That's to be expected."

"You said the crowd was different," Sam said.

"Working men fight, too."

Louanna patted her husband's thigh. "Not Jerrold. He was too smart to get involved in that silliness."

"That's not it." The older man motioned toward the ceiling. "Only thing that kept me out of a bar brawl was God's grace."

"Grace," Louanna echoed and turned to Sonja. "That's

who you remind me of—Grace Carlson."

Both Sam and Sonja stiffened, but he knew it was for entirely different reasons.

Louanna nudged her husband. "Doesn't she look like Rhoda's daughter?"

Jerrold squinted. "Now that you mention it. I suppose she does."

"Rhoda's been gone quite some time." Louanna lowered her voice. "Cancer."

"You don't have to whisper it," Jerrold said. "It's not lurking around the corner for us."

Louanna slapped the back of her hand against her husband's leg. "Haven't talked to Grace in years, but I see her around now and then. Not sure if she remembers us or not."

Sonja tapped her chest. "Grace Carlson looks like me?"

"Not sure if she still does, but a few years ago, I'd say you two were almost a spitting image."

Sonja stood abruptly. "Thank you for your time." She stepped by Sam and headed for the door.

"Something got her hair on fire." Jerrold struggled to his feet with Louanna in tow.

Louanna flinched as the door slammed behind Sonja. "Hope it wasn't something we said."

Sam rose from the couch. "We appreciate your time." He smiled. "You've been very helpful."

* * *

Sam dropped into the passenger seat and closed the door. "What're you doing?"

Sonja didn't respond. Instead, she bowed her head over her cell phone and her thumbs danced across its screen.

"Wanna start the car?" Sam asked. "It's kind of cold out here."

"Whatever." Sonja jammed her thumb against the ignition button. The Range Rover rumbled to life and air roared through the vents. It was no longer warm, so Sam turned the heater off. He tucked his hands underneath his thighs.

Outside, snowflakes fell in the early darkness of night. The snowfall was heavier now than earlier.

"Doesn't she look like Rhoda's daughter?" Sonja mockingly muttered as her thumbs continued to bounce about the phone. "I better not."

"I'm sure there's a reasonable explanation," Sam said half-heartedly. Bruce's admonition to never let Sonja meet Grace now clanged in his brain like a battleship siren.

"That dirty—" Sonja's lip curled, and she uttered an ugly expletive. She followed this with a string of swear words with Bruce's name sprinkled liberally amongst them. Sonja held up the phone so Sam could see a picture of a redhead who looked oddly similar. "Here."

"I see."

"That's Grace Carlson," Sonja said, except she shoved an unnecessary expletive in the middle of the woman's name.

"So what?" Sam shrugged as nonchalantly as he could. "Bruce has a type."

"A type?" Sonja shouted. She pushed the phone closer to Sam's face. "This is the love of Bruce's life."

He leaned back, away from her hand. "It was high school."

Sonja waggled the phone. "He said *I* was the love of his life."

"I'm sure you are," Sam said, feeling stupid for coming

to the tooth mangler's defense. He gently pushed her hand away.

"It says she's a geology professor." Her upper lip curled. "What a nerd."

"Listen," Sam said. "Going down this path isn't going to help."

"Where's she live?" Sonja grumbled. Her thumbs blazed over the phone's screen.

"I'm serious." He reached out to touch her, but Sonja swatted his hand.

"Don't." She glared at him. "Now is not the time."

Sam lifted his hands in mock surrender. "Fine."

In a moment, Sonja looked up and started the car's GPS. She typed in an address.

"This is a bad idea," Sam said gently.

"Keep it to yourself," Sonja snapped. She mashed the accelerator, and the car lurched into the street, its tires struggling for purchase. "I'll drop you at the airport if you want."

Sam pulled his seatbelt on. He didn't want to leave Havre now, just when the investigation was getting interesting.

***

The Range Rover slid to a stop in front of a small brown home on Fifth Street. A leafless tree loomed overhead; its branches bowed from the weight of snow. The driveway was empty. Across the street was a large brick apartment complex. Snow fell faster and thicker now.

"Maybe we should talk about this," Sam said.

Sonja turned off the engine and nearly jumped out of the SUV. She slammed the door behind her.

Sam climbed out of the car and immediately stepped into a snow berm. He struggled to get out of the way as he closed the door. He dropped onto his butt with his feet still stuck in the snow. "Sonja, wait."

She walked around the front of the Range Rover, through the recently shoveled driveway, and up the sidewalk. Sonja lifted her hand. "Not a word, Sam."

He pulled a leg free and rolled off the berm. The twisting action dislodged his second leg. He sprawled on the sidewalk and pellets of deicer dug into his fingers. Sam scrambled to his feet as Sonja continued toward the house. He brushed the chemical salt from his clothes and hands as he hurried to catch up.

"She's probably not even home," Sam said hopefully.

Sonja climbed the few stairs, then banged on the screen door. The noise reverberated through the neighborhood. "We'll go by the college if she's not here."

"You know where she works?"

"She's a professor, Sam. It's on her LinkedIn page."

Sam had no idea what LinkedIn was. He turned and surveyed the neighborhood, wondering if anyone was watching them. Only the apartment community was across the street, and no one there seemed to take notice of their presence.

Sonja banged on the screen door again. The aluminum frame rattled loudly under the flat of her fist.

"There's a doorbell," Sam said.

"I don't care." Sonja kicked the bottom of the screen door. "She's not home."

"Can we go?"

Sonja scooted past Sam as she left the stairs. "We're going to the school."

"Can we talk about this?"

A car drove down Fifth Avenue, its headlights illuminating the way. Sonja paused at the driveway as a Lexus sedan turned into Grace Carlson's driveway and stopped. The headlights flicked off, and the engine quieted.

"Sonja," Sam said. "This is a bad idea."

"You can go." Sonja's gaze never left the car in the driveway.

"Where am I gonna go?" Sam turned his palms upward and glanced around.

The driver's door opened, and a woman stepped out of the car. She was moderately tall, but it was hard to tell much more since she was bundled in a coat, scarf, and beanie. The early evening's darkness and falling snow helped mask her appearance.

"May I help you?" the woman called.

"Yes," Sonja said, her voice suddenly dropping to a pleasant level. "Are you Grace Carlson?"

Sam eyed Sonja, surprised at her sudden change in demeanor. It was as if she stood before a movie camera and a hidden director had yelled, "Action!"

"I'm Grace," the woman said. She walked around the sedan and stood before them. Grace clutched her purse to her waist. "If you're recruiting for election season—"

"We're friends of Bruce Bloom," Sonja interrupted respectfully. "We'd like to ask you some questions." Her words were filled with plastic sweetness.

"Bruce?"

"We understand you two used to be friends," Sonja said. She smiled and a mask of hopefulness descended over her face.

Grace's attention swung to Sam. He nodded dumbly as he tried unsuccessfully to ignore Sonja's whiplash behavior.

"I read about what happened," Grace said. "I'm not sure how I can help."

"We're trying to get some background information." Sonja motioned to Sam. "We're not from around here, so anything you could tell us would be helpful."

Grace's expression tightened. "We knew each other back in high school."

Sonja looked toward the sky. Snowflakes landed on her face. "Mind if we step inside?" Her gaze dropped pleasantly to Grace. "It's getting messy out here."

"Of course," Grace said.

***

Grace Carlson's home was warm both in temperature and tone. The living room walls were sandy brown, and the hardwood floors were rich oak. Four brown chairs sat around a circular coffee table. An oval rug with burnt umber tones brought the whole scheme together. A smell of fresh paint hung in the house.

"How do you know Bruce?" Grace asked as she closed the door behind Sam.

"We met in Spokane," Sonja said over her shoulder. She studied a picture on a wall.

Sam moved closer to the photo. A red-haired teenager stood in front of a large tree. She wore a flannel shirt and khaki shorts. The girl smiled broadly at the camera and spread her arms wide. The teenager looked surprisingly like Sonja did in school.

"You came all the way here to help him?" Grace asked.

"That's what friends do." Sonja's upper lip curled as she leaned toward the picture, examining it more closely.

"If I'm ever in trouble," Grace said, "I hope I have friends like you."

Sam faced Grace now, the first time he'd gotten to look at her in full light. She pulled the beanie from her head, exposing shoulder-length red hair. The cut was different and her face was slightly fuller, but other than that, Grace Carlson was Sonja's doppelgänger.

Sonja turned around now. Her plastic smile returned as she tugged the hat from her head. "We could be twins."

Grace Carlson smiled sweetly. "I can't hold a candle to you."

"That's kind of you to say."

Sam stared at the professor. Grace was an alternate reality version of Sonja. A copy of a copy, not quite exact. Her eyes were slightly different, as was her nose. The longer hair certainly added to their differences. None of that took away from her beauty, though.

Grace opened her winter coat and shrugged it from her shoulders, catching the garment in her left hand. She wore a tight beige sweater, green slacks, and green boots. The clothing highlighted her curves in all the right ways. Sam never had any teacher that looked like her. She turned to a nearby closet to put the coat away.

Sonja angrily bumped his elbow. "Close your mouth," she whispered.

Sam sheepishly did as she ordered.

"Well," Grace said over her shoulder, "what can I tell you?"

"How well did you know Bruce?" Sonja asked.

Grace closed the closet door and turned. She motioned toward the chairs in the center of the room. "I knew him pretty well. We used to go together in our junior year."

Sonja moved toward one of the chairs and settled into

it as gracefully as she could. Sam sat in the neighboring chair and leaned on the armrest.

"Go together?" Sonja asked.

"You know," Grace said, sitting across from Sam and Sonja. "Boyfriend and girlfriend. High school sweethearts."

"Yeah?" Sonja tried to hide her anger, but it slipped out in that single word. She must have heard her tone because she smiled wider and raised her eyebrows expectantly. "What happened?"

Grace's gaze bounced between the two. "I'm sorry. How's any of this supposed to help Bruce?"

"Like I said." Sonja motioned toward Sam. "We're trying to get some background information. That's all."

Sam nodded, throwing his nonverbal support behind Sonja's claim.

"To prove Bruce's innocence?" Grace asked.

"That's right." Sonja nodded. Her plastic smile remained affixed. "So, what happened between you two?"

Grace crossed one leg over the other, then she interlaced her fingers around the top knee. "We broke up."

"Uh-huh. And?"

"And nothing. It was high school."

Sonja's smile slipped. "Was there another guy?"

Grace stared at her for a moment before saying, "Unfortunately."

Sonja leaned forward. "Unfortunately, how?"

"I'm sure you know. Bruce became a dentist. A successful one, from what I hear."

"Was he the love of your life?"

"Bruce? Heavens, no." Grace chuckled. "We were kids. It was nothing more than a high school fling."

"And the other guy?" Sonja asked.

"What about him?"

"Was he the love of your life?"

Grace's leg bounced as she talked. "He was..." Her voice trailed off as she searched for a description. Finally, she said, "He was a bad habit."

Sonja cocked her head. "So it was a reoccurring thing?"

"Listen," Grace said, "I'm really not comfortable talking about this." She stopped bouncing her leg and stood. "I think I'd like to stop."

Sam was about to ask a follow-up question, but Sonja beat him to it.

"Was this other guy Topher Anderson?"

"I don't like what you're implying."

"We're not implying anything," Sonja said, her plastic smile cracked. "We just want to know about your connection to Bruce Bloom and Topher Anderson."

Grace walked toward the front door and opened it. "I'd like you to leave."

Sam put his hands on the armrests, prepared to propel himself to his feet.

Sonja had other ideas, though. "If it was a high school fling—" She flopped back in her chair and crossed her legs. "—why won't you answer our questions?"

"I'm calling the police if you don't leave now."

"Call them." Sonja crossed her arms and pouted. "We'll wait."

Sam mashed his lips together in what he hoped was a smile. It was unlikely the cops had talked with Grace Carlson yet. He didn't want them talking to her and learning additional reasons why Bruce might have wanted to attack Topher.

"Just a minute," Sam said. He faced Sonja and whispered, "We should go."

She pulled away from him. "I'm not leaving."

"Trust me." He stood.

"Let her call."

Sam reached for Sonja.

"Don't touch me," she said.

He hooked an arm underneath hers and lifted her from the chair. "We're leaving."

"Not until I get an answer." Sonja tried to drop to the floor, but Sam held on to her. Her weight, while not much, almost pulled him over.

"We've got to go," Sam said, his voice straining to hold her up.

"No."

"Yes." He pulled Sonja to her feet, then lifted her in the air.

"Put me down!" Sonja shouted. "I'm warning you!"

"I want you out of my house," Grace yelled, pointing toward the door.

"Trying," Sam groaned.

He waddled toward the door with Sonja clutched in his arms.

"Answer my question!" Sonja screamed at Grace. "Answer me!"

When they were outside, Grace shut the door behind them. The lock set and the porch light went out.

Sonja kicked Sam in the shin with the heel of her boot. He let go of her and she stumbled down the stairs.

She pointed at him. "Traitor!"

"What'd I do?"

"You know what you did." Sonja spun and clomped toward the Range Rover. "I should never have asked for your help."

Sam started down the path after her. The falling snow

continued at a heavy pace.

Sonja climbed in the Range Rover, the engine fired up, and the headlights snapped on.

He stepped into the snow berm and reached for the passenger door. It remained locked. Sam tapped on the window.

She never looked his way before the car pulled away from the curb. It zoomed to the end of the block, then disappeared around the corner.

"Great," Sam muttered.

He shoved his hands in his pockets. He had a vague idea of how to get back to his hotel. He definitely knew where First Street was, though. Sam headed in the direction of the city's main arterial. Once he made it there, he could easily determine how to get to the hotel.

Sam shook his head as he walked.

I should never have asked for your help.

Yeah, Sam thought, she shouldn't have. His life was nearly perfect until that moment. Like a chump, he jumped on a plane—several of them, actually—so he could play the hero. Perhaps if he had a job like he normally did in the winter, he wouldn't have dropped everything to run to Sonja's rescue.

Sam scoffed. Bruce needed rescuing, not Sonja.

"You're an idiot," he muttered to himself.

A couple of houses away from Grace Carlson's, the sidewalk was no longer clear. Its homeowner obviously took a moral stand against shoveling. Sam moved into the street as it was a clearer path.

When he got back to the hotel, he'd work on getting out of Havre. He wondered how many flights a day left the city. If there weren't many, perhaps he could rent a car and drive to Billings. There had to be more options to escape

Montana there.

Sam kicked a ball of frozen snow, and it skittered away. The falling flakes wetted his hair.

Lights brightened the roadway from behind him. Sam moved as close to the curb as the plowed snow would allow.

The Range Rover pulled up next to him and the window rolled down.

"Get in," Sonja said.

Sam stopped walking and stared at her. He thought about saying no, that he'd walk the rest of the way to the hotel. However, it was cold, and he was getting wet. The night was a perfect reminder of why he created his first rule.

Always be where flip-flops can be worn.

Sam opened the passenger door and climbed in.

***

Sonja pulled into the Best Western's lot and found a parking spot. She slipped the transmission into Park but let the engine idle.

She stared straight ahead. "Let's call it a night."

"Probably a good idea."

Sonja gripped the steering wheel. "I really lost it back there."

"Understandable," Sam said.

"It's weird, right?" She looked at him now. "How much she looks like me?"

"Or you look like her."

"Yeah," Sonja muttered. "I look like her."

They sat quietly for several moments. Sam held his hands in front of the heater vents.

"You ever do that?" Sonja asked.

"Do what?"

"Date someone who reminds you of someone else?"

Sam shook his head. "Can't say I have."

"I thought Bruce was special."

"Maybe he is." Sam hated the taste of those words.

"He must not think I'm special," Sonja said. "I'm just a copy of Grace Carlson." She added the expletive between Grace's full name again.

"You should probably allow him a chance to explain." Sam wanted to know how the tooth mangler would wiggle his way out of this trouble, especially after Bruce warned him to not let Sonja and Grace meet.

"I don't know if I want to hear it."

Silence descended over the car again. Sam watched the sporadic traffic on First Avenue.

"There's still time for us to interview someone," Sam said.

"It's dark."

"Maybe I was overthinking that."

Sonja shook her head. "I think I'm good for the day."

"Okay." He grabbed the door handle. "Same time tomorrow morning."

"Sam?"

"Yeah?"

Sonja reached across the center console and grabbed his coat. She pulled him closer, and he didn't fight it. Sonja kissed him and Sam fell into it fully. Her dark and spicy perfume invaded his nose, and memories of their past lovemaking exploded in his brain. He kissed her harder.

Her fingers slipped into his hair and held Sam tightly. Sonja moaned into his mouth before pulling away. She put her lips against his ear. "Let's go to your room." Her hot breath wreaked havoc with the chemicals in his body.

Sam swallowed with great difficulty and tried to clear the rush of thoughts in his head.

All it would take was a simple agreement, and he'd get another night with Sonja. Just by the kiss, he knew it would be wonderful. It always was with her.

Where would it lead, though? Feelings would quickly follow. Yet the inevitable truth remained—Sam wouldn't stop chasing the sun and she wouldn't leave Spokane behind.

A night with Sonja would have lasting repercussions. He was already violating his *No Drama!!!* rule by getting involved with Bruce's legal problems. Sam didn't need to go off the deep end and really make a mess of things.

He moved away from Sonja, an action he didn't want to take but knew he must. Sam said, "It's not a good idea."

"I think it is." She pushed forward, her lips straining to find his again.

Sam put his hands on her shoulders to hold her at bay. "You won't think it's a good idea in the morning."

She stared at him. "You're telling me no?"

"I have to." He popped open the door. "I'll see you at nine."

Tears brimmed at the edges of Sonja's eyes.

Sam closed the passenger door and headed for his hotel room. He didn't dare look back.

Chapter 13

Sam sat in his hotel room. He spent a few minutes flipping through the meager number of channels available on the television. When he didn't find anything worth watching, he clicked off the set.

It was a couple of minutes after six, and he was restless. Kissing Sonja had that effect.

He didn't want to spend his night locked in a room, especially now. He probably shouldn't have told Sonja that interviewing someone after dark might lead to problems.

As a deputy, he contacted many people after the sun went down. Of course, he had the power of the badge behind him. That brought him immediate respect from most people. With those few who ignored the law, the threat of a trip to jail often made them cooperative.

Sam had nothing but his charm at his disposal now. Unfortunately, he didn't feel that charismatic. Would folks really be disinclined to talk with him because of the late hour?

It didn't matter now.

Sonja was gone, and the kiss happened. He had no idea how it would be in the morning. Maybe she'd come to her senses and tell Sam he was no longer needed. Perhaps he'd be back in Hawaii tomorrow night or the next day, depending on how hard it was to get a last-minute flight.

He moved to the window and opened the curtains. The weather had turned for the worse as the snow fell harder. Sam watched its quiet descent as he recalled Sonja's perfume.

Was it too late to call her and invite her back to his room?

Sam noticed his reflection in the window and frowned. That's not the man he wanted to be, particularly not with Sonja. He'd never really thought about a love of his life, but perhaps she was his.

If he was still in Hawaii, he might pass the time by reading on his apartment's deck. Unfortunately, he didn't have a book now and the thoughts of Sonja would likely block the enjoyment of any story.

He could go down to the hotel's gym. Running on a treadmill would help burn off some of the energy coursing through his veins. Jogging gave him time alone with his thoughts, something he usually enjoyed. He wondered if he'd be able to outrun the memory of Sonja's most recent kiss.

He doubted it.

Sam turned away from the window and the theatrical snowfall. He flopped into the room's lone chair.

He often went for late-night walks under the Honolulu moon. Nothing was stopping him tonight except the cold and snow. His gaze drifted toward the window, and he groaned. He hated the weather, but he shouldn't let that stop him from getting outside. Besides, some voluntary hardship might distract him from Sonja.

Sam made up his mind. He put on his new boots, grabbed his coat, and headed for the door.

***

Sam walked to the back of the hotel property and stared at the BNSF railyard. Falling snow and the darkness made it hard to see very far. The moon was out but only a slice of it, so it added little radiance. Light poles were scattered about the railyard, but they were placed at great intervals. This resulted in rings of lit ground surrounded by large swaths of shadows.

A short wall prevented Sam from walking right onto the railyard. He could easily climb over it, but he hesitated to do so. The hotel's front desk clerk had advised Sam to walk around the train facility to get to The Grizzly Den. It seemed like an unnecessary trip, particularly in this cruddy weather, when Sam could cut right across the railyard.

No trains moved at this time of night. He studied the halos of light and their corresponding auras of darkness. No figures moved through the illuminated areas and no headlights or flashlights could be seen in the darkness. Sam believed the railyard was guarded by security personnel; it was too big of an operation not to be. Perhaps the guards were on break which gave him an opportunity if he was brave enough to take it.

Without further consideration, Sam glanced left and right before heaving himself over the wall. He landed on the other side and crouched. His heart raced and blood pumped in his ears.

Sam wiped the snow from his hands, then trotted across the railyard. He remained in a crouch as he went. His head swiveled, searching for trouble. Each clomping step was louder than he intended.

As soon as he started running, though, he realized this was a bad idea. If he was caught sprinting through a railyard, how would that look? He had no excuse for being there. He'd probably be arrested for trespassing. That would be the icing on the proverbial cake.

Darting across private property was sure to attract

attention. If not from a security guard, perhaps from a neighbor or guest at the hotel.

Better to look like he belonged, he thought. He slowed to a walk and straightened. Sam shoved his hands in his pockets and strolled directly across the yard. Act like you're supposed to be there, Sam thought. He pretended to inspect the motionless trains as he passed them. Sam fought the desire to whistle nonchalantly, feeling that might take his act too far.

On the opposite side of the railyard, he arrived at a fence comprised of three strings of barbed wire. He could see the rear of The Grizzly Den from where he stood. Sam didn't know how far the fence ran to the east or west, and he didn't feel like finding out.

He gently pushed down the middle string of wire and swung a leg over. He crouched as he passed through the first and second strands, but the barbs from the upper line snagged into the back of his new coat. The sound of ripping fabric was hard to ignore.

Once he was off the railyard property, relief flooded through Sam. He hurried toward the bar, thankful he'd managed to avoid getting caught for trespassing.

He decided then to take the long way back when he was done.

***

Darry Hartill leaned on the bar. "Where's your lady friend?"

"Home," Sam said.

"Come to do some drinking?"

"Maybe a beer and some food."

Darry slid a single-page menu in front of Sam. He

grabbed a clean glass and walked to a line of tap handles. "Care about the brand?"

Sitting on a bar stool, Sam leaned to better examine his choices.

"We don't carry those fancy craft beers," Darry said. "Beer snobs are encouraged to drink elsewhere."

"Whatever you got is fine."

Darry filled the glass and set it on the counter. Sam quickly found what he wanted on the menu and ordered a plate of chicken tenders. Darry nodded once, then headed toward the kitchen.

The Grizzly Den was busier than Sam imagined it would be. He wrongly thought the snow would keep some people home. However, those who lived in Havre were used to the weather. Sam had been that way prior to snowbirding. Spokane County often had harsh winters, yet that didn't stop most of her citizens from continuing with their lives.

Many of the tables were occupied and several men sat at the bar with Sam. A basketball game played silently on a hanging television. The Beatles "Come Together" rocked from the jukebox.

Sam pulled the folded police report from his pocket and smoothed it out on the bar. He sipped his beer as he studied the witness list.

He and Sonja had already interviewed six of the eight listed witnesses.

Carl and Pamela Buckenberger.

Norlan Wisner.

Willow Dawson.

Jerrold and Louanna Dellar.

Sam tapped the report. Correction, Sam thought, they only contacted Willow. They didn't interview her. She'd left before they could. They'd have to go back and interview her later.

So, they questioned five of the listed witnesses. Not a bad day, Sam thought, especially when they made additional contacts. They chatted with Bruce's parents, a neighbor of Topher Anderson's, and Grace Carlson.

Sam sipped his beer as he thought of Grace. He felt a smile creep onto his lips. Ol' Bruce, the dirty dog. Sam had to hand it to the tooth mangler. The guy had great taste in women.

If Sam met Grace at another time and in another place, would he have made a play for her because she looked like Sonja? He knew the answer. Having anything in common with Bruce didn't make him happy.

Darry returned and slipped a plate onto the counter, along with a napkin and some silverware. "That's ranch on the side. Need anything else?"

"These folks here tonight?" Sam turned the report so Darry could see the names of the last two witnesses.

The bar owner leaned in. "This the police report from Topher's murder?"

"Start of it," Sam said.

"Pete's here." Darry mashed his forefinger into the report. "End of the bar. Want me to make an introduction?"

***

Peter Renz leaned an elbow on the counter as he watched Sam eat a chicken tender. He was in his mid-fifties with a balding pate. His belly strained against his black T-shirt, which read *Trailer Park Legend* in bright red. "Those tenders are my favorite. They're pretty good, huh?"

Sam nodded as he chewed.

"Is it true?" Pete asked. "You really a private detective?"

Darry had introduced Sam as such. It didn't seem necessary to correct the bar owner, given the situation. Sam would have preferred for the introduction to wait until after he ate his dinner, but Darry jumped on it immediately. Pete wasn't in a hurry, so Sam continued to eat. He dipped the tender into the little dish of ranch dressing before biting into it again.

"I like mine with barbeque sauce." Pete lifted his chin toward Sam's plate. "Never been a fan of ranch. Always reminded me of mayonnaise." He sipped his beer. Afterward, his tongue darted out and ran over his lips. "You know, I once thought about being a private detective."

"That so?" Sam said through a mouthful.

"Didn't want to take the test, though." Pete shrugged a single shoulder. "Not that it'd be hard or nothing. I got straight As when I was in high school. Could've even skipped some grades if I wanted. Glad I didn't, though." Pete nodded sincerely. "Would have meant I'd have to leave my buddies behind. I couldn't do that. They needed me. You know what I'm saying? I was like the president of our crew."

Sam swallowed before asking, "What can you tell me about the fight you witnessed?"

"I saw the whole thing," Pete grinned. "What do you want to know? The lady cop who interviewed me said she'd never met anyone who gave such great testimony."

"Testimony?"

"That's what she said. Testimony. All official like." Pete sipped his beer again, then dragged his tongue across his lips. He held up the nearly empty glass. "I'm gonna need another." He turned to the bartender. "Yo, Darry. Hit me one more time."

Darry lifted a hand in acknowledgement.

Pete turned back to Sam and his smile faded. "You're picking up my tab, right?"

Bruce Bloom was covering the expenses related to proving his innocence, so Sam shrugged. "Sure."

"Nice." Pete eyed Darry again. "Hey, this guy said to move my tab to his account." He thumbed toward Sam.

Darry lifted an eyebrow, and Sam nodded his acceptance.

"Man, this is great," Pete said, as his head bobbed enthusiastically. "Really great. Where were we?"

"The police officer said you gave great testimony."

Pete snapped his fingers. "That's right. The lady cop. Boy, she was cute, let me tell you. Back in the day, she'd have gone for me."

Sam didn't bother telling Pete his math was all wrong. Back in Pete's day, Officer Riley Malone would have been a child if she'd even been born at all.

The song on the radio changed to Night Ranger's "Don't Tell Me You Love Me." It was a rocking song that Sam knew from his father's music collection. Pete nodded along to the tune.

"The fight happened right over there," Pete said, motioning toward the opposite end of the bar. "Topher was minding his own business, not doing nothing, when this lunatic came up and whacked him with a pool stick."

"You knew Topher?"

Pete barked a single laugh. "You kidding? Everyone knew Topher. Guy was the coolest, you ask me. Shame he's gone."

Darry put a fresh glass of beer near Pete's elbow and picked up the empty. The bar owner didn't hang around for their conversation.

"Did you meet Topher here?" Sam pointed at the ground.

"Met most of my friends here." Pete bobbled his head as he seemingly reconsidered his statement. "Actually, I got friends all over the city if you wanna know, but the ones I like the most are here." He took a healthy sip of beer, then wiped his mouth with the back of his hand.

"You said Topher was minding his own business."

"That's right. Wasn't doing nothing. Then this redhead, a real looker, started hitting on him."

Sam was about to bite into another chicken tender, but he paused. "A redhead hit on Topher?"

"For real. She made a go at me, too, but I turned her down."

"She made a pass at you?" Sam lowered the untasted morsel to the plate. "Really?"

"I might have changed the whole course of history if I just gave into her. Nuts, right?"

"Nuts is right."

Pete nodded. "How was she to know I don't go for gingers? Pretty sure there's something genetically wrong with the whole lot of them."

Sam brushed his hands together. "So when she didn't get satisfaction with you, the redhead moved on to Topher?"

"Happened just like that." Pete toasted Sam with his beer. "Thanks for the beer, by the way."

Sam's gaze traveled Pete's length. He tried to hide his disbelief, but he obviously failed.

"I know what you're thinking," Pete said. "How's a guy

like me get a real looker? I'll tell you." Pete toasted Sam with his beer again. "It's confidence, my friend. I'm not bragging or nothing, but I've been with a lot of ladies in my time. Like hundreds."

"That's a lot."

"Maybe even more." Pete grinned. "Women can tell when a man's experienced. They like that sort of thing." He sipped his beer, and his tongue peeked out to run along his upper lip. "They appreciate when a man's learned a thing or two in the bedroom."

Sam picked up the chicken tender, dunked it in the ranch, and bit into it.

"So anyway," Pete continued, "the redhead's boyfriend got mad she was flirting with Topher and—"

"You're lucky he didn't see her talking to you." Sam motioned toward Pete with the half-eaten tender.

"It's the other way around." Pete shimmied his shoulders. "I wouldn't have gone down like a sack of potatoes the way Topher did. Not a chance. I'd have made the boyfriend eat that pool stick." He waved his arms around like a karate practitioner. Beer sloshed over the sides of his glass.

"You trained in the martial arts?"

"Two systems." Pete nodded. "Jeet Kune Do and Tang So Do. Black belt in both."

"Impressive," Sam said through a mouthful of chicken.

"Thank you." Pete sipped his beer. "Those are Bruce Lee's and Chuck Norris's styles, in case you didn't know. I'm what they call a natural."

"At everything, it seems," Sam muttered.

"What's that?"

Sam waved away the question, then sipped his beer.

"Might have to get myself some of those tenders," Pete

said. He glanced over his shoulder at Darry but didn't order any.

"How many times did the boyfriend hit Topher?" Sam asked.

"With the stick?" Pete faced him again. "Five. Maybe six."

"That's a few more than the police wrote in their report."

"Yeah?" Pete's eyes flicked toward the papers on the bar top. "The lady cop must've written it wrong. I saw what I saw. She mention the boyfriend kicking Topher a couple three times, too?"

In the police report, Pete reported Bruce struck Topher three times with a pool cue, then kicked him twice. Sam didn't need to ask any more questions about the fight. Anything he learned from Peter Renz was going to be treated as suspect.

Sam dunked the chicken morsel in the cup of ranch dressing. He asked absently, "What happened after the fight ended?"

"Darry kicked the boyfriend and the redhead out. Things calmed down then."

"Anybody come up to Topher?"

Pete took a healthy swig of his beer. "Everybody wanted to talk with Topher. Like I said, he was a good guy."

"That's what I've heard."

"Oh, yeah. The redhead came back a few minutes later."

Sam didn't bother hiding his confusion. "She did?"

"Got all close to Topher, right up in his business. Told you she had something for him."

"What happened then?"

"Nothing. The redhead left. Probably had to get back to her boyfriend."

That's not how Sonja relayed the story. However, everything Pete had said so far needed to be considered with a grain of salt.

"Were you here when Topher left?"

Pete nodded. "I saw him check his watch, then he went outside."

"Like he was meeting someone?"

"I guess." Pete shrugged. "Not too long after that, someone found him dead, and Darry called the cops. From what I heard, it was the boyfriend who hit Topher with the stick that done it. Now that I think about it, that could've been me had I given into the sweet little ginger. You believe that?"

Sam didn't. He waved toward the bar owner and motioned for his check. He slipped off his stool and stood. He grabbed his coat from the hook under the bar. White stuffing peeked out from several tears on the back.

"You like being a private investigator?" Pete asked.

He shouldn't back out of the lie now, so Sam said, "It's got its days." He swung the coat around and slipped his arms into it.

"I bet you make good coin. I'm in between jobs right now. Maybe I should think about taking the test."

"You should," Sam said. "I bet you'd score a hundred."

"You know it." Pete laughed and lifted his nearly empty glass as a salute.

Darry slid the bill onto the bar. Sam glanced at the total, then handed over his credit card. The bar owner walked off.

"Hey, man," Pete said. "Mind if I get another?" He waggled his glass. "Seeing as how I helped you and all."

Sam sighed. Bruce was going to pay him back for this. "Yeah, fine."

Pete waved at Darry. "Hey, yo. Add another beer to that tab, and some chicken tenders, too." He glanced back at Sam. "That's okay, right?"

***

The snow fell harder now as Sam left The Grizzly Den. He zipped his coat up to his neck and shoved his hands into his pockets. He had set his mind to not cross the railyard and take the long way back to the hotel. He was having second thoughts now.

Sam walked around the building and headed toward the barbed wire fence. He stopped walking when he saw a truck parked near one of the trains. The vehicle's headlights illuminated the falling snow.

Two men with flashlights slowly searched underneath each railcar. Sam could hear their voices but couldn't make out what they were saying. He had a pretty good idea what they were doing. Someone had probably seen him cross the tracks and the guards were making sure only they were on the property.

Sam turned and headed toward First Street North. He passed through the bar's parking lot. Several trucks were parked there with snow-covered loads in their beds.

He trudged westward along the road with his head bowed against a light wind. He walked in the lane of traffic since a snow berm prohibited him from using the road's shoulder.

The street wasn't well lit; the only illumination came from light poles inside the railyard and a sliver of the moon above.

A vehicle approached. From its headlight configuration, Sam knew it was a Jeep. He left the road and stepped into the berm. It was impossible to continue walking, so he stood still until the vehicle passed. The driver honked twice.

Sam waved, then stepped back into the roadway.

He tried to work on Bruce Bloom's problem, but his thoughts kept returning to the immediacy of the moment. It was cold, dark, and snowing. If something happened to him now, would anyone know where he was?

Sam wasn't prone to worry like this. He wouldn't have been concerned if he was on an evening walk while in Hawaii. The streets were well lit, and the nights were comfortable. His sweatshirt always kept him warm enough.

Perhaps he should call Sonja and let her know where he was. Was his safety the real reason he wanted to talk with her? Their recent kiss remained not only in his thoughts but on his lips. The beer and chicken tenders hadn't lessened its echo. Chatting with her now would send the wrong message, especially if she had regretted their earlier embrace.

What if she didn't regret it and Sam called? Who knew where things might end up?

His fourth rule—*No Drama!!!*—dictated he not get involved with her now for a variety of reasons.

Sam laughed self-consciously. "You idiot," he said to himself.

Being in Montana was nothing but drama. He also violated his first rule by traveling to snowy Havre and the fifth rule by working with Chuck Palmer, the attorney. With how much credence Sam gave his list of rules, he might as well crumple it up and throw it away.

Headlights lit the road behind him.

Sam didn't bother leaving the street. The approaching vehicle had plenty of room to pass him. Yet it slowed to Sam's pace and pulled alongside. Red and blue lights now flashed back and forth, illuminating the trees and snow. A searchlight snapped on and focused on Sam like he stood centerstage in a theater.

He stopped walking, faced the police car, and lifted a hand to protect his eyes. The spotlight clicked off, and the driver's window of the patrol car rolled down.

Officer Riley Malone smiled. "Fancy meeting you out here."

* * *

Sam sat in the passenger seat after Riley unbelted her duty bag and moved it to the trunk. If the Havre Police Department was anything like the Spokane County Sheriff's Office, then allowing Sam to sit there was a violation of policy and officer safety protocols. She didn't seem bothered by either.

He leaned forward and warmed his hands in front of the heater vent. Snow fell through the beams of the headlights. It appeared to be falling heavier than a few moments before.

"Where's your girlfriend?" Riley asked.

"She's not my girlfriend," Sam corrected. "We're just friends."

"Just friends," Riley parroted. "Where is your friend, then?"

"Back at her cabin, I suppose."

Riley dropped the car into gear and accelerated leisurely, much slower than the posted speed limit. "What were you doing out here?"

"Went to the Griz for dinner."

"Not exactly Havre's finest."

Sam shrugged a single shoulder. "I've had worse."

"I suppose we all have."

"You usually patrol back here?" Sam asked.

"Most nights." She thumbed toward the railyard. "We got a call from BNSF security about a trespasser."

Sam stopped rubbing his hands together. "That so?"

"Suspect in an orange puffy coat. They didn't catch him before he slipped through a barbed-wire fence."

"Lots of orange puffy coats, I'd imagine."

"Not with rips in their back." She smiled. "I saw them when I drove up."

Sam turned his hands in front of the vents. "Going to take me in?"

"Had I planned on that, you wouldn't be sitting in the front."

"Thank you." It was stupid to say, and Sam mentally winced.

"We know you're staying at the Best Western."

"How do you know?"

Riley cast a sideways glance. "Memory problems?"

"Right," Sam said. "I told Agent Hathaway."

"Since the Griz is right behind the hotel, I figured you took a shortcut through the railyard."

"Something like that."

"Trespassing is illegal, Deputy."

"Former."

"Still illegal, though." Riley tapped her thumb on the steering wheel. "Why'd you quit?"

Sam didn't feel like sharing the story with Riley. There probably wasn't time anyway, even at the easy pace she drove. He said, "Police work turned out to not be my thing."

"I get that." Riley's thumb banged harder on the steering wheel. "Some days I'm not sure how much longer I want to do this."

"Not liking it?"

She shrugged. "It's not a bad job, but I think I want to do something else."

"Like what?"

Riley eyed him. "I don't know you well enough."

First Street curved the way an on-ramp does. Riley slowed for a Stop sign, then turned left onto Seventh Avenue. A bridge ahead would take them over the railyard.

"Learn anything from all your running around?" Riley asked. She tried to make the question sound nonchalant, but a hint of eagerness peeked out from behind it.

"Not sure if I should share it with the police."

She glanced at him, confusion in her eyes. "Why not?"

"I'm trying to get Bruce out."

Riley nodded. "You're afraid you're going to make me look bad."

"That's not it."

She waved off his denial. "You don't have to worry. I'm already kicking myself, afraid I missed something."

Sam relaxed then. He understood her eagerness now. There'd been more than a few times as a deputy that Sam worried about a decision's correctness. He said, "Topher might've had some woman trouble."

"What woman?"

Sam lowered his hands and leaned back in his seat. "Hard to tell. Maybe there were multiple."

"More than one woman?" Riley frowned. "Sounds like Topher was a scoundrel."

People in glass houses shouldn't throw stones, Sam thought, especially not men prone to wearing flip-flops.

Riley glanced at him. "Not much to go on, is it?"

Sam shrugged. "Not really."

They stopped for the light at First Street. A truck with a Pepsi logo on its side whizzed by.

"These streets are confusing," Sam said.

She scoffed. "How so?"

"Everything's numbers."

"Avenues run north and south. Streets run east and west. The numbering system starts over once you pass the train tracks. All the roads up here get labeled north. What's so hard about that?"

"When you put it that way."

The light changed and Riley turned left. They were headed back toward the hotel now.

She asked, "You always go to Hawaii when you snowbird?"

"Not always."

"What other places have you been?"

"Phoenix. Corpus Christi."

Riley cast a sideways glance. "Not exactly glamorous."

"They're warm, and I can find work easily."

"I thought you were independently wealthy."

"Hardly."

They slowed for a Subaru as it turned into a gas station.

"How long are you hanging around Havre?" Riley asked.

"Until I figure out what really happened."

"So you do think I made a mistake." She didn't look at Sam when she put it out there. "You can say it."

"The way the facts laid out that night," Sam said, "I'd have probably done the same."

"Probably?"

"Likely," Sam corrected. "However, I can't trust Agent Hathaway to have Bruce's best interests at heart now."

"You're something," Riley said. "A friend calls you to save her boyfriend and you come running. Where do I find a guy like you?" The question was filled with playfulness.

"We're around."

"Not where I can find them." She tapped her thumb on the steering wheel again and a seriousness returned to her eyes. "What happens if you can't prove Bruce's innocence?"

"I don't know."

"Haven't thought that far ahead, huh?"

Riley spun the steering wheel, and they pulled into the hotel's parking lot. She stopped the car at the front entrance.

"Thanks for the ride," Sam said. He popped open the door.

"Hey."

He looked over his shoulder.

"Tomorrow starts my days off." Riley smiled. "You think if you're still around, you might want to grab dinner or something?"

Chapter 14

The phone beeped and ripped Sam from a dream.

He'd been sitting with Bruce at a banquet table. Food was displayed from end to end. There was turkey and ham, mashed potatoes and yams, and vegetables of various sorts. There were even a couple of pies. Perhaps it had been Thanksgiving. It'd been years since Sam celebrated the holiday with anyone.

In the dream, Sonja prepared Bruce a plate. She piled his dish high with a variety of fixings, then carefully placed it on the table in front of him.

Sam waited patiently as Sonja prepared a second plate. She carefully, almost lovingly, selected slices of turkey and ham. She skipped the yams in favor of the mashed potatoes. Sam wasn't a fan of yams. She knew him well.

When Sonja finished stacking the plate with food, she winked playfully at Sam. Then she sat next to Bruce and started eating.

Sam looked down at the table in front of him. There was no plate and there weren't any utensils.

The phone continued beeping. Sam rolled over and turned off the alarm.

Stupid dream, he thought.

He pulled his running shorts from his bag and slipped them on. He put on the T-shirt he'd worn yesterday. He only had enough clean underwear and T-shirts to last for four days. If this little adventure went longer than that, he'd have to do some laundry somewhere or buy additional clothes.

The hotel's gym was well stocked with machines promoting cardiovascular health. There were treadmills, stationary bikes, and elliptical machines among others. A universal machine sat in the corner. Mirrors lined one wall.

Sam climbed onto the treadmill and set an easy pace. He usually didn't run in the early morning. Many experts suggested working out at that time of the day, but Sam ran when the spirit moved him. Running was for his health, but it was also cathartic. It allowed him to get outside and away from his troubles.

Unfortunately, he stayed in a fixed position this morning and stared into a mirror while his legs churned. His troubles remained constantly in front of him. Sam lowered his gaze and watched the beeping red dot move around a simulated track on the treadmill's monitor. However, the reflected version of himself continued to run in Sam's peripheral vision.

After only two miles, Sam stopped.

***

He ate breakfast in his room again. Just like yesterday, he snatched a pre-read copy of the *Havre Daily News* from an empty table. There was no mention of Bruce Bloom or Topher Anderson in that morning's newspaper.

He hoped for something that might help with the investigation, but there wasn't anything germane. Outside of some national news stories, there were a handful of nice articles. A local yarn shop changed ownership after forty years. The town's 4-H chapter shoveled sidewalks for housebound senior citizens. A woman celebrated her hundredth birthday.

Sam spun a spoon around a container of yogurt when his phone buzzed—a signal for a text message. He checked it.

Sonja had texted a single word. OUTSIDE.

***

"Morning," Sam said when he settled into the passenger seat.

"What happened to your jacket?" She grabbed Sam's shoulder and pulled him forward. "How'd you get tears in it?"

"Snagged it."

"How?"

"It was stupid. I'll tell you later." He grabbed the seatbelt but didn't pull it fully across his body. "How was your night?"

"Terrible," Sonja said.

"Because we kissed?"

"We're not talking about that."

The Range Rover lurched forward, and the dashboard beeped a warning that Sam hadn't put on his seatbelt. He pulled it across his waist and clicked it in place to quiet the motherly alert.

Sonja scowled as she waited to turn onto First Street. Even angry, she was still attractive. He wanted to ask her why she wouldn't make him a plate on Thanksgiving, but he already knew the answer. Besides, he never brought up what happened in his dreams. That was something only she did.

The car moved into the roadway and Sonja turned right, westbound. The fresh snow from last night had been plowed. The berms along the sides of the road appeared larger than before. The sun was climbing over the horizon now, and the sky was clear. It had the makings of a nice, albeit cold day.

"It should never have happened," Sonja snapped.

Sam eyed her. "I thought we weren't talking about it."

"Don't." Sonja held up a single, threatening finger. "Don't make a joke."

"I'm not. You said we weren't talking about you kissing me and I was going to respect that."

She gripped the steering wheel with both hands, her knuckles quickly whitening. "You kissed me back."

"If you give a man a cookie, he's going to eat it."

Her face pinched. "What's that mean?"

"It means I had no choice but to kiss you."

"Because it was so awful?"

Sam threw his hands in the air. "That's not what I said."

"You said you had no choice." Sonja turned the car south, and they left First Street.

"Where are we going?" Sam asked.

"To see Chuck."

"What for?"

Sonja shook her head. "Because I can't see Bruce for another hour." Her jaw flexed and her cheeks blossomed red.

At least he knew what was in store for the morning.

***

Chuck Palmer grinned and shook a finger at Sam. "Boy, oh boy. You're kicking up some dust around town."

Sam touched his chest. "What'd I do?"

"Havre's big, but it ain't that big." Chuck's hand fell to his chest, and he smoothed his tie over his bulging stomach. He sat in the chair he was in yesterday when they met.

Sam and Sonja were on the couch. Sonja pressed her back into the corner and sat with her arms crossed and her expression tight. Sam wondered if she stewed all night about Grace Carlson.

The deer's head watched the proceedings from its position on the wall.

"I've gotten all sorts of calls," Chuck said. "The rumor mill is in full swing."

Sam leaned forward and rested his elbows on his knees. "Anybody asking us to back off?"

The lawyer smirked. "Hardly. They want to know why I'm using a big city fella and not my normal investigator."

"Guess it was too much to hope the killer would try to strong arm our silence."

"You want that kind of trouble?" Chuck asked.

"Not really." Sam flopped back and looked up at the deer's head. This morning, its stare seemed to be less disapproving.

"He wants to be done," Sonja said.

Sam's gaze swung to her.

She kept her arms crossed and lifted her elbows in Sam's direction. "He misses Hawaii."

The lawyer chuckled. "Can you blame him? Now's the time when the winter blues set in."

Sonja tsked and shook her head once.

"Why are you making this about me?" Sam asked.

"I'm not," she snapped.

Chuck's gaze bounced between them. "Bad morning?"

"Bad night," Sonja said, facing the attorney. "We met Grace Carlson."

"She's a beauty, huh?" Chuck raised his eyebrows a

couple of times.

Sonja asked, "Why didn't you mention she looked like me?"

"She does?" The lawyer stiffened. His expression bounced between Sonja and Sam. "I never noticed."

It was a horrible lie. Sam hoped Chuck never lied like that in front of a judge or jury. It certainly wouldn't go well.

"I guess I can see some resemblance," Chuck said after a moment of pretend thought. "You're prettier, though."

"Grace two-point-oh." Sonja frowned. "Great."

"Look here." Chuck flipped his hand airily. "Grace can't hold a candle to you. You're an actress, and she teaches kids about dirt." He rolled his eyes. "Boring."

Sam leaned forward again, hoping to bring the conversation back to the task at hand. "With all those phone calls yesterday, did anyone say anything useful?"

Chuck's grin melted. "Yeah, the prosecuting attorney."

"What'd he want?" Sonja asked.

"We've known each other for some time." Chuck's gaze slid to Sam. "You understand?"

"Sure," Sam said.

Sonja cocked her head. "Well?"

"He wanted to let me know when this goes to trial—"

"If it goes," Sam interrupted.

"Right," Chuck said. "If it goes to trial, he's going to ask for the death penalty."

Sonja jumped to her feet. "The death penalty?"

Chuck nodded solemnly. "They've charged Bruce with Deliberate Homicide. Like it or not, it's an appropriate outcome."

"Appropriate outcome?" Sonja threw her hands in the air. "What're we paying you for?"

"Bruce is my friend," Chuck said. "I'm going to get him off." He motioned toward Sam. "We're going to get him off."

Sam nodded. "We'll get him out, Sonja. Sit down."

She eyed both men. "We have to."

"We will." Chuck motioned for her to sit.

Reluctantly, she settled back on the couch. "The death penalty," she muttered.

"That's still a long way out," the attorney said. "We need to focus on now."

"What else did the prosecutor say?" Sam asked.

"He mentioned he'd likely bring up your unlicensed status if you get called to testify."

Sam stiffened.

"Oh, great," Sonja said. She looked up at the ceiling. "We should have gone with a licensed guy even if it meant we had to wait. This morning keeps getting worse."

"What's that mean?" Sam asked, dreading the answer. "Testify?"

"Just because we find evidence exonerating Bruce, doesn't mean the D.A. is likely to let him go. We're gonna need to go through the whole dog and pony show, which means putting you on the stand."

Sam shook his head. "Coming back wasn't part of the deal."

"What'd you think was going to happen?" Chuck asked. "Investigators testify to what they find. How else do we introduce evidence to the court?"

"I've got a life," Sam said weakly.

Sonja scoffed. "They want to take away Bruce's life, so maybe you should just get over it."

"Maybe we can convince the judge to hold a video call," Chuck offered. "Argue hardship or something."

"It's definitely a hardship," Sam said.

"You're worried about your tan when Bruce is on death row?" Sonja pointed toward the street. "We should be out there now, instead of in here doing nothing."

"We'll be out there soon," Sam said, his words soft.

Sonja abruptly stood. "Why'd you ever leave? If you stayed home, none of this would have ever happened."

She spun on her heel and left the office. The door slammed closed behind her.

Chuck turned sheepishly toward Sam. "She does sort of look like Grace. I probably should have warned you."

Chapter 15

The ride to the county jail was spent in hostile silence.

Sonja gripped the steering wheel like she wanted to strangle the life out of it. Sam did his best to stare straight ahead.

First Street, which served double duty as Highway 2, was mostly clear of snow. Plows and repeated traffic had removed most of it from the roadway. The Range Rover left the arterial and worked its way toward the jail. The snow on this back road was compacted like that on most of Havre's city streets and muted the sound of the spinning tires.

"She's a beauty," Sonja muttered.

Sam eyed her. "What's that?"

"Chuck said, 'She's a beauty.'" Sonja's nose wrinkled, and she clucked. "Grace isn't even that pretty."

Had anyone else made that statement, Sam probably would have argued with them. However, Sonja's pride was at stake now. He didn't want to get sucked into her self-esteem vortex. He'd made that mistake before and ended up shamelessly groveling to appease her feelings, all but ignoring the wounds to his pride.

No, Sam thought, he should let Sonja spin alone in this crazy cycle and remain as calm as he possibly could. He recalled something his grandfather said many times: better to remain silent and be considered a fool than to open your mouth and prove it. Sam thought he understood his grandfather's meaning, yet he often said something wrong and immediately regretted it. Right now, the best course of action was to remain silent. No need to provoke an angry lioness.

A large swath of unimproved land lay to the south. The rolling hills were covered with undisturbed snow. It was beautiful under the blue sky, and Sam focused his thoughts on that.

"Oh, great," Sonja said, glancing at him. "Sit there all silent like. Guess you think she's pretty, too."

He did, of course, but he didn't say that. He wasn't stupid. "I wasn't thinking that."

Sonja waved a hand. "You haven't said she wasn't."

Sam knew she was trying to drag him into the weeds of her one-woman quarrel. Unfortunately, she couldn't because Sam was too smart this morning. He imagined himself a shifty gazelle that the arguing lioness would never catch.

"I was listening to you," he said. Sam turned slightly in his seat to better see her. "Isn't that what you want?"

Her hand dropped to the steering wheel. "I want you to *agree* with me."

"Fine." Sam shrugged. "Grace is ugly." He wasn't going to argue with her. Better to agree to something he didn't believe in and let the matter die a quick death.

Sonja's gaze snapped to him. "You think I'm ugly?"

"I didn't say that."

"Yes, you did."

The Range Rover weaved toward the side of the road.

"Watch it!" Sam called and pointed ahead.

Sonja corrected the vehicle's path. "Grace and I look alike."

"You misunderstood me," Sam said.

"How was I supposed to take that?"

Sam stared at her. He had opened his mouth and proven himself a fool.

"You think she's ugly, which means you think I'm ugly." Tears welled in Sonja's eyes. "This day keeps getting better."

Sam cocked his head, a feeling of indignation rising in his chest. "You said she wasn't pretty. How's that any different from what I said?"

"I said she wasn't *that* pretty." Sonja's head bobbled left and right. "Meaning she's not as pretty as me." She glanced at him. "You said she was ugly. Meaning I'm ugly, too."

Sam had been sucked into the self-esteem vortex. He needed to get out of it. There was only one thing to do. "You're beautiful, Sonja. No one compares to you."

"Stop falling on your sword."

"I'm not."

Tears streamed down her cheeks. "This isn't about Grace."

"It's not?"

"They want to give him the death penalty." She sucked air in sharply.

Sam sighed. "There's a long way to go before that. Hathaway's not even done with his investigation."

"Still." Her hands relaxed on the steering wheel. "We need to get him out."

"We will," Sam promised.

The Range Rover bounced into the county jail's parking lot. Sonja slipped the vehicle into Park.

She brushed the tears away from her cheeks. "Are you going to wait out here?"

"I'll reread the police report while you two talk." He reached into his coat pocket.

Sonja popped open the driver's door and slid out. She turned back to him. "Sam?"

He looked at her.

"Thank you for saying I'm beautiful."

Before he could say she was welcome, Sonja closed the door.

He watched her walk toward the jailhouse.

***

Sam reread the police report for a third time. He skipped the list of names and only focused on the narrative. Nothing stood out since they were the same words he'd read before. He was starting to memorize pieces of Officer Riley Malone's report. That wasn't good because it meant his brain was filling in parts of the story. When he caught himself expecting certain words, he stopped and went back to the start of the narrative.

This time, he read out loud. Speaking the words helped focus his attention and kept his brain from helping by filling in words.

The night of the incident, Bruce exited the restroom to find Topher Anderson talking with Sonja. He became enraged and snatched a pool cue—Sam stopped reading. Where had the stick come from? Was it stored in a rack, lying on a table, or did Bruce pull it from someone's hands?

Sam decided where the cue came from really didn't matter. All that did matter was Bruce grabbed it and hit Topher twice. Then the bar owner kicked Bruce and Sonja out of the establishment.

The report didn't mention the trip back to Bruce's cabin or the argument he had with Sonja. Obviously, Bruce hadn't revealed any of that to Officer Malone the night she responded to his 911 call. She found Bruce near the now-dead Topher, blood on his left hand, and a bloody rock nearby.

A helicopter flew overhead, and Sam looked up from the report. He watched it fly over the jail until it landed on the pad next door to the border patrol offices.

The sun glinted off snow and wet surfaces. Sam lowered his eyes back to the report.

After detaining Bruce, Officer Malone and a couple of deputies stood by until members of the Division of Criminal Investigations took over the crime scene to conduct their investigation.

Sam rubbed his chin with his thumb. He wondered when Chuck might get a copy of Agent Hathaway's report. Had he even filed one yet, since the investigation was ongoing? For that matter, when might a defense attorney see the autopsy report? That, at least, had to be finished.

He realized Chuck would probably receive those reports as part of the formal discovery process after they were sent to the prosecuting attorney. Who knew how long that would be? It might be days. Sam couldn't wait that long.

He frowned as his thoughts drifted to Chuck's comments about Bruce's trial. Sam didn't want to return to Havre after he left, especially if he was still in Hawaii. His window for island time was closing. In a few short months, Sam would head back to his cabin in Newman Lake.

Sam pulled his phone from his pocket, prepared to call Nina Wilder. There was a three-hour time difference. She'd probably still be sleeping after last night.

Nina worked the graveyard shift. When her weekend

came around, she'd transition to more normal hours. Sam remembered doing that when he worked shift work, too. He wondered if Officer Riley Malone did that as well.

Whenever Sam was in a relationship with a woman, he stayed monogamous. Messing around with another was a good way to create drama in his life. Luckily, most of his relationships remained short term due to his snowbirding schedule. Sometimes, the women he met wanted nothing more than a night or two. Sam hadn't had a liaison like that in some time. He preferred a deeper connection. However, Nina's apparent lack of concern about his sudden absence bothered Sam. He wished it didn't since he wanted to be a bigger man.

That's why he agreed to meet Riley tonight when she asked. It was something he would never have done had he been in Hawaii with Nina. Now, in the light of day, he regretted the decision.

Even though Riley was attractive and probably very interesting in a social setting, Sam didn't have to make it romantic. He could simply have dinner with her, enjoy the conversation, then call it a night.

He stared at the phone a moment longer, wishing he could talk with Nina just to say hello. Sam slipped the device back into his pocket.

His thoughts returned to the report, and he focused on the witnesses. Sam and Sonja interviewed six of the eight listed. Only two remained, one of which was Willow Dawson.

Could she have lied when she refused to talk with them yesterday? Maybe she didn't have a class. Perhaps she knew Topher Anderson in a more intimate way.

Sam grunted. The cars didn't fit what he knew. Willow drove a red Honda Accord, and the woman who supposedly argued with Topher in front of his house drove a red Toyota Tacoma. The colors matched, but it was hard to confuse a car with a truck. Still, Willow's abrupt departure from her house seemed suspicious.

He started the report again, reading aloud. He changed his voice to that of a television announcer. It sounded different in his head and helped him pay closer attention to the words.

When he got to the section describing how Officer Riley Malone discovered Bruce, Topher, and the bloody rock, Sam paused. He reread the paragraph slower in the announcer's voice.

Afterward, Sam said, "Huh."

He looked up. Sunlight reflected off the snow-covered field in between the county jail and the border patrol office. Sam's gaze swung around his immediate surroundings. Compacted snow covered the parking lot. Mounds of the white stuff were visible in various truck beds.

Movement caught his eye. Sonja strode out of the jail with a stern look on her face. Sam watched her cross the parking lot. She jerked open the driver's door, climbed in, then slammed the door shut. Sonja's hands settled on the steering wheel, and she stared forward.

"How'd it go?" Sam asked.

"Bruce wants to see you."

***

Bruce Bloom seemed much thinner than yesterday. Sam didn't know if that was physically possible. Perhaps it was an optical illusion based upon his tired eyes and mussy hair. His orange jumpsuit was wrinkled. A splotch of ketchup lingered on his chest.

At least, Sam hoped it was ketchup.

"Why'd you let Sonja see Grace?" Bruce asked. His eyes filled with desperation as they searched Sam's. "I asked you not to let them meet."

"Don't you want to talk about the death penalty?"

Bruce waved him off. "That's not going to happen."

"Are you sure?"

"I could lose Sonja over this."

Sam had never spoken with anyone who might face such a fate. Perhaps it was a human condition to ignore the worst outcome and focus on something more immediate. Sam didn't think so. If he was in Bruce's shoes, he'd certainly be focused on the death penalty, especially since he didn't know how Montana carried out that judgement. Electric chair? Poison? Firing squad? None of them sounded as good as dying peacefully in his own bed. Even that sounded dreadful.

He refocused on Bruce, who waited expectantly for an answer. Sam said, "You should have told me they looked alike."

Bruce tossed his hands in the air. "Why else would I tell you not to let Sonja see her?"

"I thought it was because you reconnected on Facebook."

"Don't remind me." Bruce's voice strained with frustration. "Wait. Did you tell Sonja I did?"

"Give me more credit than that."

Bruce raised an apologetic hand. "Sorry."

"It's all right. Got to be hard in here."

"Why'd you go see Grace?"

"One of the witnesses we interviewed said Sonja looked like her."

"Of course." Bruce looked at the ceiling. "Havre strikes again."

"You can imagine her reaction."

"I don't have to." Bruce's gaze slowly lowered back to Sam. "She let me have it when she came in. Both barrels."

Sam didn't respond. Bruce knew Sonja well enough to have predicted how she'd react. Hiding Grace's resemblance was his own bad decision, so Sam let him wallow in it for a few moments.

"Why didn't you talk her out of it?" Bruce asked.

"There's no talking Sonja out of anything."

"You could have tried," Bruce whined.

Sam raised an eyebrow.

The dentist scoffed. "Look at what I'm saying."

"You want to talk about anything pertinent to your case?" Sam asked.

"You like her, don't you?"

Sam opened his mouth to speak, but Bruce cut off his denial.

"I get it. Now that I'm out of the way, you can finally be with her."

The guy had it all wrong, but Sam wasn't about to correct him.

Bruce continued. "I saw the way you looked at her."

"When?"

"At the golf course where we met. I haven't forgotten how you watched her."

Sam frowned. He didn't remember looking at Sonja with anything that revealed romantic intentions. If he correctly remembered the events at the Coeur d'Alene Resort's golf course, he teased Sonja. They bantered back and forth with Bruce in the middle of the conversation. Sam didn't want to get involved with anyone last summer, let alone Sonja. He was trying to cleanse himself by swearing off women for the season. It hadn't work out as planned, but Sonja wasn't part of that.

"Is that why you asked to see me?" Sam asked. "So you could accuse me of trying to take Sonja from you?"

Bruce's expression hardened. "Well?"

Sam leaned forward. "I flew nineteen hours to help you."

"That's what I mean." Bruce waved his hand in Sam's direction. "Who does that? Who gets on a plane to help someone they barely know?"

"A friend," Sam said. "Sonja called and asked if I'd help."

"That's all it took? She called, and you came running?"

Sam shrugged a single shoulder. "She said you'd cover my expenses."

Bruce stared at him a moment longer before his face relaxed. His eyes drifted to the table, and he sighed. "You're in it for the money."

"Getting my expenses covered isn't making money."

"You're not charging me for your time?" Bruce looked up but didn't lift his head.

"I can," Sam said, "if it'll make you feel better."

"Proving me innocent is all that'll make me feel better."

"That's what I'm trying to do. Now, are we done talking about Sonja?"

Bruce reluctantly nodded.

"You want to talk about what we've learned?"

"Not really." Bruce rubbed the table with his hand. "I wanted to know why Sonja met Grace."

"Now you know," Sam said. "I was along for the ride."

Bruce sighed heavily but didn't respond. He slouched in his chair as his gaze grew distant. It was as if his thoughts had fled from the moment.

Sam knocked on the table to get his attention. "I've got a question."

"What's that?" The dentist blinked several times and pushed himself back up in his chair.

"It's about when you found Topher."

"Ugh." Bruce shook his head. "Please, don't remind me."

"I've got to. That's why you're paying me."

Bruce smirked. "Walked myself into that one, didn't I?"

"Tell me about the rock," Sam said.

"It was a rock." Bruce held out his palm. "About this big."

"That's not what I want to know." Sam rested his elbows on the table. "Where was it when you found it?"

***

Sam settled into the passenger seat and closed the door. "Feeling better?" he asked Sonja.

The Range Rover lurched from its parking spot, pinning Sam into his seat. The tires spun, and the backend fishtailed. Sonja's hands jumped about the steering wheel as she tried to straighten the vehicle's direction.

"Guess not," Sam said as he yanked the seatbelt across his body and clicked it into place.

The car bounced onto Second Street and headed back toward Havre. The morning sun beamed through the window. Sam flipped down the visor above his seat.

"Where to now?" Sonja asked icily.

"Not going to tell me how it went with Bruce?"

Sonja slapped down the sun visor above the driver's seat. It thunked into place. "I forgave him."

"Doesn't look like that's sitting well with you."

"It's not." She glanced at him. "I had to do it because of you."

"Me?"

"Us," Sonja muttered. "That stupid kiss."

"Hey," Sam said, "I would never—"

"We're not talking about it."

"You brought it up."

Her eyes cut to him. "So you'd know why I was in a bad mood. Doesn't mean I want to relive it."

Sam wouldn't mind reliving the kiss. Although, it would mean adding more drama into his life and violating the fourth rule, which he seemed to be doing daily, maybe even hourly.

Sonja angrily flipped the sun visor up. "Who're we seeing?"

"We've got two options," Sam said. "There's one witness we haven't contacted yet, or we can go back and try to interview Willow Dawson."

"Willow."

"I'll get you the address." Sam slipped his hand into his coat for the report.

"I remember how to get there."

"Yeah?"

"I'm not stupid, you know?"

"I know." Sam pulled his empty hand out. "I never said you were."

Sonja's knuckles whitened as she choked the steering wheel.

The muted sound of spinning tires on the snowy road overwhelmed the vehicle's interior. Sam wanted to hear Sonja's side, but he didn't push her. Based upon Bruce's reaction, he already knew their conversation didn't go well. Sam was surprised Sonja forgave Bruce for the whole Grace debacle. Maybe she hadn't told the jaw mangler that to his face, though. Sonja could be that way at times—decide something but keep its outcome to herself. She had done it occasionally when she and Sam were together. It didn't happen often, but it did occur.

Her forgiving Bruce didn't change much in how Sam viewed the situation. He wasn't going to get back together with Sonja if her relationship with Bruce imploded. Yeah, they might have a romantic interlude, but he was still heading back to Hawaii. Sonja knew that and would surely get upset. She wouldn't keep those feelings to herself.

Maybe she'd come with him to Honolulu. Sam gnawed on his lip as he thought. Would he want that? His short-term relationship with Nina was fine. More than fine, actually. There were no strings attached. Although, as Sam discovered by his recent hasty departure, he might have liked one or two strings. Loosely attached, that is. Just to know she cared. So maybe the relationship with Nina wasn't as fine as he suspected.

If Sonja followed him to Hawaii, they'd return to Spokane County in early May. Another summer with Sonja would be great. Sam's forehead relaxed as he smiled. Sonja looked amazing in a bikini. They'd spend days at his cabin, get some waterskiing in, then hang around a campfire at night. There'd surely be passionate evenings spent under the stars.

Of course, all summers eventually end. Sam's smile melted and his forehead corrugated once more. Whenever fall arrived, Sam would begin his preparations to snowbird. That's when Sonja would get mad, and he'd be forced to once again explain why they could never be together—his dreams and her dreams didn't align. She'd yell at him for his rational explanation, while he'd get frustrated with her emotional reaction.

Still, spending a summer with a scantily clad Sonja might be worth one more spin on the crazy ride. His smile returned as memories of their many sexual escapades flooded his thoughts.

"Why are you grinning?" she asked.

His expression flattened. "Huh?"

"You were smiling."

"I didn't know I was," Sam lied.

Sonja clucked. "Probably thinking about Hawaii."

Nothing he said would help the situation. Sonja was mad which meant she wanted to argue. His best bet was to stay silent.

His cell phone buzzed, and he removed it from his pocket. He hoped for a text message from Nina. It didn't have to be anything long. Something as short as "thinking of you" would be nice. She could abbreviate to "thinking of U" if she wanted. Even though he disliked truncated text messages, it'd still be enough for Sam. Her lack of strings bothered him. Every woman he'd been involved with for any length of time had some sort of commitment requirement.

Sam opened the message and sighed. It was from the wrong woman. Maybe because of how Sam lived his life, they would always be the wrong women.

She glanced at him. "What is it?"

"Nothing."

"Something important?"

He slowly shook his head. "Not really."

Sam stared at the phone's display. STILL ON FOR 7?

Sonja couldn't be the right woman because their dreams didn't align. Nina didn't seem to care that he'd dashed away in the night. Even if she was a perfect match emotionally and physically, Riley Malone would never be the right girl geographically. There was no way Sam would live in Havre.

He was getting ahead of himself. She'd invited him to dinner. That's all. She didn't have to be the right woman to share a meal. Besides, if the conversation ever stalled, he could bring up Bruce's case. It'd be a pleasant way to spend the evening.

His fingers bounced over the keyboard. SOUNDS GOOD.

LET'S MEET AT THE DUCK INN, Riley responded. IT'S ACROSS FROM YOUR HOTEL.

***

Sam and Sonja returned to the small rancher on Seventeenth Street. The red Honda Accord wasn't in the driveway.

She pulled the Range Rover to the curb. "Looks like she's not home."

"I see that."

"What do you want to do? Wanna go interview the last witness?"

Sam didn't need to pull the report from his pocket to remember Willow wasn't employed. She'd told Officer Riley she was a student. Sam remembered seeing an MSU-Northern sticker in the back window of the Accord.

"Do you know where Montana State is?" he asked.

"We're in it."

Sam waved his hand. "The college."

"Oh," Sonja said. "Isn't that in Bozeman?"

"How would you know that?"

"I dated a guy who went to college there."

"When?"

"Why does that matter?"

It probably didn't, but it still bothered Sam. Sort of, he thought and tried best to relax his expression. Unfortunately, it didn't work, and a smirk lingered.

Sonja dipped her chin. "Don't you dare say something about me dating a lot of guys."

"I wouldn't." He'd think it, though.

"Before pointing a finger at me," Sonja said, "take a look in the mirror."

Okay, maybe she hadn't dated as much as Sam had, so he definitely should keep quiet on this matter. He held up an apologetic hand. "I think there's a northern branch of MSU around here somewhere."

"Right." Sonja nodded. "Willow said she was headed to class."

Sam pointed at the vehicle's display screen. "See if you can find it."

Sonja started the GPS function. Her finger tapped the screen twice, then stopped. "Do you think she knows her?"

"Who?"

"Oh my God." Sonja's eyes bulged. "*Her*. Do you think she knows *her*?"

Sam stared at Sonja for a moment as he tried to interpret her question.

Sonja clucked. "She's a teacher."

"You mean Grace Carlson?"

"Ugh." Sonja exaggeratedly rolled her eyes. "Don't say her name."

"Fine," Sam said, "but I think she's a professor."

Sonja's upper lip curled. "Really?"

"Doesn't matter."

"No, it doesn't."

Sam waggled a hand. "Maybe they know each other. I mean, Willow is a student and—"

"Don't," Sonja interrupted.

"Can I call her Sonja two-point-oh?"

"Not funny."

Sam shrugged. "You called yourself Grace two-point-oh."

Sonja shot a final dirty look at Sam, then finished typing the college's name into the GPS system. The result pinged immediately. They were only a couple of minutes away.

Chapter 16

The campus of Montana State University—Northern sat in the southwestern part of Havre. It appeared like most state colleges. Impressive old buildings mixed with state-of-the-art structures. All were surrounded by large swaths of open ground and a multitude of trees. Sam suspected during the non-winter months that the ground was carpeted in a lush green lawn that provided plenty of opportunities for students to lounge and play in the sun. Today, though, the campus was covered in snow.

Sonja slowly guided the Range Rover down Cowan Drive. A line of vehicles parked haphazardly along the curb. Sam assumed this to be a row of normal parking spots during the dry months. However, a berm stopped cars from getting close to the curb and the compacted snow on the ground covered the lines of any stalls.

"This is like finding a needle in a haystack," Sonja said. Her head swiveled left and right as she searched for Willow Dawson's car and continued to keep an eye open for approaching traffic.

"It's not that bad," Sam said. "It's like half a haystack."

Montana State University—Northern was small in comparison to campuses like Eastern Washington or Washington State, the only two colleges Sam had been around. However, it was likely the size of eight or ten high school campuses. At least, that's how Sam imagined it to be.

They crept past Donaldson Hall; a campus sign

identified the aged structure as such. A student shuffled across the street toward the nearest building, her books clutched to her chest and her feet never leaving the slick road. Sonja slowed their car, allowing the girl to pass.

To the south was a small lot marked *Faculty Parking*.

Sam motioned for Sonja to pull in there.

She cast a sideway glance at him. "Willow wouldn't park in there."

"I know," he said, "but do it for me."

She tsked, but spun the steering wheel, nonetheless.

There were only a handful of spots, all of them occupied. None of the cars were Grace Carlson's Lexus.

"Why are you looking for you-know-who's car?" Sonja asked.

"Curious if she was here."

Sonja stomped on the brake and the Range Rover slid a few feet. "Are we talking to her again?"

"I hadn't planned on it."

The SUV lurched forward, and Sonja directed it back to Cowan Street. They continued westbound.

"Aren't there phone numbers on the police report?" she asked.

"If Willow didn't want to talk with us at her home," Sam said, "you think she'll want to talk with us on the phone?"

"Text her."

Sam bobbed his head. It wasn't a bad idea. "Let's see if we can find her car first."

They continued past the stately Cowan Hall. Sam believed this might have been the first building built for the college. It had the appearance of something constructed in the early 1900s. Of course it was only speculation, and he didn't have the time nor inclination to look up the history of the building or the school.

The Range Rover quickly reached the western edge of the campus, and Sonja turned them south onto an unmarked road. A row of haphazardly parked cars was on the right side of the street, and a small parking lot was on the left.

"Let's try there," Sam said, pointing at the lot.

It took less than a minute for them to find Willow Dawson's red Honda parked between two lifted pickups. Sam knew it was hers due to the MSU-Northern sticker in the back window. Both trucks had mounds of snow in them.

"What now?" Sonja asked.

"Find a parking spot."

Sonja pulled into the nearest opening and stopped.

Sam shifted in his seat and looked over his shoulder at the red Honda. "Maybe back us in?"

She clicked her tongue against the back of her teeth. "You should've told me that in the first place."

Sonja backed the Range Rover out of its spot, then reversed in. Now they sat facing Willow's car. "Better?" Sonja asked.

"Much."

A sign at the corner of the parking lot identified the nearest building as Hagener Science Center. "Willow's probably in there," Sam said.

"Are we going to search from room to room?"

Sam pulled his cell phone and the police report from his pocket. "I'll text her like you suggested."

He figured a short message would suffice. THIS IS SAM, THE GUY YOU MET YESTERDAY. I'D LIKE TO ASK YOU ABOUT TOPHER ANDERSON. Maybe it wasn't short, Sam thought, but the message was simple.

"Now what?" Sonja asked.

"We wait for her to respond."

"What if she doesn't?"

"Then we wait for her to come out to her car."

Sonja slumped in her seat. "This is so stupid."

"It's police work."

"Really?"

Sam shrugged. "Some of it. There's more waiting around than people know."

He checked his phone to see if a message had arrived. It was silly because the phone would have buzzed had Willow texted.

A couple of minutes passed in silence. There was no movement in the parking lot. Sam checked the time. It was the middle of the hour. Class was likely still in session.

"Going to tell me how it went with Bruce?" Sam asked.

"No."

He probably begged for forgiveness, Sam thought. Bruce seemed the type, especially with a woman who looked like Sonja. Sam wondered if Bruce ever behaved that way with Grace Carlson back in high school.

Sam's phone buzzed, and he checked the text message from Willow Dawson.

I'M IN CLASS.

I KNOW, Sam replied. I'M AT YOUR CAR.

"That her?" Sonja asked.

"Yeah."

Another text arrived. LEAVE ME ALONE, CREEPER.

Sam chuckled as his thumbs bounced over his phone's screen. I DON'T MIND WAITING.

Sonja glanced at his phone, obviously hoping for another message. Finally, she said, "I'm meeting Bruce's parents for dinner tonight. You can come."

Sam shook his head.

"Let me rephrase that," she said. "You should come. They need to know we're doing something."

"I can't."

"Why not?"

"I've got plans," Sam said.

Sonja turned in her seat and faced him. "Avoiding his parents isn't a plan."

Sam would have argued if he didn't really have something better to do. "I've got a date."

"A date?" Sonja stiffened. "With whom?"

"A date is the wrong word."

"What is the right word?"

"I'm meeting someone for dinner."

Sonja's nose crinkled. "That's a date."

The phone buzzed in Sam's hand. I CALLED SECURITY. NOW LEAVE.

"That's aggressive," he said.

Sonja leaned toward Sam as she tried to get him to look at her. He kept his attention on the cell phone. "Who're you seeing tonight?" she asked.

"Why's it matter?"

"You know why."

"No, I don't."

She pulled back. "We kissed."

He looked at her now. "I thought we weren't talking about it."

Sonja shrugged. "We can talk about it. This seems a good time."

"Okay, then," Sam said. "If we're gonna get technical about it, you kissed me."

"I didn't."

"Those weren't your lips mashing against mine?"

She dismissively flicked her hand. "Whatever. Who started it doesn't matter."

"Bruce would think differently."

Sonja's eyes widened. "You didn't tell him, did you?"

"About how you accidentally stuck your tongue in my mouth?"

"Don't be gross."

"It wasn't gross."

"You know what I mean."

Sam shook his head. "I didn't tell him."

A white truck with yellow lights on top pulled into the small parking lot and started down the far row of cars.

"Anyway," Sonja said, "you kissed me, too. I felt it."

Sam lowered the back of his seat, his attention still on the truck.

Sonja pushed back against the driver's door. "What do you think you're doing? I'm not climbing over there."

He glanced at her. She wore a horrified expression.

"I'm not kissing you again," she said.

Sam's gaze returned to the white truck making its way through the parking lot. "Face forward and act natural."

"Why?"

"See the security vehicle?" Sam asked.

Sonja looked out the window. "Yeah."

"Willow called them on us."

"She did?" Sonja turned in her seat. "That's rude." In a moment, she smiled and waved.

"What're they doing?" Sam asked.

"Leaving," Sonja said.

Sam returned his seat to its upright position. "That was close."

Sonja faced him again. "I haven't forgotten."

"About our kiss?"

Her face soured. "About your date."

Sam brought out his best roguish smile, the one he thought worked with all the ladies.

"I'm not falling for it."

"Falling for what?"

"You kissed me."

"You started it."

"Seemed like you enjoyed it."

Willow Dawson appeared at the edge of the science building and headed in their direction. Sam motioned out the window, but Sonja didn't seem to notice. Her concentration remained on Sam.

"You don't have a date," she said. "You're just trying to get out of dinner with the Blooms."

"That's not it."

"Of course it is."

"If you really want to know," Sam said, "I'm seeing Riley."

Sonja cocked her head. "Who?"

"Officer Malone."

"What for?"

"Dinner. I already said." Sam opened his door. "When I get out, block her car in."

"Who? Riley?"

Sonja's head whipped about as she tried to catch up with what was occurring.

***

"This is harassment," Willow Dawson said, stepping out of her car. She pointed at the Range Rover, which now blocked her car into its parking stall. "She can't do that."

Sam raised his hands to show he meant no harm. "We

need to talk."

"Maybe I don't want to talk with you." Willow crossed her arms and thrust her hip to the side, banging the inside of the car door. She wore a red parka and rainbow-colored gloves. "Maybe I don't wanna get involved."

"You're already involved," Sam said, lowering his hands. "You're listed as a witness in a police report."

Sonja exited the Range Rover and started around the vehicle. She stopped at its hood and listened in on the conversation.

Willow glanced around. "I should've kept my mouth closed."

"You didn't," Sam said, "and an innocent man is in jail."

"That guy's not innocent. He hit Topher." Willow sneered. "Everyone saw."

"We're not disputing that." Sam thought about moving closer but figured that might spook Willow. He stayed rooted in his spot. "We want to know what happened after."

"After what?" Willow's gaze swung to Sonja. "Wait. I know you. You're the one who started the whole thing." Willow's eyes snapped back to Sam. "Hey. What's the big idea? You said you were working with the defense."

"I am," Sam said.

"What about her?" Willow lifted her chin toward Sonja. "She's not with the defense."

"She's my driver."

"That's convenient."

Sam shrugged. "Havre's a small town."

Willow groaned. "Ain't that the truth." She leaned slightly so she could look past Sam. "Never seen anybody with a driver before. Let alone a Range Rover."

"Now, you have."

"Whatever you're doing must pay well." Willow waved a hand at Bruce's car. "What's something like that cost?"

"More than a college student can afford." Sam jerked his head toward Sonja. "What happened after she and her boyfriend were kicked out of The Grizzly Den?"

"Nothing." Willow glanced back at the science building, then looked around the campus. "I didn't see anything."

"A couple of people reported seeing a woman talking with Topher later."

Willow rested her arm along the top of the open car door and slouched slightly. It was an attempt to appear relaxed, but her expression betrayed her worries.

"Was it you?" Sam asked. "Were you the woman who talked with Topher?"

"Wasn't me." Willow's eyes flicked to Sonja. "It wasn't."

Sam stepped forward now. Not terribly close, but he closed the distance to make the conversation more intimate. He lowered his voice when he said, "You saw someone, though."

Willow tried to back up but only succeeded in wedging herself into the sharp corner created by the Honda and its open door. "I didn't see anyone."

"You don't have to tell us," Sam said.

"She doesn't?" Sonja blurted from behind him.

He held up a hand, hoping she'd understand the signal to be quiet. "You don't have to tell us," Sam repeated, "but we know you saw someone. When we get the camera footage from the Griz—"

Willow grabbed the top of the door and pulled herself out of the wedge. "They've got cameras?"

"Yes," Sam lied.

"I've never seen them."

"Darry doesn't want the customers to know," Sonja said. "He said it'd be bad for business."

Willow's jaw dropped. "You bet it would. Wait 'til this gets out."

"When we see the video," Sam repeated, "we'll know who the woman is who talked with Topher."

"So will the cops," Sonja added.

Sam thumbed over his shoulder. "We'll share everything we learned with the prosecuting attorney. It's called discovery. Maybe the cops will talk with you about interfering with a police investigation."

Willow glanced around the campus again. "I didn't interfere with anything."

"Not telling the truth is interfering."

"I didn't do anything wrong." Her protest was weaker this time.

"I guess that'll depend," Sam said.

"On what."

"On what you really saw. If withholding information helps someone get away with murder, you're definitely going to have trouble with the law."

Willow gnawed on her lower lip as she thought. Her eyes darted about the parking lot for several seconds. "If I tell you what I saw, can you keep it… like, unofficial?"

"Depends," Sam said. "How bad is it?"

"I don't know, but I don't want to get in trouble if she sees my name." Willow tapped her chest. "It's the only class I'm getting an A in."

"Grace Carlson?" Sam asked.

"How'd you know?"

"I knew it." Sonja clapped her hands once. "She

murdered Topher.”

“What?” Willow glanced back at the science building before whispering, “I didn’t say that. Don’t put words in my mouth.”

“She was at the Griz that night,” Sam said, recalling Peter Renz’s story about a redhead coming back into the bar to talk with Topher. It’d be easy for him to confuse Sonja and Grace, especially if he was drinking.

“Listen,” Willow said. “All I saw was Grace walk in and talk with Topher for a few minutes. Maybe not even that long, then she left.”

“Did Grace see you?” Sam asked.

“I don’t think so.” Willow cocked her head as she eyed Sonja. “Are you related to Grace?”

Sonja’s expression soured. “No.”

“You sort of look alike.”

“So I’ve heard.”

Sam held up a hand to interrupt the path the conversation was taking. “What happened after Grace left the bar?”

Willow shrugged. “Topher hung around for a bit more, then he went outside. I figured he was leaving.”

“What were you doing there?” Sam asked.

“Hey.” Willow’s lip curled. “I’m answering your questions. Don’t drag my name through the mud.”

“The police report didn’t mention you being there with anyone.”

“So? Sometimes I go to the Griz to study.”

“In a bar?”

Willow folded her arms over her chest. “Maybe I wanted a beer while I did it. That a crime?”

Sam wouldn’t have been able to study inside the Griz, but he’d read plenty of books while seated at bars. Perhaps

Willow had better concentration skills than he did.

He eyed Sonja. "Anything else?"

"No." She looked at the science building. "I want to find Grace. Let's go." Sonja moved around the Range Rover.

"She's not there now," Willow said. "At least, I don't think so."

"Why's that?" Sam asked.

"Because class is over. I don't think she has another one today."

"I still wanna check," Sonja said. "I'll park the car."

She climbed into the Range Rover, and it rolled backward from its resting spot.

"Thank you for your time," Sam said.

"Just keep my name out of any reports, okay?"

Sam shuffled backward. "Got it."

"Hey, wait," Willow said. "If the Griz had cameras, why didn't the police get the footage?"

"What's that?"

"Wouldn't the police have gotten the camera footage the night Topher was murdered?" Willow rolled her hand while she spoke. "They would have seen Grace and talked with her already, right?"

"Yeah," Sam said, feeling sheepish. "There were no cameras."

"You lied?"

"I stretched the truth."

"Not cool, man." Willow turned to her car. "Not cool."

***

It took less than five minutes to find Grace Carlson's office in the science building. A row of professor offices was clustered on the first floor. Small black placards attached to the wall announced the occupant of each room. The door to Grace's office was locked but they could see into it courtesy of a small window. No one was inside.

Sam eyed Sonja, ready to suggest they ask someone about Grace's whereabouts, but she had walked away. He hurried up to her. "Where you going?"

"Maybe she's teaching a class."

"Willow said she wasn't."

Sonja smirked. "She said she didn't know."

Sam walked with Sonja as they headed toward the opposite end of the first floor. Their gazes bounced right and left. When they came to a closed door with only a number placard, Sonja opened it and stuck her head in.

Several times, she discovered people working. Most didn't bother to look up from their duties. Those who did noticed her and smiled. Sonja would close the door and they'd continue their stroll.

Had Sam done that, stuck his head into a room full of strangers, he doubted he would have gotten the same result. Life was different for attractive women. They could get away with certain behaviors that others couldn't. People usually forgave whatever transgressions an attractive woman committed simply because of her beauty. Sam wondered if the same was true for attractive men. He doubted it.

Sonja yanked open another door and stuck her head in. An older man in the room pulled his attention away from his computer screen to notice Sonja. He grinned. "Yes?"

"Wrong room," she said.

"Not for me."

Sonja smiled politely and closed the door. She turned and headed back toward the center of the building.

For several more minutes, it went like this on the second and third floors. Sonja yanked open the doors and peered into classrooms. Some were occupied. Others were empty. No one seemed bothered by her interruptions.

During the search, Sonja's face reddened, and she unzipped her coat.

Sam tried to stay engaged with the hunt for Grace Carlson, but with each failure, he lagged a little further behind. Sonja, on the other hand, seemed extremely focused. She silently strode from classroom to classroom, jerking open the doors with expectations of finding her quarry. Not doing so, she quietly closed the doors and moved on to repeat the scenario.

When they reached the last classroom on the third floor, Sonja closed the door. "She's not here." Sonja brushed past him and headed for the stairwell.

Sam followed but remained silent.

She stopped and turned. "Can I ask you something?"

"Sure."

"When did you talk to what's-her-face? The cop."

"Riley?"

"That's the one." Sonja put her hand on her hip, pushing her unzipped coat aside. She wore a tight black sweater that highlighted her attributes. "So, when did you talk to her?" Sonja asked again, trying her best to sound calm.

"Last night," Sam said with a nonchalant shrug.

Sonja frowned.

Sam held up his hands in surrender. "It wasn't like that."

"It's okay," Sonja said, but it was clear it wasn't. "I'm not accusing you of anything. It's your life, remember?"

"She picked me up at the Griz."

"The Griz?"

"Not picked me up, picked me up," Sam said hurriedly. "I was leaving. I went there for dinner."

"You don't have to explain." Sonja's jaw flexed, obviously holding back a comment she really wanted to say.

"She was working." Sam pushed his hand out, like a car in a race. "Driving by the bar when I was leaving." He talked faster than necessary, but he felt guilty for some reason. "She works the graveyard shift, remember?"

"It's no problem." Sonja glanced around, her expression darkening again. "Any idea how we can find Grace?"

She turned and started walking. Sam relaxed his shoulders, thankful the conversation about Riley was over. Unfortunately, she abruptly spun back to him before he could even take a step to follow her.

"I want you to know," Sonja said.

Here it comes, Sam thought.

"I appreciate you flying nineteen hours to help Bruce." Before Sam could protest, she added, "Help me."

"You're welcome," Sam said carefully.

"It's just this whole Grace situation has me freaking out. I'm not doing a good job of holding it together."

"Understandable."

They started down the wide stairwell. Their boots clomped and echoed with each step. Neither spoke until they exited the building. Sonja zipped up her coat as they walked. When they reached the sidewalk, Sam said, "I had a thought."

"About?"

"About the murder," Sam said, still not looking directly at Sonja. Her perfume invaded his nostrils and played havoc with his memories.

"Well?"

He eyed her. "It has to do with the rock."

"What rock?"

"The one used to kill Topher."

"What about it?"

"Where'd it come from?"

"Where do you think?" She rolled her eyes. "Maybe the ground, which is where every rock in the history of rocks comes from."

"Yeah?" Sam asked. "Find me a rock."

Sonja looked around. Two feet of snow covered everything that hadn't been purposefully cleared away. "Where do I get a rock?"

"That's what I was wondering," Sam said.

Almost immediately, Sonja's expression tightened once again. "Grace is a geology professor."

"She is."

"Which means rocks."

"I think there's more to it than rocks."

Sonja pointed at the science building. "She did it."

"We don't know that."

"Let's call the cops."

"And tell them what? We don't have any proof."

"The rock is all the proof we need."

Sam shook his head. "That's not how it works," Sam said.

"Where would she get the rock?" Sonja looked back at the building. "Did you see any in there?"

"No."

"Were you looking?"

"A little."

Sonja frowned. "Well, I wasn't."

She turned and headed back toward the science building.

Chapter 17

"See any rocks?" Sonja's nose was pressed against the window of Grace Carlson's office door.

Sam peered over Sonja's shoulder and into the small room. "No."

She cupped her hands around her eyes. Sam wasn't sure how that might help, but he wasn't close enough to the glass to bother trying the same.

Her breath fogged a small portion of the window. "Maybe they keep that stuff in a classroom."

Sam doubted it, but he wasn't a geologist, let alone a professor of the subject. Keeping rocks and dirt around seemed like overkill when they could walk outside anytime and get the stuff. He realized the irony in that statement as soon as he thought it. Professors and students couldn't go outside in the winter to collect rocks and dirt. That's why the issue of the rock that killed Topher seemed like such a big issue right now.

"Let's check the rest of the building," Sonja said.

She abruptly turned to Sam, her lips nearly brushing his.

He inhaled her dark and spicy perfume which caused his cheeks to warm and his heart to race. A playful smile hinted at the corner of his mouth. It was a natural reaction to the situation. Flirting with Sonja was bad mojo, especially now. He planned to return to Hawaii and her boyfriend—almost fiancé—was still in jail.

"What're you doing?" she asked. She put both of her hands on his chest and pushed him back. "I've got a boyfriend, and we've classrooms to search."

Sam blinked twice. Didn't she feel the excitement of them being so close to each other? Hadn't she felt the danger of another possible kiss?

"Don't just stand there," Sonja said. She headed toward the stairs.

***

Students filled the second-floor hallway as they hurried toward the stairwell. Sam and Sonja proceeded through the mass of undergraduates like salmon swimming upstream.

Several male students slowed their gaits enough to gawk at Sonja. When Sam made eye contact with them, they showed no shame at their brazen ogling. One guy even had the guts to say, "Cougars are the best," as he walked by Sam. His buddies slapped hands with the oversexed twenty-something.

Sam watched the guys disappear down the stairwell.

Sonja emerged from a nearby classroom. "No rocks in there. What's wrong?"

He thumbed down the hallway, then thought better of mentioning the younger guy's comment. A cougar was an older woman who sought romantic relationships with younger men. Sam didn't thing reminding Sonja of her age right now would be helpful. "Nothing," he said.

"Come on," she said and headed down the hall.

Sam poked his head into the empty room that Sonja had just exited, didn't immediately see any rocks, and decided his effort was good enough. He joined Sonja in the next classroom.

Rows of desks faced a whiteboard. Sonja stood in the middle of the room, her head swiveling and legs bending as she searched for anywhere a geology professor might store some rocks.

A student peered into the room. She noticed Sonja and Sam, then closed the door.

"We're spinning our wheels," Sonja said.

"We're making good progress. Only one more floor to go."

"Maybe Grace keeps some rocks at her house."

"It's probably natural for a geologist to do that."

"Did you see any when we were there?" Sonja asked.

"I wasn't looking."

"Then we should go back."

Sam sighed. "I figured we would."

"Fine." Sonja headed for the door. "Let's go now."

"You don't want to finish searching the building?"

She stopped and faced him. "Are you trying to waste time?"

"No."

"Seems like it. I saw how you tried to kiss me downstairs."

"That was an accident. You bumped into me."

She pointed at him. "You had your chance, Sam Strait, and you blew it."

"I thought we weren't talking about last night."

"You broke up with me so you could wear flip-flops," Sonja said. "Tell me I'm wrong."

"The flip-flops are a symbol."

Sonja snapped her fingers. "That's right. They're a symbol of how you couldn't be bothered to stay with me."

Sam didn't like how the conversation devolved into a critique of his relationship with Sonja. He needed to get things back on track. "You're getting mad at me because we can't find Grace."

"Probably." She walked out of the room, and Sam trotted behind her.

"We'll find her," he said.

"You bet we will."

A woman in her early sixties walked down the hall. Her silver hair was pulled back tightly, and she wore blue slacks and a light green sweater. She carried a walkie-talkie in her right hand. "You two," she said. "What are you doing here?"

"Looking for Grace Carlson." It might have been the nicest way Sonja had said the professor's name since learning about her connection to Bruce.

"She's gone home," the woman said. She pointed the walkie-talkie's antenna at Sam. "We've received complaints of non-students walking the halls."

"We're leaving," Sonja said.

She walked by the woman, not bothering to look back for Sam.

"Sorry for the inconvenience," Sam said.

***

Sam rested his head against the passenger door window as Sonja drove toward Grace Carlson's house.

"She did it," Sonja said. "I knew it. I knew it!"

Sonja slowed the car for an uncontrolled intersection. She glanced in both directions before stomping on the accelerator. The tires spun briefly on the snowy road. When they caught traction, the Range Rover rocketed forward.

"We don't know Grace did anything," Sam said.

"Yes, we do," Sonja snapped.

He raised an apologetic hand.

"When did you figure out the thing about the rock? Was it last night with Officer Malone?"

He opened his mouth to explain but didn't get a word out before she interrupted him.

"Wait. You don't have to tell me." Sonja lifted her hand from the steering wheel and let it fall back with a thud. "It's your life."

She didn't bother slowing for the next intersection. The Range Rover blew through it, which caused an older pickup coming from the right—the passenger side—to slam on its brakes.

Sam pulled his head away from the window and stiffened, prepared for impact.

The two vehicles missed each other by inches. Sam checked the side mirror and watched the truck spin through the intersection.

"You can do what you want," Sonja said. "Doesn't bother me."

"You almost hit a truck."

She checked the rearview mirror. "He should've stopped."

Sam returned his head to the passenger door window but only briefly. Sonja didn't seem concerned about slowing down on the snowy roads and the image of the sliding truck still lingered in Sam's thoughts. He sat upright.

"Maybe slow down," he said.

"We should call the cops." She glanced at him. "She's a murderer, you know."

"We haven't proved that."

The brakes on the Range Rover locked, and the vehicle slid to a stop. Sonja glared at him. "What about the rock?"

"We don't know Grace killed him."

"Why are you protecting her?"

"I'm not,' Sam said. "The rock might not be anything."

Sonja exaggeratedly rolled her eyes. The move included a head roll, too. "It's the murder weapon!"

A car honked from behind them. Sonja eyed the waiting vehicle, then spun in her seat. The Range Rover rocked forward.

"What I'm saying," Sam said, "is the rock might just be a rock."

Sonja strangled the steering wheel. "You were the one who asked where it came from."

"I'm sure Agent Hathaway asked the same question."

"Stop defending her."

"I'm not defending anyone."

Sonja pulled to the side of the road. They were across the street from Grace Carlson's house. No cars were in the driveway.

"Maybe she parked in the garage," Sam said.

Sonja slipped the SUV into Park and jumped out. She trotted up to the house and banged on the front door.

Sam pulled the police report from his pocket, along with his cell phone. He located Grace Carlson's number and called her.

As the phone rang in his ear, Sonja pounded on the door. She even kicked it once.

Grace answered the call. "Hello?"

"Hi," Sam said, then introduced himself.

"Not again."

"I've got a couple follow-up questions."

There were other voices in the background of the call. Some ambient noise suggested she might be at a restaurant. "I'm having lunch," Grace said.

"We can meet you."

"I'm almost done."

"We'll meet you anywhere."

Sonja slapped the front door once before heading back toward the Range Rover.

Grace sighed into the phone. "Fine. I'm at Fifth Avenue Grind."

"We'll be there in five minutes."

He ended the call as Sonja climbed back into the SUV.

"She's not home," Sonja said, then slammed the driver's door.

"She's having lunch."

Sonja faced him. "How do you know?"

"I called her."

"Why didn't we do that before?"

"Because you wanted to drive here."

Sonja's lips pursed as she thought. Finally, she said "You're right."

"She's at Fifth Avenue Grind."

With great restraint, Sonja slowly entered the business name into the GPS. "It's not too far from here."

"Nothing in Havre is far from here."

***

"Maybe let me do the talking," Sam said.

"I can keep it together."

They were in the parking lot of Fifth Avenue Grind located on the arterial of the same name. The lot was crowded with vehicles, including Grace Carlson's Lexus.

"It's okay," Sam said. "She's a touchy subject."

"I'm not going to lose it in there."

"Listen, this is an interview. That's why you asked me to fly out and help."

Sonja nodded several times before muttering, "Whatever. The goal is to get her arrested, right?"

"The goal is to prove Bruce is innocent."

"That's what I meant."

Several cars waited in the drive-through lane as Sam and Sonja entered the cafe.

Inside, the small eating area was filled with a mixture of high-top and regular-height tables. A cacophony of customer conversations and poppy music bounced off the tiled floor. A woman smiled at them from behind a counter.

Sam returned the pleasantry, then scanned the restaurant.

"There," Sonja whispered.

"Wait," Sam said but the request went unacknowledged.

Grace Carlson sat alone in the farthest corner. She looked over the lip of her coffee cup as Sonja and Sam approached. A winter coat was draped over the back of her chair. She wore a tight beige sweater that Sam could never imagine any of his professors wearing. Grace lowered the cup and set it on the table, then motioned toward the counter with her chin. "Get something if you want. Everything's good."

"We're not eating with you," Sonja said sternly.

"Have it your way."

Sonja crossed her arms and scowled. She looked like a mother about to scold a disobedient child.

Grace ignored Sonja's disapproval and picked up the remaining portion of her sandwich. There was only a sliver remaining. She studied it briefly before looking up at Sam who stepped around Sonja. "You said you had more questions."

Sam's stomach growled as Grace tossed the bit of sandwich back on the plate. It was after one now and he could go for something. Even a small snack would tide him over. It would have to wait though. Business first.

"Thank you for meeting with us," Sam said. He pulled out a chair, but Sonja held out her arm to stop him from sitting. He looked questioningly at her, but Sonja's gaze remained locked on Grace.

"Where'd you get the rock?" she asked.

Grace brushed her hands together over the plate. "What rock?"

"You know." Sonja sniffed. "The one you killed Topher with."

The other conversations in the cafe stopped abruptly and Sam became more aware of the music. It was an '80s pop song but he couldn't remember the name. It wasn't something in his father's collection since most of those albums tended toward rock and glam metal.

Grace glanced around the restaurant. "Take that back."

Sonja put her hands on her hips. "I won't take it back. It's the truth."

"I'm done talking," Grace said to Sam. "She leaves, or I leave." The professor pulled a napkin from her lap and threw it on her plate.

"Whatever," Sonja said. "We'll call the cops." Her head bobbled as she spoke.

Sam touched Sonja's arm, and her gaze snapped to him.

"What?" she asked.

"Go outside," Sam said calmly.

Sonja's face soured. "You can't be serious. Bruce is going to get the death penalty—"

"Please," he interrupted. "Let me do my job." He did his best to keep his tone even.

"I lost it, didn't I?" Sonja's attention returned to Grace. Her lips trembled as if she fought back saying something. Eventually, her shoulders relaxed. "I like your sweater." She spun on her heel and left the cafe.

Sam, Grace, and the other customers watched her go. When Sonja was outside, the cacophony of conversations slowly returned. Sam watched Sonja through the windows until she reached the Range Rover, then his attention dropped to Grace.

"I'm sorry about that," Sam said as he finally sat. "She's upset."

"Death penalty?" Grace asked.

"His attorney said the prosecutor was leaning that direction."

"Chuck Palmer, right? I read about that in the paper. We went to school together."

"That's what he said." Sam nodded. "You all knew each other."

"Go Blue Ponies." She half-heartedly pumped her fist in the air.

"I've got a question," he said.

"Sounded like you had a few."

Sam smiled politely. "This should be an easy one. How'd you end up at Northern?"

Grace seemed confused by the question.

"You grew up here, went to school somewhere, obviously."

"Oregon State," she said. "Earth Sciences."

"Then you came home to Havre to teach at MSU-Northern?"

"It's not that hard to figure out. I love being here. I got my education, saw there was an opening and applied for it. Most professors want to be in places like Billings or

Missoula, where the action and supposed culture are. I didn't worry about any of that. I just wanted to be home. That answer your question?"

It did.

Grace continued. "I'm sure you didn't come here to talk about my resume. What's this about a rock?"

"It was the murder weapon."

"That wasn't in the news."

Sam rested his arms on the table. "The cops do that to keep the crazies out of the investigation."

"I don't think you can say crazy anymore."

"You're probably right."

Grace removed a tin of lip balm and applied some to her lips. "I'm getting the impression you think I had something to do with Topher's death."

"A witness said you were at the bar that night."

"That so?" She set the tin on the table and rubbed her lips together. "I didn't think Willow saw me, but I guess she did. She didn't tell the police or they would have interviewed me by now. Isn't that right?"

Sam thought so.

"It's not what you think," Grace said.

"What was it then?"

"He did some work at my house."

Sam recalled the smell of fresh paint in Grace's home. "And?"

"And nothing." She leaned back in her chair and crossed her arms. "I was unhappy with his work."

"So you went to The Grizzly Den to complain?"

"What's wrong with that? People complain all the time. Topher was at the Griz every day."

"The hour seems suspect." Sam didn't know the exact time she went, but his comment seemed nebulous enough to get away with bluffing.

Grace looked away. Her head bobbed while she thought. When she looked back, "What'd Willow say?"

"She said it looked like more than business." It was another bluff, but Sam felt like he was on a roll now.

"How would she know?"

"She's a woman."

"She's a girl."

Sam didn't bite on the distinction. "She knows how certain communications are supposed to look. You and Topher didn't look like business."

Grace exhaled heavily and brought her attention back to Sam. "Why didn't Willow tell the police she saw me?"

"She didn't want you to flunk her."

"I wouldn't do that." She leaned in. "I've got my ethics."

"Then tell me what happened."

Grace pulled back. "I don't want to get involved."

"Not very ethical."

"I guess my ethics are more situational than I thought."

"Bruce is in jail."

"Maybe he did it," Grace said.

"He didn't."

"How do you know? I don't, therefore, I'm going to trust what the cops say."

"They're making their assumption because they don't know about you and Topher talking right before his death."

She blinked twice but didn't look away.

"If they did," Sam continued, "maybe you'd be considered for the murder."

"I didn't want to hurt Topher, let alone kill him." She leaned forward with a look of earnestness. "The cops seriously wouldn't consider me just because I went there to talk with him.”

“They might when they put the rock in your hand.”

“What rock?” She crossed her arms. “What’s so special about this stupid rock?”

Sam motioned toward the window. “Look around.”

Grace’s gaze swept toward the street. “What am I supposed to be seeing?”

“Snow.”

Her nose crinkled. “What about it?”

“It covers everything.”

“Yeah, so? It’s winter. That’s what happens here.”

“Where would a killer get a rock at this time of year?”

Grace’s expression slackened. “That’s where you’re going with this? Are you serious?”

“You see any rocks out there?” Sam asked with more than a bit of satisfaction. “I don’t.”

She pointed at her chest. “You think I have a rock? Because why? Because I teach geology?” She laughed once, a sharp chuckle filled with disbelief. “Tell me that’s not true.”

“I think a prosecutor could argue a geology professor is exactly the type of person who might have access to rocks in the winter.”

“You’ve been in the sun too long. It’s melted your brain.” Grace’s eyes darkened. “We’re in Northern Montana. There are rocks everywhere. On the side of the road. In landscaping projects. In the fields.”

Sam raised an eyebrow. “Covered by several feet of snow.”

Grace continued, undeterred. “Every old pickup—” She thumbed over her shoulder. “Heck, even some of the newer ones have extra weight in their back end at this time of year. Some use sandbags. Others use dirt, wood, whatever they can find. Wanna guess what that includes?"

"They'd be covered with snow. Just like everything else."

"I'm not saying the rock came from a pickup. I'm just saying rocks are everywhere." She tapped her temple. "Think. I'm not the keeper of all rocks come winter."

"Maybe you aren't." Sam cocked his head. "But you had an argument with Topher at the bar that night. What was that about?"

Grace put her hands on the edge of the table. She nodded several times before saying, "Fine. Doesn't matter. It's not like I killed the guy." She looked at the customers at the other tables. "Topher and I had a thing."

"We know," Sam said.

Surprised, her attention swung back to Sam. "How'd you—?" A realization occurred to her, and her expression flattened. "Bruce must've told you about high school. Or maybe Chuck."

"Back at your house, you said the guy you left Bruce for was a reoccurring bad habit."

"You can say that again." She scrunched her nose. "The thing I'm talking about with Topher was new." Grace waggled her hand. "Newer. Should never have gotten involved with him again."

"Why did you?"

"He was around the house, working on projects that I'd let go for too long." Grace gnawed on her lower lip. "I don't want to sound shallow, but that sort of did it for me."

"What did?"

"I'm not one of those types who loves tinkering on her house. Maybe if I'd gotten married along the way." Grace abruptly sliced the air with a karate chop that would've made Chuck Norris proud. "No. Can't go down that path."

An embarrassed smile formed on her lips. "I like men," she said. "I just don't need them. Understand?"

He did.

Grace grabbed her coffee cup. "Where was I?"

"Having Topher around the house did it for you."

"Yeah," she said remorsefully. "Him and his toolbelt. It was like a cheesy romance novel or something."

"Why'd you call him in the first place? What with your history and all?"

"Have you ever tried to hire a handyman?"

Sam hadn't.

"It's hard to get a good one, especially one that isn't condescending to you because of your gender."

"So you called him up and what?"

"It wasn't like that." Grace considered the contents of the mug, then put it back on the table. "I hadn't intended to hire Topher because of our history together. Then I saw him at the grocery store, and we got to talking. Don't get me wrong. I saw him around town a fair bit. It was hard to miss Topher. He still looked good, even after all these years." She studied Sam. "I'm guessing you and I are about the same age."

Sam nodded.

"Men, a lot of them anyway, let themselves go when they get in their mid-thirties." She cocked her head. "Although you look like you take care of yourself."

"Thank you."

"Topher didn't exercise. Not that I know of, anyway. He just had that lean physique. Probably because he didn't eat well, but it worked for him." She glanced at the ceiling. "He also had this sexy vibe. Like he was dangerous in a way that didn't make him scary. Does that make sense?"

"I think so, but I'm still trying to understand why you'd

call him for work when he treated you so badly in high school.”

“Bruce and Chuck told you a lot.”

“It’s a small town,” Sam said, choosing not to rat out either man.

“So you got the scoop from others? That’s fair, I guess.” Grace pushed her plate away. “Ever been dumped?”

“We all have.”

“Ever been dumped in a way you couldn’t comprehend? Like, you did nothing wrong. That everything seemed perfect. Then one day it wasn’t, and you were disposable?”

“No.”

Grace tapped her chest. “Let me tell you, it sucks, and that pain sticks with you. It eats at you. You can tell yourself whatever you want—you’re a good person, you matter, it’s their issue and not yours.” Her lips pursed. “It won’t make a difference. When the person you loved— thought you loved—treats you like trash, they never fully get out of your system. There’s a part of you that wants to show them what they missed out on.”

Sam’s eyes cut to the window and the Range Rover. He couldn’t see Sonja since the SUV faced the other way, but he wondered if that’s why she still pursued him. Was she still infatuated with him because she couldn’t tie him down? Did Sam remain fascinated with her because she represented the life he rejected? Maybe it was simpler than that—Sonja was hot.

“Anyway,” Grace said, “I saw Topher in the grocery store a few months back. The cereal aisle, if you can believe it. Me with my granola. Him with his Lucky Charms. That describes us perfectly.”

“Did you hire him with romantic intentions?”

Her brow furrowed. "Of course not. My kitchen faucet needed replacing and my gutters needed repairs, what with winter coming on. I knew he had a handyman business because he had a sticker on the side of his truck." She waved her hand in the air like a salesman describing a new appliance. "Mr. Sure Hands."

Sam raised an eyebrow.

"He loved that name. Probably because he slipped between the sheets with more than one of his clients."

"When did the new relationship start between you two?"

"Hate to admit it, but it happened pretty quick." She inhaled deeply, held the breath for a couple of seconds, then let it out. "It wasn't anything more than an occasional tumble when he was around the house."

"You never went anywhere?"

"God no." Her face tightened. "I wouldn't want to be seen around town with Topher. I have a reputation to maintain."

"Then why show up at The Grizzly Den that night? A witness clearly saw you talking with him."

"Because a woman threatened me."

"Who?"

"I don't know," Grace said. "She knocked on my door and told me to stay away from Topher. She said she'd kill me if I didn't."

Sam leaned forward. "What'd she look like?"

"Mean, nasty."

"Was she white, black, or…"

"Oh." Grace nodded. "I see what you're asking. She was white."

"How old?"

"Younger than us. Maybe she was our age. I don't

know. I'm sorry. I was focused more on her anger than anything else."

"What color hair?"

"She wore a baseball hat. That's all I noticed besides the hatred in her eyes."

Sam set his hands on the table. "You didn't want to hurt Topher."

"Are you kidding?" Grace said. "I know how shallow this is going to sound, but there were more repairs I wanted fixed in my house. Besides, Topher was good for an occasional no-strings-attached roll in the hay. Why would I want to mess that up?"

"Why not tell the cops this?" Sam asked.

"Telling you about my booty calls with Topher is one thing. Getting that fact into a police report is something different. I haven't gotten tenure yet. Maybe if my career was on solid footing, I'd speak up, but the college can let me go for any reason right now."

"I thought Bruce was your friend."

"I haven't spoken to him in years."

"What about Facebook?" Sam asked. "Didn't you just reconnect?"

She stared at him. "You know how many old boyfriends or guys I work with friend me just to see if they have a shot? I can't tell you how many of them are married, but know this, it's a lot. Do I want Bruce in jail? No. But if he killed Topher—"

"He didn't," Sam interrupted.

"If he did," Grace continued, "then he's where he should be. If he didn't, Chuck will get him out. He's a good attorney from what I read in the paper."

"You should call the police and tell them what you know."

"Yeah, okay," Grace said. "I'll do that when I get back to my office."

Sam didn't believe her.

***

Sonja smiled at Sam when he climbed into the passenger seat of the Range Rover. Hot air blew gently through the vents as the SUV's engine idled. Country music played on the radio. Sam turned the volume down.

"I'm sorry," she said.

"It's okay. Everything worked out."

"Did she admit it?"

"No, but I've got a new lead."

She looked straight ahead at the small stucco building on the next lot.

"What's wrong?" Sam asked.

"I'm acting like a lunatic. You don't have to tell me. I know it."

"Your boyfriend is in jail."

She eyed him. "He might get the death penalty."

"He's not," Sam said. "We're going to get him out."

"With this new lead?"

"I don't know. Maybe."

Sam needed to let the police know about the woman who threatened Grace Carlson. He pulled out his phone, prepared to call Riley Malone, but he stopped. She responded to the murder scene, but she wasn't investigating the case. Agent Hathaway had that responsibility. Besides, Sam could always bring Riley up to speed when they met later in the evening.

He dug the state investigator's business card out of a

jacket pocket and dialed the number.

Sonja glanced at him with a questioning look.

"Agent Hathaway," he said.

Sam looked out the passenger window and noticed an old yellow truck parked next to them. The bed of the small Toyota held a large mound of something which caused its backend to sag. Perhaps it was just snow. Maybe there was something underneath it. Vehicles with two-wheel drive required extra weight during the winter, just like Grace Carlson had suggested. Even some of the four-wheel-drive pickups needed additional weight.

The call rang a third time before it was answered. "DCI. Hathaway."

"This is Sam Strait."

"Wondered if I'd hear from you."

Sam opened the passenger door.

"What're you doing?" Sonja asked.

As he slipped from the Range Rover, Sam held up a single finger, silently asking her to wait. He didn't bother looking back, though. He could picture the face she was making now.

"Just wanted to pass along a couple tips," Sam said.

Hathaway chuckled. "You wanna pass along tips—to me?"

"Yeah." Sam swiped some of the fluffy snow away from the mound in the truck with his bare hand. The action revealed only more snow.

"Little odd for the defense to call the lead investigator and clue them in on their leads. Unless you're trying to muddy the waters."

"That's not it," Sam said. He wiped away a heavier layer of powder from the top of the pile to reveal a layer of crusty snow underneath. "There are a couple folks you might want to talk with."

"Who's that?" Hathaway asked.

Sam dug deeper into the snow mound and hit something hard. His cold fingers dug at it until he realized what it was—a chunk of wood.

"The first you already talked with—Harvey Mayer."

"Topher's neighbor."

"That's right. He told you about a woman arguing with Topher."

Hathaway muttered, "This isn't a tip."

"She drove a red Toyota Tacoma."

"How's that?"

"A red—"

"I heard you," Hathaway said, obviously irritated. "He didn't tell me that."

"That's why I'm calling."

"Anything else about her?"

"Just the red baseball hat."

The detective tsked. "Mayer said it was a hat."

"Probably worth a follow-up call."

"Thank you for telling me how to do my job, Strait." Hathaway grunted. "All right, who else should I talk to?"

"Grace Carlson," Sam said. "A professor at the university."

"What's she got to do with anything?"

"She had a relationship with the victim."

Sonja leaned across the passenger seat. "What're you doing out there?"

An older man stepped out of the cafe. "Hey, you! Get away from my truck." He angrily motioned Sam back.

Sam smiled and waved at the upset man, then climbed into the Range Rover.

"How'd you find this Grace Carlson?" Hathaway

asked.

Sam thought about making a snarky comment about his superior investigative skills, but he didn't. Not only was it an exaggeration, but he never knew any cop to take teasing well. When he wore a uniform, Sam was the same. Cops needed to be in control of everything. Things changed when he aspired to spend his life in flip-flops. His gaze dropped to the boots he now wore.

"Well?" Hathaway said. "I'm waiting."

"It was luck."

Sonja motioned toward the phone with her finger. She mouthed something that Sam interpreted as, "Put it on speaker." He lowered the phone and activated the device's speaker setting.

Hathaway's tinny voice rang out. "—gotta hear how it was luck."

"We stumbled on her," Sam said. "How is not important."

"Tell me, former Deputy Strait, what exactly is important in your estimation?"

"Topher Anderson's been working on her house. She started having—" Sam struggled to find a polite way to describe what Grace Carlson had been doing with her handyman. He settled on, "—intimate relations with him."

Sonja rolled her eyes. "Of course."

"Who's that?" Hathaway asked.

"Sonja Boyd."

"I'm on speakerphone?"

"Yes, sir."

Agent Hathaway growled—literally. Sam had never heard a man do such a thing. "You warn someone when you put them on speaker, Strait."

"I understand."

Hathaway cleared his throat. "You think this Carlson woman had something to do with the murder?"

"I don't."

Sonja rolled her eyes again.

"Then why even bring her up?" Hathaway asked. "You're trying to muddy the waters, just like I said."

"A woman came to Grace's house and said she'd kill her," Sam said, "if Grace didn't stop seeing Topher."

"Well, now," Hathaway said. "That's interesting."

Sam stared at Sonja who looked genuinely surprised. "That's what I thought."

"How do I contact this Grace Carlson?"

It took a moment for Sam to relay the information to the investigator.

Hathaway asked, "She know you're calling me?"

"I told her she should call the police. I'm just making sure it happens."

"Uh-huh." Hathaway sighed audibly. "All right, Strait. I'll call her. We'll see what happens."

"We appreciate it."

"My money is still on your guy doing it, though."

"Of course it is. Have a nice day." Sam hung up.

Sonja studied Sam. "Should we have kept that clue to ourselves?"

"This is the best way," Sam said. "Hathaway and his DCI pals will look for this other woman, too."

Sonja motioned in the direction of the cafe. "You think she told the truth?"

"I do."

"Some woman threatened her to stay away from Topher?"

"That's what she said."

"I don't get it." Sonja frowned. "He didn't seem like

such a catch when he came onto me."

"You only talked to him for a minute."

"A minute was all I needed."

Sam shrugged. "Maybe it's a bad boy vibe."

"He was a handyman."

"Handymen can be bad boys." Sam cocked his head after hearing the words come out of his mouth. "Handymen can be bad men."

"Whatever." Sonja grabbed the steering wheel and shifted in her seat. "Bad boys only break your heart." She dropped the SUV into gear and headed toward the exit. "Where to?"

Chapter 18

Sam bit into the hamburger he'd just purchased at the Dairy Queen drive-through. It might've been the best burger he'd ever eaten. Of course, that might have something to do with his hunger.

"You're spilling crumbs," Sonja said, glancing at him.

"I am?" Sam continued to chew as he brushed crumbs away from his pant leg.

"That's not helping." She shook her head.

He didn't see what the big deal was. First, cookie crumbs lingered in the passenger seat's crevices. The snickerdoodle fragments that made it to the floorboard were mixed with melted snow. It was impossible to keep a car clean in the winter.

Sonja slowed for an uncontrolled intersection, looked both ways, then accelerated smoothly through it. They were on their way to see Reagan Dobson, the last witness listed on the initial police report.

Sam pulled a cluster of French fries from the box tucked between his legs. He wished he had some ketchup to dunk them in, but Sonja forbade him from spreading the condiment on an opened burger wrapper.

"We're not getting anywhere," she said.

He shoved the fries into his mouth. "Sure we are," came out muffled and uninspired. He swallowed quicker than he should have so he could repeat his statement.

"Ugh." Sonja's nose crinkled. "Look at you."

"I'm not dropping anything." He held the half-eaten

burger in his right hand and another bunch of fries in his left. He lifted them for emphasis and a small fry slipped from his fingers, tumbling between his seat and the center console.

"How can you eat at a time like this?"

"How can you not?"

"I'm too upset to eat."

The GPS screen flashed an alert that an upcoming turn was in one hundred feet.

"You know," Sam said, stuffing the burger in his mouth, "we should ask ourselves a question."

"Could you not?"

"What?"

"Talk with your mouth full."

"We're on a schedule." Sam waved at the GPS screen with the French fries pinched between his fingers. "We've only got a minute until we arrive."

"Fine." Sonja pulled the Range Rover to the side of the road and parked. A snow berm stopped her from getting any closer to the curb. According to the GPS, they were around the corner from their destination. She turned in her seat as much as her seatbelt would allow. "Now, finish chewing, then speak."

Sam slowed his chewing, hoping to enjoy the fries more than when he first started. Unfortunately, the latest cluster of fries weren't as good as the first when they were at their warmest and his hunger was at its peak. It went for the burger, too. The initial bites were always the best.

He swallowed, slightly depressed at the diminished enjoyment in his lunch.

"We should ask ourselves a question," Sam said.

"What's that?"

Sam hesitated as he struggled for a delicate way to put

his thought. "Is there a chance Bruce did it?"

She cocked her head. "Really?"

"It doesn't seem likely, but we should consider it."

"No." Sonja faced forward, then dropped the car into gear. "He didn't do it."

"What if he did?" Sam was about to take the last bite of the burger but refrained.

"Stop it."

"Sonja—"

Tears welled in her eyes as she gripped the steering wheel. "Why are you doing this?"

"It's something we haven't considered."

"Maybe I have." Her gaze cut to him. "Ever thought about that?"

He hadn't.

"Bruce isn't a murderer. He doesn't even have a temper."

Sam raised an eyebrow. "He hit Topher with a pool cue."

"Because he was afraid of losing me." A tear ran down her cheek.

"I think it was a little more than that," Sam said. "He and Topher had a history back to high school."

"Bruce didn't do it, and that's final." The Range Rover leaped forward, then turned the corner.

"So be it," Sam said. He shoved the last bite of burger into his mouth and balled up his wrapper.

***

The Black Bear Apartments were on Tenth Street SW across from Havre Middle School. Seven two-story buildings huddled around a single shared parking lot.

Sam scanned the assembled vehicles, hoping to find a red Toyota Tacoma. He didn't.

Reagan Dobson, a taller woman in her early forties, opened the door to her apartment after Sam rang the bell. No make-up covered her clear complexion. A messy bun held her blond hair on top of her head. She wore a black Pittsburgh Steelers sweatshirt and yellow leggings. Her feet were bare.

"What's this about?" Reagan asked after Sam and Sonja introduced themselves.

Sam thumbed over his shoulder, not really knowing what direction he was indicating. "We'd like to talk with you about the fight you witnessed a couple of nights ago."

"Are you cops? Because I already talked to them twice."

"We're with the defense," Sam said.

"Private investigators," Sonja added.

Reagan nodded twice. "Cool." She glanced into her apartment. "I'm on a Zoom call right now for work. You can come in, but I've got to get back in front of the screen. You understand, right?"

The apartment was larger than Sam imagined with a staircase to a second level.

"In here." Reagan led them to the kitchen. A laptop computer sat on the table and a man's voice droned on from its speaker. A notepad and pen were nearby. Arm's reach from the table, a baby crawled inside a square playpen. It was filled with toys and a blanket.

"My granddaughter," Reagan said as she settled into the chair facing the laptop screen. She motioned for Sam and Sonja to sit across from her. Reagan put her elbow on the table and covered her mouth with her hand. Her eyes remained on the computer. "We can talk, but I have to be on this training call. It's mandatory." The final word caused her face to pucker.

Sam and Sonja sat quietly.

From the computer, the man continued to prattle on about the importance of completing all the fields assigned to the database.

"What do you do?" Sam asked.

"Medical billing and tracking for small offices. We're outsourcing for doctors, dentists, and what not." Reagan continued to speak into her hand. It reminded Sam of how pitchers talked into their baseball gloves when communicating with other players, so the opposing team couldn't lip read their intentions. "Our company is all remote. Welcome to the new world order, right?"

Sam eyed Sonja. "Does Bruce use outsourcing?"

She shrugged.

The baby cooed from her playpen and rattled a toy shaped like an egg on a stick. Reagan reached over the pen and wriggled her fingers.

"We could come back later," Sam offered. "After the call."

"I'm good doing it now if you are. It'll be more fun than staring at the screen for the next hour."

The man leading the training call blathered on about saving their work frequently. *"We go forward by backing up,"* he said.

Reagan eyed Sonja. "You look familiar. Where do I know you from?"

Sonja smiled politely. "The bar that night."

"Right, right." Reagan nodded as her eyes dropped to the laptop screen. "Your fella knocked holy hell out of Topher."

"Unfortunately."

"Don't be upset," Reagan said into her hand. "Nobody deserved it more than Topher. He had no business looking that good and never having to work for it."

"You knew him?" Sam asked.

"You could say that." Her eyes cut to Sonja now. "Topher had that look. You probably know the one. The type of guy that is guaranteed trouble."

Sonja nodded. "Sure."

"That was Topher. He was basically the same guy I'd fallen for since I first discovered boys. The same type that knocked me up in high school. I should have known better, but I just couldn't help myself."

Reagan nodded at the screen as the instructor continued lecturing.

"What happened with you two?" Sam asked.

"I played mother hen to him for a while. This was a few years back before I became a grandmother." She motioned to the baby. "This is my second grandchild." Her eyes cut back to the laptop, and she again spoke into her hand. "I might've been a little older than Topher, but he didn't care as long as I was tending to his needs."

"What happened?"

"What always happens with guys like Topher."

Sonja harrumphed. "Another woman."

"You can say that again." Reagan dropped her hand from her mouth. "I forgave him once. I sure as hell wasn't going to do it a second time. There was no changing him. Topher was known as a dog—"

"*Ms. Dobson*," the instructor for the training call asked, "*are you paying attention?*"

"Crud," Reagan whispered as she tapped something on her keyboard and leaned toward the screen. "Yes, sir. Totally."

"It appears you're distracted."

"I'm sorry. My daughter is sick and I'm babysitting my granddaughter today."

Several women chimed in and requested to see the baby.

"Really?" Reagan said with a smile. She turned toward the playpen.

"We don't need to do that," the instructor said loudly.

Reagan straightened and faced the computer once more.

"You may have other duties today, Ms. Dobson, but do your best to pay attention."

"Yes, sir."

"Now, where was I?"

Reagan tapped the laptop's keyboard, then covered her mouth once more. "We're muted. Sorry about that."

"No problem," Sam said.

Sonja added, "We get it."

The instructor chattered on about the need to understand how the function keys worked.

"We were talking about Topher being a dog, right?" Reagan lifted her chin in Sonja's direction. "I suspect more than a few guys smacked Topher over a woman. Can't act that way and not make some enemies."

"Ever see anyone?" Sam asked.

"Not really, but I was only in Topher's orbit when we were at the Griz. Who knows what happened with the rest of his life? After we ended, he tried to get together more than once." She chuckled. "Any time he got drunk. Got to say, I thought about it. Fool me once, they say. Well, he fooled me twice. I wasn't going to fall for his act a third time."

"We'll take a five-minute break," the instructor said. *"Stretch your legs and come back ready to finish the last*

hour strong."

"Finally," Reagan said. She turned the laptop away from her. It faced the corner of the room. "I thought he'd never stop talking."

Sam scooted forward in his chair and rested his arms on the edge of the table. "What else can you tell us about that night?"

"Not much, really. The fight happened and Darry tossed her and her boyfriend out." Reagan waved at the baby, who smiled back. "Although." She frowned as she looked back at Sonja. "For a moment, I thought you came back to make nice with Topher. It wasn't you, though. Your clothes were different."

"Grace," Sam said.

Sonja frowned. "Yep."

He eyed Reagan. "How'd the conversation look between Topher and this other woman?"

"Stilted," Reagan said. "You know. Like old lovers who are forced to talk about child support."

"What makes you say that?" Sam asked.

"Because I've seen that argument before. I've been in it and around it." She motioned toward the baby. "You be polite, but there's something underneath."

"Anger?" Sonja asked.

"Could be. Could also be remorse with a twist of lust. The conversation just never looks right. Understand?"

Sam thought he did.

"Were you there alone that night?" he asked.

"I met my girlfriend for a drink, but she had to get home to her husband. I didn't want to leave when she did because, well, it's more fun to have a beer around others than do it in an empty home."

"You were there when Topher's body was discovered?"

It was an obvious question, and one Sam didn't need to ask. Reagan was there because she was in the police report. Even though it was unnecessary, the query did the trick.

Reagan nodded. "Someone came in and said the cops were outside. There was a body on the ground. I didn't know it was Topher until the interviews started."

"Were you upset?"

"Why wouldn't I be?" Reagan asked. "We used to hook up. Just because we didn't work out, didn't mean I wanted the guy dead."

"What kind of car do you drive?" Sam asked.

"Why?"

"A witness said they saw a woman arguing with Topher outside his house recently."

"Not me," Reagan said, "Me and Topher have been done with our escapades for some time."

"We've got a vehicle description."

Reagan rolled her eyes. "Whatever. I drive a Subaru Outback. It's ten years old." She looked toward the ceiling. "Make that eleven." Her gaze dropped to Sam. "It's got almost two hundred thousand miles on it."

Sam looked at Sonja. "Anything we forgot to ask?"

"I don't think so."

"I told the cops everything I knew," Reagan said. Her attention swung to Sonja. "I read about your boyfriend getting arrested. I sure hope he didn't do it."

"He didn't," Sonja said firmly as she got to her feet.

Sam stood. "Thank you for talking with us."

"No problem." Reagan smiled. "You helped pass the time." She pulled the laptop to its position in front of her. "Now if you'll excuse me."

She unmuted the speaker, and the instructor's droning returned.

"What'd we get from her?" Sonja asked.

Sam rested his head against his seat. "Nothing new, I think."

They were driving northbound through a nearby neighborhood. Snowflakes fell gently from the sky.

"She saw Grace," Sam said. "I guess that's something."

"We already knew that."

Sam thought about pulling the initial police report from his pocket, but he'd read it so many times he felt he had it memorized.

"Are there any more witnesses to interview?" Sonja asked.

"Reagan was the last."

The vehicle slowed, but Sonja kept her face forward. "What do we do now?"

"Find more people to interview, I guess."

"Where? How?"

"We still have Topher's other neighbors to interview."

"Yeah," Sonja said softly.

The Range Rover picked up speed.

"We could also start over," Sam said half-heartedly. He really didn't want to do that, but he was running out of options for people to question.

"You'd do that?" Sonja looked at him. "You'd really start over."

"Detectives do it all the time when they hit a roadblock."

"If you say so," she said.

The vehicle slowed for an uncontrolled intersection.

He faced her. "Let's interview Topher's neighbors, then

we'll call it a day."

Sonja's expression tightened as the car accelerated on the snowy road. "What if we don't find anything?"

"We will." Sam waved at the windshield. "Slow down."

"He'll get the death penalty."

"That's not guaranteed."

The Range Rover blew through an intersection. A man standing on the corner shouted at them and waved his fist in the air.

"Slow down," Sam said.

"Bruce is counting on me." Her voice rose with panic. "I don't want to be responsible for his death."

"You won't be, but we need to be alive to help him. Slow down."

The SUV approached the next intersection. A Ford Escape loaded with teenagers sped through before them. Heads turned in their direction, all with wide eyes and open mouths.

Sonja slammed on the brakes. The Range Rover slid into the intersection, barely missing the other vehicle. The SUV fishtailed, and Sonja fought for control. She over-corrected and the car spun. Sonja screamed.

Sam grabbed the door handle and flinched as he prepared for a collision.

The Range Rover spun a second time before its rear end collided with a snow berm along the roadway with a horrible sounding crunch. Their spin stopped abruptly, and they bounced into the middle of the street. They faced the opposite direction from which they'd been traveling.

Silence overtook the car.

A moment passed before Sam asked, "You okay?"

"I'm afraid to look."

He leaned over and checked her out. "You look fine."

"Not me." Sonja stared straight ahead. "The car."

"Bruce's baby," Sam said.

"Don't remind me," she whispered. "Will you look?"

Sam slipped out of the car and walked around to the back. The right rear was crumpled, and the brake light was shattered. Pieces of red glass littered the snowy road.

He returned to his seat and pulled the door closed.

"How bad is it?"

"Broken taillight."

"That's it?" she asked, her eyes wide with hope.

"You probably shouldn't look."

She put her head against the steering wheel. "He's going to hate me."

"No, he's not." Sam put his hand on her shoulder. "He loves you." He didn't want to say those words, but he thought they might comfort her.

"Do you think we could get it fixed before he gets out?"

"Guess that depends on how long Bruce stays in there."

Sonja dropped back in her seat. "I should probably slow down."

"I'd appreciate it."

The SUV crept forward. "Topher's neighborhood, then?" Sonja asked.

Chapter 19

Sam opened the door to his hotel room and stepped inside. He sat on the edge of his bed for a moment before flopping onto his back. He spread his arms wide and stared at the ceiling.

He and Sonja had interviewed four of Topher's neighbors. They hadn't learned anything new. Most of the neighbors commented on how Topher kept his lawn and home. They didn't provide much more than that. They wanted to talk about the murder in the way neighborhood gossip grows.

"Maybe Topher owed someone money," one neighbor suggested. "I bet he got whacked because he wouldn't pay. He seemed that type of fella."

"I bet it was random," another offered. "Havre's getting more dangerous every year."

"He looked the type for trouble," one woman implied. "Look at all those cars. What kind of man has all those cars?"

In the end, Sam and Sonja wasted a couple of hours. It needed to be done, though. One of Topher's neighbors might've held a clue to Bruce's innocence.

Sam sighed and sat upright.

He checked his phone for a text or missed call from Nina. There was neither. He started to message her but stopped. He dialed her number, and she answered on the third ring.

"There you are," she said pleasantly. There were voices

in the background, maybe some music, too.

"What're you doing?" Sam asked.

"Grocery shopping. Exciting, huh?"

"How's the weather?"

"Sunny and seventy." She sounded distracted.

"So, terrible?"

"Exactly." Nina chuckled. "Hey, do you like mushrooms? I've never seen you eat one."

"They're fine."

"What're you doing?"

Sam waved his hand. "Getting ready for dinner."

"What do they eat in Montana? Elk and buffalo?"

"I think you can get that."

"Really?" Nina said. "Is that what you're eating?"

He didn't want to tell Nina about the burgers and fries he'd eaten earlier. "You haven't forgotten about me already, have you?" Sam grimaced. It was a needy question, and one he wasn't prone to make. He wasn't sure how to deal with her lack of remorse at his absence. Maybe he was a narcissist, after all. Sam hated the idea of that.

"Not sure how to respond," Nina said.

"Forget I asked."

"You doing okay?"

"The weather's got me down."

"Ever heard of seasonal affect disorder?"

"SAD?" Sam said. He'd heard about it, of course. He believed a majority of Spokane County suffered from it during the winter. It's one of the reasons he routinely fled Eastern Washington before the gray skies and snow arrived.

"Maybe you've got it," Nina said.

"That's probably it."

"What's keeping you there?"

Sam shrugged. "An innocent man is sitting in jail."

"If I'm ever in trouble, I hope you'll come to my rescue."

"Count on it."

"What more could a girl want?"

Sam thought about Sonja. She wanted plenty he couldn't give her. Long-term commitment being the biggest hurdle. What he could give her now was staying focused on Bruce's plight and not worrying about his own happiness.

"I should go," he said.

"Sam?"

"Yeah?"

Nina said, "I miss you."

He was still trying to think of a response when she broke the connection. Before he put his phone down, another call arrived. It was a 406 area code, but Sam remembered this number.

He answered, "Hello, Agent Hathaway."

"Strait," the detective said, "you might be on to something."

∗∗∗

Sam's phone buzzed once—the signal for a text message. *Here.*

He responded with ON MY WAY.

A heavy snow fell and nearly six inches had accumulated on the sidewalk. Sam hunched his shoulders, lowered his head, and shoved his hands in his pockets as he shuffled across the parking lot. Puffs of snow launched from the toes of his boots with each step.

He waited at the corner for the traffic light to change,

cocking his head slightly to see the crossing sign. The snow muffled the sound of cars speeding through the intersection.

When the sign illuminated the signal to walk, Sam scurried across the intersection. He wasn't proud of his silly trot, but warmth and dryness were a higher priority right now than looking cool. Sam continued with his head down until he reached the entrance of the Duck Inn.

This is why I created the first rule, Sam thought ruefully.

He shook the snow from his head, brushed it from his shoulders, and stomped his feet.

Sam jerked open the door and entered.

Chapter 20

Riley Malone sat in a booth near the back of the restaurant. She smiled as Sam approached.

"It's really coming down out there, huh?" she asked.

"Hasn't stopped since I got here."

Sam slipped off his coat, tossed it to the far end of the booth, then sat across from her. Two menus and glasses of water were on the table.

Riley's smile broadened further. She wore a black knit sweater that highlighted her hair. She wore makeup tonight. Not much, though. Just a hint of mascara and some clear lip gloss.

Red neon looped around the restaurant's ceiling. Green vinyl chairs and booths accompanied oak tables. A printed carpet lay underfoot. "You Can't Hurry Love" played softly overhead. Sam didn't know who sang it, but it was a song he'd heard with his grandfather.

The restaurant was partially full, maybe a third. Empty plastic glasses with napkins and silverware stood guard on the unoccupied tables. Sam wondered if the weather dampened turnout or if this was normal for the time of night. It seemed the type of restaurant the early-bird crowd might like. He imagined senior citizens got a discount for eating there.

A server walked over. The older woman clasped her hands in front of her. "Your other half has finally arrived."

Riley nodded. "He has."

Sam raised an eyebrow.

"Can I get you started with some drinks?"

After securing their selections, the older woman left them alone again.

"I already know what I want," Riley said.

Sam opened the menu. "Come here a lot?"

"More than I should. It's not good for my waistline."

He smiled. From what he could see, she had nothing to worry about.

"Getting along okay in the snow?" she asked.

"It's not a problem when I'm not driving."

"What's your friend doing tonight?"

"Visiting her in-laws."

Riley leaned in. "What's the deal with you two?"

Sam set his menu down. "What do you mean?"

"I don't believe you're just friends. Men and women can't be that."

He studied her for a moment. If he told her the truth, could she use it to hurt Bruce? To coerce some sort of admission from him. Sam decided it wouldn't matter. "We used to date."

"Before Bruce?"

"That's right."

"Does he know?"

Sam shook his head. "I don't think so."

"That's some secret to keep from the guy."

"It's Sonja's choice."

"I disagree." Her tone was sharp, as if she carried hurt from a past relationship. "Bruce should know."

Sam regretted telling her now. He sipped his water instead of responding.

Riley glanced around, presumably checking to see if anyone heard her. When her gaze returned to Sam, her eyes softened. "I'm sorry about that."

"It's okay."

She waved off his comment. "I've had some bad boyfriends in the past. Those memories sting at inopportune times."

"I get it."

The server returned with their drinks. She put a glass of iced tea in front of Riley, then slid a beer in front of Sam. The older woman pulled a notepad from the half-apron she wore. "Ready to order?"

Riley sipped some tea through the straw in her drink, then ordered a BLT with fries. Sam ordered a grilled cheese sandwich and a side salad.

When Riley eyed him questioningly, he explained, "I had a late lunch."

The server finished writing, took the two menus, and left.

"Can I ask you something?" Riley moved the ice in her drink with the straw. "What's your family think about you snowbirding?"

"I don't have any family."

"None?" Riley stopped stirring the ice. "Not even grandparents or aunts and uncles?"

Sam shrugged. "My maternal grandparents are in Florida. I haven't seen them in more than twenty years."

"How come?"

"They're in Florida."

"Sounds like a perfect place to snowbird."

It did actually, but Sam had never been close to his mother's parents. Spending a summer in the same state with them might prompt some guilt-related visits. It probably wouldn't be good for any of them. Sam sipped his beer.

"Your parents passed away?"

"When I was a baby," Sam said.

"That sucks." Riley slowly turned her glass of tea. "How?"

"Car accident."

"Who raised you? Your grandparents?"

"My paternal, yeah."

"They're gone, too?"

Sam nodded.

"Were you snowbirding before they passed?"

"After."

"Ever take your friend with you?" Riley jerked her head toward the restaurant's exit. "The ginger?"

He shook his head as he took another sip of beer.

"Anyone ever go with you?" Riley asked.

"No."

"Has someone come back with you? You must have met someone, right? I mean, here we are. You were in town two days and got a date with me."

"You asked me out," Sam said.

"I didn't have time to waste." She forced a smile. "Ever have a long-term relationship? Something that lasted beyond a snowbird season?"

Sam set his glass on the table. "What's with the twenty questions?"

Riley studied him. "Trying to determine how damaged you are."

"Damaged?"

"All that loss, you're going to be emotionally wounded."

"I'm fine," Sam said. "I got over everything years ago."

"You built up scar tissue."

Sam stared into his beer. "You ever ski?" he said, hoping to shift the conversation away from his past.

"Don't change the subject." Riley reached across the table but didn't touch his hand. "This is interesting."

It wasn't to Sam. He didn't like where this exchange was going.

"You don't want to get hurt again," Riley said.

He shook his head, still not looking up. "No one's hurt me."

"Maybe not on the conscious level, but subconsciously they have. Your parents abandoned you when you were young."

Sam looked up now, but Riley lifted her hand to stop his protests.

"They died," she said. "They didn't want it to happen, but it did. Then your grandparents passed. You're all alone."

He leaned back in the booth and crossed his arms.

"You don't want anyone to get close," Riley said, "so you leave before they can."

Rule three, Sam thought. *Leave when it's time.*

He became aware of a new song on the radio. "Midnight Confessions" was one of his grandfather's favorites. Sam almost smiled at the memory of the man who was his surrogate father.

"I can see by the look on your face I'm right."

He pointed at the ceiling. "Listening to this song."

Riley's gaze drifted toward the ceiling. "Don't know it."

"Doesn't matter," Sam said. "My turn."

She brought her attention back to him. "Not going to respond to my hypothesis?"

"What would you rather do than police work?"

"Where did that come from?" Riley asked.

"You said you didn't know me well enough to share. I

think now might be a good time for some quid pro quo."

"Right. I did say that." She pulled her iced tea closer to her. "Fine." Riley inhaled deeply, then exhaled. "It's going to sound stupid."

"It won't."

"Trust me, it will."

She grabbed the straw and jabbed it in and out of her drink. Riley focused on the bobbing ice cubes. "I want kids."

"You can do that and still do the job."

"Let me clarify. I want to be a stay-at-home mom." She looked up now. "Pretty stupid, huh?"

"No."

"I need a husband for that."

Sam stared at her, an uncomfortable worry growing in his stomach.

"Relax, Romeo." She laughed once and let go of the straw. "I'm not looking to tie you down."

He didn't want to breathe a sigh of relief, so he played it off with a smile and a dismissive wave. "I know."

"It's just I've had lousy luck with men. Either it's me or it's this town."

"Ever think of leaving?"

"I have."

"Where would you go?"

"Someplace warm, that's all I know."

The server returned to the table with their orders. The conversation turned lighter as they ate.

***

Sam pushed away his plate. The grilled cheese was excellent, although it was a pretty hard entrée to screw up.

He'd made them plenty, and they always came out fine. Once he finished that, he discovered he wasn't in the mood for a salad. The lettuce and other vegetables remained untouched on his plate. He should have gotten the fries, double calories notwithstanding.

His phone buzzed once, the signal for a text message. He checked it, then set the phone on the booth next to him.

"By the way," Riley said, cavalierly waving the remaining sandwich portion in her left hand, "how's your investigation going?"

"It's going."

"That good, huh?"

Sam said, "I thought we had something when we found a woman who had a casual relationship with Topher."

Riley set the last bite of her sandwich on the plate. "Casual, how?"

"They hooked up occasionally."

"Yeah?" She picked up a French fry but didn't bite into it. "What's her name?"

"Grace Carlson."

Riley rolled her lower lip down as she studied the fry. "Never heard of her."

"Why would you?"

"Havre's a small town."

"I suppose, but you don't have to worry about Grace."

"Why's that?"

"I told Agent Hathaway about her. He's interviewing her."

"Ah." Riley dropped the fry onto the plate and grabbed a napkin. "This Carlson woman give you anything?"

"She went to the Griz the night Topher died and talked to him shortly after the fight he had with Bruce Bloom."

"No one said anything to me about it."

"Don't take it too hard," Sam said. "She's a dead ringer for Bruce's girlfriend."

"That so?"

"The witnesses who saw Grace thought it was Sonja who had come back in." Sam's head bobbled. "Well, except one. She knew it wasn't because the clothes were different."

Riley's expression soured. "Guess I didn't ask the right questions."

"You had a lot going on that night."

"I guess," she said. Riley wiped her hands with a napkin. "Anything else?"

"Maybe. Hard to tell."

She watched Sam silently, waiting for him to continue.

"A neighbor saw a woman arguing with Topher in front of his house."

"You've done pretty well for two days." Riley checked her fingernails. "You get a description?"

"White woman in a red baseball hat."

"Not much to go on."

"She drove a red Toyota Tacoma."

"Could be anyone." Riley wiped her fingers a final time and balled up the napkin. "An upset customer or something."

"Yeah. Maybe."

The server walked over to their table then. "How was everything?"

Sam smiled. "It was good."

"You didn't touch your salad," the older woman said.

"Had a late lunch." He patted his stomach and felt silly for it.

"Did you save room for dessert?"

"None for me." He eyed Riley. "You?"

She shook her head. "I've got to get going."

The server pulled a long black book from her apron and set the bill on the table. "Whenever you're ready."

"Hold on." Sam reached for his wallet.

"I'll get it," Riley said. "I invited you."

"On a normal day, I'd let you." Sam pulled a credit card from the billfold.

"A normal day?"

"Bruce is reimbursing me for my expenses."

The server slipped the plastic from Sam's fingers, grabbed the receipt, and hurried away.

Riley frowned. "Feels strange for the man I arrested to pay for my dinner."

"If it bothers you," Sam said, "I won't ask for the reimbursement."

She looked toward the exit. "What're you going to do now?"

"Go back to my room. Watch some TV."

Riley smiled. "I mean with the investigation."

He shrugged. "I'm not sure there's much more I can do. I've interviewed everyone listed on the report. Talked with Topher's neighbors. Never found a friend of his or any family, but Hathaway's probably doing that."

"Yeah," she said. "He probably is."

"If I had access to Topher's business records, maybe I'd go through them and interview recent clients. Hathaway will do that, though."

"I reckon." Riley grabbed her coat and stood. "Listen, thank you for tonight."

"You're welcome." Sam slid out of the booth, taking his coat and phone with him. "Did I say something to offend you?"

"No," she said. "I'm just tired."

She didn't look it. Also, this was about the time when she'd normally start her workday.

Riley patted Sam's arm. "I'll see you around." She headed for the exit.

He slipped his coat on and took one final glance at the table. That's when he noticed Riley left something behind on the seat next to where she sat. He picked up a Boston Red Sox cap.

"Riley," he called, lifting the red baseball hat in the air. "You forgot this."

She paused at the front door and glanced over her shoulder at Sam. Then she was out the door.

Sam didn't bother chasing after her.

Chapter 21

Riley Malone stood next to a Hill County Sheriff's car. Two deputies, both large men, stood on opposite sides of her. They wore brown winter coats and similarly colored beanies. Behind the patrol car was a red Toyota Tacoma. A parking lot light beamed down on the shiny truck, highlighting it.

Agent Hathaway walked over to Sam. He wore boots, jeans, and a dark blue coat. He was dressed casually for this time of night. "Why don't you wait inside? I'll come in and get your statement in a couple of minutes."

Sam gave Riley's red hat to the investigator. "She left this."

Hathaway took the cap. "Like the neighbor described."

He nodded, took a final look at Riley, then went inside.

The older woman who served Sam earlier stood at his table with his credit card and receipt. "I thought you forgot this."

Sam dropped into the booth. "Just had to run outside."

"Everything okay?"

"It is now."

The server put the card and receipt on the table. "Let me know if you need anything."

"You wouldn't have pie, would you? I'm suddenly in the mood for a piece."

After Sam decided on dessert, the server left him alone.

He placed two phone calls then.

The first was to Sonja.

The next was to the airline.

***

Sonja slid into the booth. "They're still outside."

"Might take some time." Sam dragged the tines of his fork through the remnants of his apple pie. "That's my guess."

"You think she did it?"

"We'll find out."

"When did you know?"

Sam set his fork down. "Hathaway called right before I met her for dinner. He found Riley owned a red Toyota Tacoma."

"That was lucky," Sonja said.

"Just good police work."

She smirked. "Lucky we found out about the truck, I mean. So Riley's been arrested."

"Not sure she's been arrested yet. She's definitely been detained while Hathaway interviews her."

A man said, "I heard my name."

Agent Dale Hathaway stopped at their table. He held a notebook in his right hand. "Got a few minutes?"

"Whatever you need."

Sonja slid over and made room for the detective to sit. Hathaway sat across from Sam.

"I need to formalize the stuff we talked about on the phone. When and where you learned certain details, and who you talked to in the process."

Sam asked, "Did Riley admit to anything?"

Hathaway flipped open his notepad. "Admitted to it

all."

"Why would she do that?"

"Now that we've homed in on her, she knew she was cooked. She said there were calls between her and the victim. We've already requested Topher's cell phone records, but they haven't arrived yet. When we get them, we'll confirm she had contact with him. It was only a matter of time before the connection came to light, and Riley knows that. She said she met Topher when she hired him for a bathroom remodel. I'm sure we'll find payments to him when we subpoena her bank and credit card statements."

"It's fortunate Sam called," Sonja said.

Hathaway considered her statement, then nodded. "It certainly sped up the process. We'd have found the connection, eventually. We got Topher's business records, if that's what you can call them, courtesy of a search warrant. The guy kept horrible records."

Sonja shifted her position in the booth to better look at the investigator. "You weren't looking for Riley, though. You already arrested Bruce."

Hathaway set his pen on the table. "I understand your frustration, Miss. However, we never stop looking for other suspects or for other explanations to how a death might've occurred."

"Why do that?" she asked.

"Because the defense will." Hathaway eyed Sam. "We have to make sure we cut off every viable excuse attorneys could use to defend their clients. If we think about it first, we can debunk it, so the prosecuting attorneys won't get blindsided in court."

"So," Sam said, "Riley and Topher started a relationship she took more seriously than he did."

Hathaway nodded. "That's how she explained it."

"When she discovered Topher was messing around with Grace Carlson on the side, Riley threatened her to stay away from him."

"I haven't confirmed it was Riley, but Grace said she was threatened, yes. After we finish here, I'll take a photo array over to the professor's house and see if she can identify Riley."

The server walked over and smiled at Sam. "Looks like you've made some friends. Should I bring some drinks or menus?"

"I'll have some coffee," Sam said. "I think we're gonna be here awhile."

Sonja and Hathaway both motioned they'd take coffees as well. The older woman walked away.

Hathaway picked up his pen. "Shall we get started?"

"One question before we start," Sam said. "Did Riley tell you where she found the rock?"

The agent nodded. "She said it was in the parking lot. She picked it up during her argument with Topher and hit him with it."

"Where did it come from?" Sam asked.

"I just told you—the parking lot."

"What about the snow?"

Hathaway cocked his head. "What about it?"

"It covers everything. How'd she find it?"

Sonja nodded in agreement with his question.

"I don't know," Hathaway said. "Maybe it fell off a truck. Maybe it was there all the time and got pushed around by a snowplow. Does it matter how it ended up there? She picked it up and hit him with it. Case closed."

"She did it while on patrol?" Sam asked.

The detective nodded slowly. "Sounds like she found

out he had flings beyond Grace Carlson. He stopped taking her calls. She saw Topher's truck in the Griz's parking lot that night and waited. When he came outside, she confronted him. The rest, as they say, is history."

"As they say," Sam parroted.

"What about Bruce?" Sonja asked. "When are you going to let him go?"

"As soon as we get done with this interview," Hathaway said. "I need to have my facts straight so I can properly book Riley. Then I'll call the prosecutor and inform him of what's happened tonight."

Sonja eyed Sam. "I guess you did it."

"You can say that when we get him out of jail."

Epilogue

"I'm sorry I've been so crazy the past couple days," Sonja said.

"When?"

She turned in her seat to eye Sam. They were parked in the lot of the Hill County Jail. "What do you mean, when?"

Sonja had been upset with him plenty over the past couple of days. Sam didn't want to assume which moment she was apologizing for. Maybe she was asking forgiveness for them all. "I don't know," seemed the most appropriate answer he could give.

"The entire time," Sonja said. "Worrying about Bruce had me twisted inside. I could barely keep myself together."

Getting an apology from Sonja was rare. He certainly wasn't going to argue with her. "Thank you," he said.

She looked toward the jail's exit and frowned. "I still think you would have slept with Riley had events worked out differently."

"You said you were okay with how I live my life."

"Leopards can't change their spots, Sam. That goes for both of us."

He nodded. "Think Bruce is going to ask you to marry him now?"

Her gaze cut to him. "Why are you asking?"

"I want to know if I'll get an invitation to the wedding."

"You're making fun."

"No, seriously. You think he'll ask?"

"I don't know," she said softly as she faced forward

again.

The jail's front door opened, and the morning sun glinted off it. Bruce Bloom stepped onto the sidewalk. He wore a fresh set of clothes that Sonja had brought him, including a ski parka. The clothing he wore the night of Topher's murder was still in evidence. If Bruce wanted the garments back, it would take some time for the release paperwork to wend its way through the criminal justice system.

Sonja honked the horn and Bruce looked in their direction. A smile creased his face, and he waved.

She slipped out of the driver's seat and moved toward the front of the Range Rover. Sam met her there.

Bruce hurried over and embraced Sonja. He clung to her like a man clutching a life preserver while in the middle of the ocean. "I thought I'd never get to hold you again."

"Me, too," she said. Her arms wrapped around him. She nuzzled her head into the tooth mangler's neck.

Bruce broke the hug and lightly kissed Sonja. He turned to Sam and extended his hand. "Thank you for all you did."

Sam shook the dentist's hand. "Glad it worked out."

"Me, too," Bruce said. He put his arm around Sonja's shoulders. "What should we do to celebrate?"

"Sam has a noon flight," Sonja said, her eyes filling with sadness.

Bruce chuckled. "No time to waste, huh? Got to get back to the sun and the ladies?"

"The sun, anyway," Sam said.

"I bet you've got them lined up around the corner." Bruce playfully punched Sam on the shoulder. "Handsome guy like you."

"We should get him to the airport," Sonja said.

"Of course, of course." Bruce let go of Sonja. "Did you

give your expenses to Chuck?"

Sam nodded.

"Good. We'll get you paid immediately." Bruce's gaze cut toward the Range Rover. "As soon as I get back to the office." His hand hovered over the hood as he walked around the car. "Baby needs a bath, doesn't she?"

Sonja eyed Sam. "We didn't have time."

"No time," Sam agreed.

"I understand." Bruce looked back at her before he started around the passenger side. "We'll stop somewhere and clean her up."

"I've got to tell you something," Sonja blurted.

Bruce stopped walking, and his eyes focused on the right rear of the SUV. "What the—" He scurried around to the back. "What happened?"

Sonja lightly touched his shoulder. "There was an accident."

"Did you get the name of the other driver?"

She shrugged.

"It was a hit and run?" Bruce threw his hands in the air. "Did you call the police?"

"Well, no."

"Why not?" Bruce whined.

"You were in jail."

"Oh, man." Bruce squatted so he could stare directly at the crumpled rear end. His fingers gently touched the crinkled metal. "I guess this day couldn't get any worse."

"I ate cookies in the car," Sam said.

Sonja rolled her eyes as Bruce cocked his head.

Sam nodded. "They were your mom's."

"Her snickerdoodles?" Bruce stood.

"Got crumbs everywhere." Sam waved his hand in front of him. "Big mess."

It seemed only appropriate to admit such an offense and tweak the man.

Bruce might marry Sonja, after all.

***

"So that's how it went down," Sam said.

Nina Wilder reclined on the lounge chair underneath the afternoon sun. She wore large, round sunglasses and a black bikini she filled out nicely. It was nearly ten when Sam arrived home the previous night. Nina was at work, and he was exhausted. They agreed to meet at the pool the next day.

It was another warm late February afternoon. Nearly a record the TV forecaster said that morning.

Sam put his hands behind his head and closed his eyes.

"That's the whole story?" Nina asked.

"Yes," Sam lied. He left out the platonic date with Riley, the kiss with Sonja, and his ill-will toward Bruce, the jaw butcher.

"The lady cop did it?" Nina asked.

He opened his eyes. "You can just call her a cop. I think it's preferred, actually."

She turned toward him and lifted her sunglasses. "Did you just mansplain sexism to me?"

"Wouldn't dream of it." Sam waved a dismissive hand. "Lady cop works."

Nina dropped her glasses back onto her nose but didn't look away. "I'll say this. You're some friend."

"You said that already."

"I did, huh?"

He smiled. "A few others said it, too."

"What others?"

"You don't know them."

Nina tsked, then rolled onto her back. She lifted her face toward the sun. "Ask you something?"

"Anything."

"You meet anyone while you were there?"

"I was there like two days."

Nina frowned. "You were gone longer than that."

"Travel days."

"You haven't answered my question."

Sam shook his head. "Didn't meet anyone."

"That's good."

He eyed her. "It is?" Optimism crept into his voice.

"I didn't meet anyone while you were gone, so we're even."

"Oh," Sam said, turning his face back to the sun.

"What's wrong? I thought you wanted no strings attached, Mr. I'm Leaving When Spring Arrives."

He sighed. "Some strings wouldn't be so bad."

"For the next month or so."

"Right." Sam nodded once.

Nina uncrossed her ankles. "I guess I could live with that."

"Then it's settled."

She sat up. "I think I need a nap."

"Didn't you just wake up?"

Nina stared at him until Sam got her meaning.

"Oh," he said with a widening smile. "A nap."

The Rules

1. Only be where flip-flops can be worn.
2. No attachments.
3. Leave when it's time.
4. No drama!!!
5. Avoid people with repulsive careers—lawyers, accountants, IRS agents, politicians, real estate brokers, preschool teachers, bikini baristas, and dentists.

About the Author

Colin Conway is the creator of the 509 Crime Stories, a series of novels set in Eastern Washington with revolving lead characters. They are standalone tales and can be read in any order.

He also created the Cozy Up series which pushes the envelope of the cozy genre. Libby Klein, author of the Poppy McAllister series, says *Cozy Up to Death* is "Not your grandma's cozy."

Colin co-authored the Charlie-316 series. The first novel in the series, *Charlie-316*, is a political/crime thriller that has been described as "riveting and compulsively readable," "the real deal," and "the ultimate ride-along."

He served in the U.S. Army and later was an officer of the Spokane Police Department. He's owned a laundromat, invested in a bar, and ran a karate school. Besides writing crime fiction, he is a commercial real estate broker.

Colin lives with his beautiful girlfriend, three wonderful children, and a codependent Vizsla that rules their world.

Learn more at colinconway.com:

www.ingramcontent.com/pod-product-compliance
Lightning Source LLC
Chambersburg PA
CBHW061119310726
48974CB00002B/595